# TURKISH TRIANGLE

## A COLD WAR THRILLER

### BY BILL RAPP

coffeetownpress

Kenmore, WA

coffeetownpress

A Coffeetown Press book published by Epicenter Press

Epicenter Press
6524 NE 181st St. Suite 2
Kenmore, WA 98028,
www.Epicenterpress.com
www.Coffeetownpress.com
www.Camelpress.com

For more information go to: www.coffeetownpress.com

www.billrappsbooks.com

All rights reserved. No part of this book may be reproduced or transmitted in any form or by any means, electronic or mechanical, including photocopying, recording, or any information storage and retrieval system, without permission in writing from the publisher.

This is a work of fiction. Names, characters, places, brands, media, and incidents are the product of the author's imagination or are used fictitiously.

A Turkish Triangle
Copyright © 2023 by Bill Rapp

ISBN: 9781684920792 (trade paper)
ISBN: 9781684920808 (ebook)

LCCN 2022941090

Printed in the United States of America

# DEDICATION

Our little dogs, heartbeats at our feet and in our laps, such wonderful, loving companions over the years as I toiled away with pen and paper, typewriter and computer. We miss them all. From Edith Wharton.

# ACKNOWLEDGMENTS

There are numerous people responsible for the good in this book. Jennifer McCord, the senior editor at Coffeetown Press is one. She insisted that I keep my protagonist, CIA officer Karl Baier, consistent with the principles and integrity he had developed in his past adventures whenever I tried to have him stray from that path. He is a better character and the narrative is a better story because of it. There is also my wife, Didi, who acted not only as an editor and fact-checker, but also as a sounding board and source of encouragement throughout. And I would be remiss if I did not mention the many colleagues I worked with over the years on eastern Mediterranean affairs, who proved to be a source of expertise, insight and inspiration, and a great group to work with. Anything wrong a reader may find with the book is mine alone.

# CHAPTER ONE

"Ankara?" Karl Baier asked. "Really?"

Baier sat back against the padded cushion on his desk chair and lifted one leg to cross over and rest on the other. His ankle sat against the light brown cotton fabric of his slacks, and the pants leg hung open underneath his calve. He pulled his argyle socks back up to cover the exposed skin, then rolled his shirt sleeves up to his elbows and laid his forearms on the arms of the chair. "Why there? And what the hell for?"

"Yes, Ankara, Karl." Ralph Delgrecchio settled his rear end on the front edge of Baier's desk. The bottom seam of his plaid sports coat folded up against a stack of papers Baier had been studying. "You know, the capital of Turkey. Which is not Istanbul, not any longer. Not since 1923." His finger rose. "And don't be so damn condescending."

"I know where the hell it is, Ralph. And what it is. I am not being condescending. I'm just puzzled." He studied the rounded figure of his good friend, noting to himself how Delgrecchio appeared to be losing the battle between his dedication to exercise and the allure of good food. Like most things delicious, the bulk of it just happened to be heavy and loaded with carbs. That had been true at least since their tour together in Vienna, Central European cuisine being what it is. Delgrecchio liked to point to all the protein and nutrition, as well as the taste. But he forgot, or avoided, that it could also be fattening. Nonetheless, there was an odd sense of reassurance for Baier in this man's middle-aged spread, as though his colleague would always be there for friendship and support. He wasn't about to go anywhere fast. Not unless he embarked on a crash diet.

"By the way, nice jacket. With all those clashing colors, who needs the overhead lights?" Baier's eyes rose to the ceiling and dropped back to the desk.

"Man, you've got to get with it, Karl. That tan thing you're wearing puts you back in the Eisenhower Administration. It's 1962 already."

"Thanks for the reminder. It's what Sabine gave me to wear this morning."

"Does your wife pick out all your clothes?"

"Hey, I happen to like it. It has served me well over the years. And just so you know, I voted for Kennedy. But tell me, why Ankara and why me?" Baier's foot fell back to the floor as he leaned forward and brought his elbows to rest on the desk. "And why now?" He thought of the possibilities, but there was really only one for someone of his rank and experience. For some reason, the mandarins at CIA Headquarters must be considering sending him out as the new chief of station. But that would be even more puzzling than the sudden mention of a Turkish adventure. Changes like that normally come during the summer rotations.

"This isn't a PCS move, is it, something permanent?" Baier asked. "We've already got a station chief there, as I recall, and he's a good one. Jim Breckenridge, right? At least I haven't heard any complaints."

Delgrecchio stayed silent. He stared at Baier, and his face gave no hint of agreement or disapproval.

"And Jim's only been out there for a year or so," Baier continued. "So, there's no need for a change in station management. At least not that I can see."

Delgrecchio nodded. "Yeah, that's right. This would just be something temporary, not a permanent change for you or the station. You'd have to get Sabine's agreement, of course. Not officially, but…"

"Approval from my real boss, you mean?"

Delgrecchio nodded, then smiled. "You can always ask her to give you a list of what to wear."

"Ha, ha. Very funny. But I doubt Sabine will have any objections. She can do without me for a little while. She might even look forward to it. And I doubt she'd want to go along."

"Why is that? Doesn't she like Turkey? Lots of good shopping opportunities. Plenty to see as well. Lots of history there. They say the best Greek ruins are in Turkey. It used to be called Asia Minor, you know. Or Ionian Greece."

"Enough with the highlights, already. It's just that I'm not aware she's thought about Turkey all that much. She's finally getting to feel at home here in Virginia." Baier sat back again and loosened the collar button on his white shirt. It was early October, but Baier was still feeling the heat and humidity of the northern Virginia climate, where the CIA had decided to plant its new headquarters. The knot in the tie dropped about two inches.

He would hate to miss the Autumn, though, normally his favorite time of the year in Virginia. In fact, it was about the only season he enjoyed in that area. Up north, the colors had already begun to change, but here the trees remained full and green, as they would until almost the end of the month. Baier had to admit that the warmth and moisture here certainly made the landscape rich and verdant. In fact, that was the worst thing about his new office. Not that it was so small, but that there was only a narrow window that Baier had to approach at an angle to get much of a view of the scenery outside. For the most part, the rich countryside just beyond the glass that ran along the George Washington Parkway remained a mystery until he sat in the traffic on his way home along Route 123 about a dozen miles west of the Agency's new Headquarters in Langley. That had been finished over a year ago in March of 1961, and most people working at the Agency had moved across the river to Virginia by that September. As far as Baier was concerned, it definitely beat driving into downtown Washington.

Delgrecchio decided to follow Baier's example. If anything, he hated the heat of the Washington region as much as Baier. He may not have come from Chicago, like Baier, but his memory of the fall weather in New Jersey was a lot more pleasant than this. He popped his collar button, and his solid brown tie dropped several inches soon after. He glanced at his colleague, picking up Baier's thoughts. They had been working together on and off for fifteen years and had come to know each other well. Both men knew they could trust each other's judgment and discretion.

"It does make you wonder why our founding fathers picked this place to build their new capital." Delgrecchio said. "The Indians must have been scratching their heads at those stupid white men purchasing what was little more than a swamp for their future capital."

"Be that as it may, you still need to tell me why you want me to go to Ankara, and why now."

Delgrecchio pulled himself off the desk front, grabbed a chair and slid it to the side of Baier's desk. It was almost as though he wanted to avoid being overheard by anyone. "It seems we have a problem there."

"In Ankara? What sort of problem? And why can't Breckenridge handle it? It's what we expect our station chiefs to do."

"Well, despite the generally good marks he's gotten as chief out there, there are some of us here who believe that he hasn't been handling this one all that well."

"So, what's the problem? It sounds serious."

"Oh, it is. We've lost three agents over the last month or so." Delgrecchio looked at his hands like he was counting the fingers. "Actually, more like six weeks."

Baier leaned in closer to his guest. "Three? For Chrissakes, Ralph. Lost them how?"

"Two have been killed in Istanbul, and one was recalled to Moscow. Preliminary soundings indicated that that one was shot in the basement of Lubyanka."

"How were the other two killed?"

"One shot and one poisoned."

"So all three assets were Soviets, not Turkish?"

Delgrecchio nodded. "Yep." He frowned as his eyes studied

Baier's. "And given what's been going on down in Cuba, you can imagine how much that hurts us right now. The folks that count in the White House are not happy. This has left us almost blind as far as Soviet plans and intentions go. You know, are they really going to put nuclear-capable, medium range missiles in Cuba? What will they do with them? What will it take to get them to back down. And so on, and so on."

"Yeah, I get all that, Ralph. And I can imagine they've got worries enough right now. So, I take it these guys were reporting on Soviet policy and objectives?" Delgrecchio nodded, his face grim and the lips tight. "Don't we have any other assets in that particular stable?"

Delgrecchio sighed. "We do have some others, one of whom is a real star. But he's not plugged in to the decision making on this issue."

"What does he give us?"

"We get a lot of military intelligence from him. You know, material on the missiles, military planning, other weapons information…"

"Sounds pretty useful."

"But it doesn't give us the insight we need on the policy discussions and goals. In fact, it's not clear whom Khrushchev is talking to. If anyone."

"And we were getting that from these guys?"

Delgrecchio nodded. "Some. Which in this case means a lot. A little is always better than nothing."

"So where do things stand down there now?" Baier asked. "I confess that I haven't been following all the details of the Cuban crisis as closely as I should have. There's been a lot of back and forth, most of it speculation from what I've seen."

"Well, my friend, you will need to get smarter on this stuff now," Delgrecchio replied. "There have been signs of increased construction activity since July…"

"On missile sites?"

Delgrecchio shook his head. "Not exactly. Mostly airbases and defensive batteries."

"How reliable is that stuff?"

"On the airbases? Pretty good. The question is why are they building that kind of shit, especially now and all of a sudden. Our director told the President he believes that this is precisely the sort of thing the Soviets do to protect missile sites."

"Do we still have our U-2 flights over the island on hold?"

"Unfortunately, thanks to our Secretary of State, Dean Rusk. It's been about five weeks, during which we haven't been able to get any picture of what's up inside Cuba. People around here have been referring to a 'Photo Gap' ever since the flights were called off in early September. So, you can imagine how welcome any news is that restricts our reporting on Soviet intentions and activities even further."

"Has the station reviewed its security measures, checked on surveillance? You know, all the standard procedures?"

"Of course, they have."

"Everything okay with our Turkish hosts? I seem to remember we have a pretty strong liaison relationship there."

"Your memory is correct, and it still is a strong relationship."

"Then, what," Baier asked, "do you expect me to do? Why not send someone from the Counterintelligence Division? This sounds like a classic CI issue. One of your own, as it were. I mean, you're the deputy chief in there." Delgrecchio frowned. "Okay, so your present job is a temporary assignment," Baier continued. "I realize most of your contacts are in the Middle Eastern Division, your old home, as it were. But you are still number two in the CI office for now."

"Because, my friend, I do not want our vaunted leader to get his grimy paws on this case. That is, when those paws are not wrapped around his afternoon martinis." Delgrecchio leaned back and blew out a breath of stale air that could have matched the swamp grog outside. "And don't you dare breathe a word of my view of Angleton outside this room, or to anyone ever. And that includes Sabine."

Baier sat back in turn, a wide grin breaking across his face. "Hold on there, partner. I don't like that fucking vampire any more than you do. And seeing as how Angleton has crippled our work against the Soviets, I'd hate to see him screw this case up as well. But just how did you manage to pull off this end run around that ghoul? The guy's a power unto himself in this building. And as his deputy, that bloodsucker is the man writing your evaluation reports."

"Well, that's where you come in, ol' buddy. I convinced him that you'd have a much more deft and skillful hand to play, given your own experience with the Soviets. That, and the fact that you know Breckenridge so well."

"Ralph, I do not know the man that well. We worked together for a brief period after my banishment here to the training division when I got back from Berlin…"

"Where you still languish. I thought you'd be happy for a chance to break away. This training stuff is hardly up your proverbial alley, my friend. Given what you've accomplished in places like Budapest, Vienna, and Berlin, you should be running the European division. You've just got to stop pissing off the people on the seventh floor. Also the sixth, fifth, fourth, and third floors. That would help, too."

"Are you saying I'm okay on the second floor, though?"

"Well, it is where you're sitting now. But give it time." He studied Baier for a moment. "You know, if you do well and solve this particular riddle you could put yourself in position for a chief of station job somewhere nice. Maybe even in a posh European capital."

Baier leaned in again. "That does sound inviting, of course. But I have to admit that training new recruits has its rewards, believe it or not. I actually enjoy the work."

"Ah, but you still long for that action in the field, don't you? And this is your opportunity to break free. Get your hands dirty, just like you like 'em." Delgrecchio broke a new grin that widened quickly. "And you won't have to worry about any interference from Headquarters, like in your past assignments."

"Ralph, you always have to worry about interference from Headquarters in our job. It comes with the territory. We're a bureaucracy."

"Not on this one, Karl. You'd answer to me, and me alone. And from our time together in Vienna, you know I will give you all the leeway you need."

Baier stood and walked to the window. The early autumn sun lay like a wool blanket on the lawn outside that ran up the hill at the back of the new Headquarters building: heavy, fetid, and seemingly unmovable. He wondered if it was much the same in Ankara at this time of year. It was in Asia, after all. He wheeled around and found Delgrecchio standing just behind him.

"Just what am I supposed to do once I get out there?"

Delgrecchio shrugged and smiled again. "That's up to you, champ. You can use your valuable judgment and discretion. Just make sure that it doesn't get both of us in trouble this time."

"What sort of obstacles or opposition do you expect me to encounter out there?"

Delgrecchio shrugged. "Well, I'm sure the Soviets will start sniffing around as soon as they find out you're in town. Not sure about anyone else. I expect it will be like one of those mystery novels you like to read. You know, chasing the clues and all that." He smiled. "That is when you're not buried in some deep German tome. Who's that guy you like, Thomas Mann?" Delgrecchio rolled his eyes. "Geez!"

"Has Breckenridge been informed? Does he have a view on my arrival?"

"I am about to send off that cable now. As soon as I get back to my desk, in fact. He'll probably resist some, maybe even squawk a bit. But tough shit. You can handle him if he does."

"That's encouraging. Maybe. How long will I be gone on this temporary assignment?"

Delgrecchio shrugged. "That depends on how long it takes you to get to the bottom of this thing."

# CHAPTER TWO

"But why Turkey, Karl?" Sabine Baier did not bother to hide a concern and surprise that bordered on contempt. "It's not even Europe."

Baier and his wife were standing next to the sink in their kitchen. They had bought a house a year ago in the town of Vienna, Virginia, some fifteen miles or so west of Washington, D.C. The town and the area to its west were fast becoming a suburb of the CIA Headquarters in nearby Langley, which bumped up against the George Washington Parkway not far from houses that were well above a civil servant's pay grade. Hence, the growth of the many small towns like Vienna within easy driving distance of the CIA campus.

"First of all, Sabine," Baier began, "Europe is not the only place of importance to this country. It is on the front line of our Cold War, but significant things are happening in other spots of the globe, you know."

"That's arguable."

"Perhaps for you. But Turkey is also a western-leaning, secular democracy, thanks in no small part to Mustafa Kemal, or as he is affectionately known in Turkey, Ataturk."

"I've heard that name before. Doesn't that mean something like 'Father of the Turks'?"

"Yeah, I guess you could say he's Turkey's George Washington. Anyway, he's the guy who emerged after World War One to lead the Turks against the Greeks and the Western colonial powers that wanted to divide up the remnants of the Ottoman Empire, including what became modern Turkey, among themselves. Or at least most of it, especially along the Aegean coast."

"Oh, how wonderful. So, the victors in that war for democracy did not confine their imperialism and land grabbing to Africa and the Far East?"

"No. In fact, I'd say most of their attention in 1919 was on the Middle East, including the defeated Ottoman state. Something about the rising importance of oil. And the Greeks did invade and occupy a chunk of territory in Asia Minor, where they hoped to recreate the grandeur of ancient Greece."

"Seriously? That sounds a bit delusional."

"It was. Especially since modern Greece has been defined a lot more by the Byzantines and the Greek Orthodox Church than the ancient world of Athens and Sparta. But they were encouraged by the likes of Llyod George and other equally delusional Brits who also fantasized about Classical Greece. And they weren't alone. The Italians wanted a piece, and the Armenians planned to create their own state as well."

"Well, the Armenians at least had some justification."

"It was all in the Treaty of Sevres."

"So, what happened? I take that that treaty didn't last long."

"No, you're right. After Ataturk's success in kicking the Greeks and the others out a new treaty was signed revoking all that other stuff. I believe it was the Treaty of Lausanne. Anyway, Ataturk went on to abolish the Caliphate—you know, Islam's Vatican, sort of--and establish a western-oriented democracy to bring his country out of its role as the 'Sick Man of Europe.'"

"The late Ottoman Empire of the nineteenth century, right? I remember reading something about that in school."

"Yep. He believed it was the only way to make Turkey a modern nation state. But my real point here is that Turkey is now an important ally of ours. Just look at a map sometime. It borders the U.S.S.R, Bulgaria, Syria, Iraq, and Iran. But for now it is firmly oriented on the West. They'd like to think of themselves as Europeans, almost. They're in NATO, you know."

Sabine studied her husband as he maneuvered around her at the stove, where she was preparing a pot of spaghetti sauce—closely aligned with the popular Bolognese style—a recipe she had gotten from his mother, who, remarkably, did not have an ounce of Italian blood in her. "Since when did you get to be such a big expert on Turkey?" Sabine pressed.

"Since I started reading up on it two days ago when Delgrecchio spoke to me about going there. I also spent a good bit of time with the analysts, who gave me some great context on the Turks' view of the Western world they want to be a part of."

Baier opened the refrigerator, extracted a bottle of Italian white, a pinot grigio from the Alto Adige, or South Tirol, as it was known in his family. He poured them both a full glass, just below the brim, before replacing the bottle in the refrigerator. Baier then took his glass, splashing a small puddle's worth on the kitchen counter, to the table, where he took a seat against the wall.

"So, you needn't worry about me while I'm gone," Baier continued.

"Why not?"

"Because it will almost be like I'm in Europe."

"For how long?"

"I'm not sure. Delgrecchio left that open. It really depends on the mission, if I can get to the bottom of this case about the lost agents."

Sabine turned down the flame on their gas stove to let the sauce simmer for another hour or so, then strolled over to the kitchen table. She pulled out the chair opposite her husband and settled into a seat for what Baier knew from experience would be the start of his real interrogation.

"So, how much more can you tell me?"

"Not a lot, of course. But there have been several who disappeared under suspicious circumstances."

"And that's what you're supposed to figure out? What those circumstances are and how they came about?"

"I suppose you could put it that way."

"Who's the chief there?"

"A fellow by the name of Jim Breckenridge."

"And? Is there a problem with your people in Ankara? And the chief in particular?"

"I'm not sure. It's really too early to tell. But he has a pretty good reputation, and he appears to have been running a pretty successful operation there. At least until now. But at this point I don't want to say anymore."

"Fair enough. And I realize you can't tell me any more about the people involved. But how has station morale been?"

"Good, as far as I can tell. Of course, people are a bit shell-shocked at the moment. Everyone is checking their own security and any other cases we might have there. It's only natural to ask yourself if there was anything you might have done to betray an operation, either on countersurveillance or security at home, on the telephone. The usual suspects, as it were."

"How is the relationship with the Turks?"

"Good. In fact, very good. They can be pretty sensitive about what we're up to there. But for the most part they're pretty cooperative. They see us as important allies, and protectors even. I gather they don't want to piss us off." He paused to sip his wine. "There's a limit to that, of course. But there is everywhere."

Sabine leaned back and took a long sip of wine. Her glass was a little more than half full. Baier's, she noticed, was nearly empty. She nodded in the direction of his glass. "You'd have more if you hadn't spilled so much over on the counter. You fill the glasses too full."

Baier shrugged. "I don't like having to get up and refill it so often. It cuts into my drinking time."

"Har, har." Sabine smiled and leaned forward over the table. "And now for the real question. Will you miss me? This only the second time we've been apart because of your work."

Baier leaned forward in turn, studying his wife's face. "I know. We've been lucky."

She sat back. "You've never thought of leaving the Agency for some other kind of work, have you?"

He shook his head. "No, I haven't. I think I would miss the work, the people, the sense of mission far too much."

"I know. That's why I would never press for such a thing. It means too much to you. You would be like one of those lost souls, or that fish out of water struggling to breathe. Even if it is taking you away from me now."

Sabine sat forward again as her hand drifted towards her breast, where she undid the top three buttons of her white linen shirt. Baier's gaze was drawn immediately to his wife's cleavage. He thought back to their first encounter at the house in Berlin shortly after the war, when she had seduced him by guiding his hand inside her blouse so that he could feel her firm breast and hardening nipples. He was a goner at that point. Hell, he was gone before she even made that move. He had been captivated at his first glance, the first encounter when they had met at the battered dry-cleaning store in the ruins of western Berlin just after the war. From that point on he had never looked back. And he had never lost his desire for her.

She took his hand once more and repeated the move, as though she had been reading her husband's mind. Then again, there wasn't much else inside his head at that point. She stood and let her blouse fall open as she undid the rest of the buttons. Then she took Baier's hand and led him to the stairs.

"I think I need to make sure you'll miss me, Karl. I wouldn't want you to forget what you have waiting for you here at home in Virginia."

• • •

Baier sat up in bed and surveyed his wife's body as she lay in bed, dozing. He appreciated what the Virginia sun had done for her color this summer, leaving brown tan lines across her chest and around her buttocks on a skin that had always been light-colored, more alabaster than white. That made sense, he realized, given her north German background. He reached over to stroke her legs, and she took his hand and brought it to rest between her breasts. Seconds later, she fell back into a slumber, her light snoring giving her away.

Baier nestled down beside her and let his mind wander.

Unfortunately, it wandered to the subject of Jim Breckenridge. Baier had known the man more by reputation, then personal experience. True, their paths had crossed in the training program, but only briefly. Breckenridge had been finishing up his course on countersurveillance—which would be ironic, Baier suddenly thought, if that was the cause of their problems out there—and started the process for his departure shortly after Baier's arrival to teach the courses on asset recruitment and living your cover. Baier was surprised at the time to learn that Breckenridge was on his way to Ankara, which was considered an important posting, given Turkey's strategic location. Breckenridge had told him it was his first chief of station assignment, although Ankara was usually reserved for someone a little more senior, a little more experienced. Hell, you just had to consider Turkey's geography to recognize its importance: the country bordered the Soviet Union, as well as Bulgaria, one of the USSR's satraps in the Warsaw pact, not to mention Syria, Iraq, and Iran. Relations with those three were good right now, but when you considered the potential for trouble in that part of the world, you could never count on that continuing for long. There had already been two Arab-Israeli wars, and given the enmity between those people, another one could never be very far off. Thankfully, the Turks actually liked the Israelis, and a close trading relationship had evolved between the two countries, including with their defense industries. And the Turks had their own issues with the Arabs, seeing as how the Ottomans had ruled over the Arabs for about the past 500 years. Memories lived long in that part of the world, and neither group cared much for the other, according to the analysts.

No, Baier doubted the problems lay with the Turks meddling in and upsetting any of our operations, at least those they knew about. There had been no reporting that under Breckenridge the relationship had faltered. But the man did remain a bit of a puzzle for Baier. Delgrecchio had gotten Baier access to Breckenridge's personal file, or at least parts of it that related to his tour in Ankara, which was just a year old at this point. Breckenridge had a reputation as a solid officer with a host of recruitments in East

Asian posts. But in their brief encounters, the man had struck Baier not as a sycophant or ass-kisser so much as someone who hesitated to tell truth to power. That was a major tenet among Agency officers, the delivery of the unvarnished and objective truth to policymakers, regardless of their political persuasion or importance. Of course, that did not mean that Breckenridge was dishonest, nor could one assume that he was unique. It happened, especially when confronted or challenged by the powerful. More often, it hinted more at conflict avoidance, or even an ambition that avoided delivering bad news so that the messenger did not suffer for doing his job.

If there was one thing Baier was sure about, it was the man's ambition. It fit with his prep school and family background from Bloomfield Hills outside Detroit. Daddy had probably worked for one of the automotive giants, and Breckenridge would have been expected to succeed in whatever career path he chose, even one in his country's civil service. And that must have been especially true for a career within an institution that had been founded on the shoulders of elite private schoolers from the Ivy league and other prestigious eastern colleges. Breckenridge himself had migrated to an eastern prep school—Choate—and then moved on to Dartmouth, both of which were no doubt seen as signs of success and arrival. Then again, so what? That sort of background and breeding was hardly unique or unusual at Langley.

More to the point, there had been no reports—or even rumors—of dissatisfaction or poor morale among the personnel in the station. Or of any troublemakers. But Baier figured he would have to see about getting a look into the officers' files as well, especially those handling the assets who had been lost. That would be a challenge, though, and it would test Delgrecchio's ability to deliver on his promise of a free hand. Not to mention his pull with the seventh floor. Since the lost agents had been Soviets, then their handlers would have come from the Soviet Division. Or at least they would have had to serve a form of apprenticeships before being allowed to polish such precious jewelry. And those people were about as tight-lipped and closed-fisted as anyone in the Agency. It was almost as though the sense of camaraderie had been taken to an absurd extreme. They considered their work to be the Holy Grail of American espionage, and few were deemed worthy of entry behind the tall and thick barriers that guarded the entry to their chapels and even further, behind the sacred altars.

Baier stared at his wife, not having realized that during his brief mental journey the sheet had fallen to her waist. He pondered her body for a moment, admiring the curve of her hips and breasts. He considered himself to be an extremely lucky man for having found her and gotten her to accept him as her soulmate after the horrors of war and occupation in the ruins of the Third Reich. He shot up suddenly with a start. Sabine awoke and rolled over, her eyes wide in surprise.

"What the…?" she muttered. "Where are you going, Karl?"

"The sauce," Baier exclaimed. He jumped naked from the bed and ran downstairs. He just prayed it hadn't burned during their lovemaking. "My mother always said you should stir it every five to ten minutes or so."

# CHAPTER THREE

The desk the Soviet Affairs Division had provided was enclosed inside a narrow cubicle in a back corner of a vault that few were allowed to enter. Despite having a Top Secret and a collection of codeword clearances that probably matched those of anyone else in the room, Baier had been relegated to a corner spot that provided little more than a desktop and sparse lighting. It also had a window, although the view into the courtyard below was almost completely blocked by the side panel of his workspace. He had to ring for admission to the room and was not allowed to bring in a notebook or borrow anything to write on while he read through the files. 'No,' had been the simple response he received when he asked if he could take notes.

"Stop whining," Delgrecchio had said when Baier complained that first afternoon after spending roughly six hours plodding through a small mountain of files. "They even performed their own background check on you to make sure you could be trusted not to sell the family jewels."

"I guess they didn't look very hard."

"For God's sake," Delgrecchio exclaimed, "don't joke like that. You'll end up reading these files with a loaded pistol at your ear." A smile broke through Delgrecchio's chin that looked like a crack in a concrete façade. "It probably helped that you were the guy who brought Chernov out of Berlin. They did appreciate that, even if Angleton is still as suspicious as he is goofy. It's not every day that they get to debrief a KGB colonel." Delgrechio thought for a moment. "Hey, that might even have helped sway those people in your favor. They don't like Angleton any more than you do."

"That's good to know. I'll remind my watchdogs of that when I have to take a pee."

Baier hoped his research there would not take too long. In addition to the mistrust, there was also the factor of his physical discomfort. The metal chair they gave him, for example, was hard and cold on his rear end, presumably to induce him to engage in some speed reading. And it was working. Baier grabbed the personnel file on top of the small pile in front of him and began to read about the deputy station chief in Ankara. It wasn't long before he recognized the hallmarks of a typical Midwesterner—much like himself—if such a thing were possible. Fred Badger had come to the Agency from Dubuque, Iowa. Unlike most Catholics from there, Badger was not of German extraction, but Baier decided not to hold that against him. Instead, Badger's family came from one of the Irish-American groups that Baier guessed had migrated to the area, probably in the last century to work in the lead or tin mines. He had originally gone to Iowa State University to study to become a vet, but after a year of science classes had found his true happiness in English Literature. And Badger's success at the Agency looked like one of those mythical American stories, where the first generation of sons and daughters had been able to lift themselves up from their families' migrant beginnings into middle-class prosperity. This was Badger's third tour, and he was now Breckenridge's deputy chief of station, a pretty quick rise through the ranks. His evaluation reports from Ankara were all solid—quite positive, in fact—which hinted at a good relationship between the two.

Badger had handled the KGB officer, who had been kidnapped in broad daylight off the streets of Ankara and later executed in Lubyanka prison, the logical end in that service for anyone caught spying for the other side. The poor sap had been a mid-level officer who had agreed to Badger's pitch after a yearlong recruitment effort. The guy had been reporting on KGB activities in Turkey and occasionally elsewhere in the region for nearly a year before he was hustled off an Ankara street as Badger watched helplessly from a café nearby, just outside the medieval citadel that sat at the heart of Ankara's old city. The two had scheduled a meeting for that night, and it was clear that the Soviet swipe team had been aware and waiting for their KGB colleague, one Ivan Levkovsky, to come along. Interestingly, none of the reporting on the case showed any sign of suspicion that the KGB was on to Levkovsky. There had been no warnings of careless communications— the guy had followed Badger's instructions to the letter—or the indiscriminate spending that could prove so disastrous by pointing to an unexplained and large income. It was exactly what one would expect from a seasoned professional like Levkovsky. In fact, Badger had placed Levkovsky's salary in a savings account in London for future use, once he and his family would have been smuggled to safety—should the need arise. Rather than a life of comfort and freedom in the West, that family could now count on a dismal future in the farther reaches of Mother Russia. It was the kind of unfortunate ending that every case officer worked to avoid, but that still happened on occasion. Reading the story of Levkovsky's sad end, Baier felt inspired by the need to find out what really happened.

The second collection of cable traffic told the story of Robert Hughes, a second-tour case officer from Seattle, Washington. A graduate of the University of Washington, he almost immediately won Baier's favor as someone who had avoided the normal route of entry after serving his apprenticeship at the Harvards or Amhersts of the Eastern establishment. Most of those schools, in Baier's opinion served as little more that cookie-cutter nurseries for the sons and daughters of the Eastern elite. Hughes had focused on Soviet studies while getting a degree in international affairs, and he had passed on a Foreign Service assignment to join the Agency. As a dyed-in-the-wool Midwesterner Baier was happy to find colleagues who broke from the Agency's traditional mold, and Baier was coming to like this guy more and more as he read on. Hughes's first tour had been in Central America—Honduras, to be exact—which made as much sense as any Agency posting, given his concentration on the Soviet Union. But he got to Soviet affairs eventually once he arrived in Turkey, handling a long-time

Foreign Ministry asset, who had been reporting for almost five years. The Soviet diplomat, Alexander Kosrov, had been recruited in Paris near the end of his tour there, but had continued the relationship during his posting in Rome, and now Ankara. That had ended, sadly, after a poisoning incident at the Pera Palace Hotel in Istanbul. What made that particular ending so insulting—aside from the asset's loss of life, of course—was that it all occurred in the shadow of the American Consulate next door. Baier did not doubt that that gruesome touch had been intentional.

Again, there were no indications that Kosrov's cover had been blown at any point before his death. Hughes had been meeting him in Istanbul for over a year and a half, precisely to avoid any prying eyes from the Soviet diplomatic and intelligence community in Turkey's capital. But to no avail, obviously.

"Everything okay here?"

Baier turned to find his guardian angel looking over his shoulder, white shirt sleeves rolled up past the elbows and the striped regimental tie pulled about a third of the way from the collar. Sunlight peeked over the barrier by the window and streaked his crew cut with flashes of silver.

"Yeah, sure. Any chance I could get a cup of coffee from you guys? This kind of reading material can get a bit tiresome."

The guardian shook his head as the hands went to his waist. "Sorry. We don't have any extra cups."

"Okay then," Baier returned to file pile, "I shouldn't be too much longer here."

"Fine, then. Just let me know when you're through."

The third folder covered the longer and undistinguished career of Steve Garner, now on his fifth tour. Garner looked to be stuck at the GS-13 level and not destined for future management. His problem appeared to be a lack of recruitments, a sure path to stagnation in a career dependent on a numbers game of new assets and numerous, highly-graded field reports. Coming from Nashville, Tennessee, Baier wondered if Garner was the quintessential 'good ol' boy.' Then he read that Garner's family lived in west Nashville—some neighborhood called Belle Meade—

which Baier remembered during his brief stop in the city on a tour of Civil War battlefields with Sabine, as the more prosperous part of town. That, and his degree in History from Vanderbilt, suggested that Garner, or at least his family, was pretty well off.

He looked like a decent enough officer. His debriefing skills were allegedly excellent, something that had come across well in the many reports he filed from the other Soviet Foreign Ministry officer, Viktor Topokov, who had been recruited in Santiago, Chile nearly a decade ago. Baier found it interesting that this Topokov fellow had been stationed in Havana around the time of the Revolution and had been considered something of an expert on the new Cuban government. Well, that would certainly have helped over the last year, and now looked to be especially unfortunate, given the new crisis brewing over the Soviets' growing military presence on the island. And his material had been deemed valuable for the insight it provided on Soviet policy toward Europe and the Mediterranean region. What Baier found so puzzling was why someone like this would have been sent to Turkey just when US-Soviet relations were becoming increasingly strained—dangerous even—and his expertise would seem to have been needed in the region or perhaps back in Moscow. And at such a critical time, with the missile crisis brewing in Cuba. He had arrived in the spring of that year, late April to be exact. But instead of enlightening the top policymakers in Moscow, he had been shot in the back of the head just outside the Istanbul bazaar.

Garner did not appear to be responsible for any lapse in security or handling that would have exposed his asset. Again, the station was dealing with an experienced asset, someone whose salary had been placed in a trust fund back in the States to take care of the Soviet diplomat's children and their university education once they had all arrived in America, whenever that was supposed to happen. Garner had done a couple postings in West Africa, like the Ivory Coast and Senegal—his French was supposed to be excellent—and Europe, primarily Scandinavia. Baier wasn't sure how much good his French would be there, but he guessed Paris and Brussels had been spoken for at the time of his reassignment.

In any case, he had stumbled upon the dead Russian on his way to the meeting. And once more, the KGB hit team appeared to have been aware of the rendezvous, since the corpse was found near the café Garner had selected for the meeting.

"Yo, I'm done here," Baier shouted in the general direction of his guardians. He stood and walked to vault door, not bothering to wait for permission or to see if anyone retrieved the files. 'Fuck 'em,' he thought. He'd be more polite responding to their directions once they had been to finishing school. Or at least offered him a cup of coffee. He was stopped short by a voice from another back corner of the vault.

"Hey, Mister Baier. The chief wants to see you before you leave."

Baier turned, his fist around the door handle. "What does Ricky want?"

"You'll have to ask him. And, please, don't call him that."

Baier strolled to an office at the opposite end of the room, a small windowless chamber that felt so tight Baier wondered if the lack of space and oxygen was intended to prevent any of the secrets from circulating and possibly escaping. The walls, like the rest of the vault, were painted in an off-white color that brought to mind melted vanilla ice cream. Here, though, there were no pictures to provide some backdrop or break the monotony. Richard Spronk sat behind a nearly bare metal desk, his tie tight against the collar of a white dress shirt and the cufflinks still clinching his wrists. The man was thin--angular, actually--and Baier nearly asked if he ever ate any meat and starches. This guy was definitely not from the Delgrecchio school of fine dining. Hollow cheeks rested under a head of black hair that glistened under a thin sheen of Brylcream. Or so Baier guessed. Although he appeared at first glance to be a mixture of man and robot, two deep blue eyes looked out at Baier and everyone else they saw as if they were a pair of searchlights, penetrating enough to see right through you. The glasses set within thin metal frames failed to hide their depth. It was the first time he had met Spronk, and Baier understood now why this man had a reputation for intelligence and insight. It couldn't be any other way. Basically, he did not appear to have any other human talents. Or personality.

"Thanks for letting me spend some time here," Baier said.

"Did you find whatever it was you were looking for?"

Clever, thought Baier. He knew exactly why I was here. "Well, not everything. I still don't know why those assets of yours were lost. But I hope some time in Ankara will clear that up."

"Just what do you think you will find out there that nobody else could?"

"I wasn't aware that anyone else had tried."

"Of course, they have. We have. And Jim Breckenridge is fully capable of figuring out what happened. He has done an excellent job out there, and we will welcome him back with a position of appropriate authority."

"I take it he belongs to your division." Spronk nodded. "Then I can see why you're so defensive."

Spronk bristled at the implications of Baier's statement. His face turned red for just a moment. But seeing as how not a muscle in the man's body had moved up to that point, Baier figured he must have been rattled to display even that little bit of emotion.

"You know, if it hadn't been for your exfiltration of this Chernov character we would never have consented to you coming in here."

"So, I've heard. Just how long do you think you would have been able to ignore the instructions from the CI division and the seventh floor?"

Spronk was silent for a moment as he pondered his reply. In the end, he ignored the question. "Just see to it that you do not let Angleton and his henchmen, like your friend Delgrecchio, interfere and bury this mystery along with the others he has tried so hard to hide. We need answers, not more martinis."

"I'm glad we can agree on that much. But Delgrecchio will not be your problem. Or mine."

"And neither will Breckenridge. You would be wise not to waste your time on him. He can be touchy at times, but the man is a true patriot."

"Where do you suggest I put my attention and efforts?"

"Try the case officers. They probably screwed up. It's usually the case."

"If it is, then I will find out."

Spronk let a wisp of air escape from between lips separated by no more than a crack. His eyes did not move from Baier's face.

After what seemed like an hour but was probably no more than twenty seconds, Baier turned and marched from the vault. If the old cliché was physically possible, steam would have seeped from his ears. More than forewarned, he was angry at the attempt to direct his inquiry by someone who was clearly an interested party with an overpowering sense of turf. Some people just needed to get out more, he concluded. Which was precisely what he planned to do now. He had one more stop before he left for Turkey, and it would take a while to get there. He had to drive out past Louden County and Virginia's horse country, to the foothills of the Shenandoah Mountains to visit an old friend and former nemesis for his next discussion. Hopefully, the sun would still be shining throughout the drive. It was warm enough to ride with the window open, and Baier planned to let the scent of late summer or early fall, whichever season was alive west of the capital, clear his head of the Washington maneuvers and plotting.

• • •

The late-afternoon drive out to Berryville, Virginia took longer than Baier had expected, interrupted by heavy traffic and stop lights until he passed Middleburg. The sunny weather, though, was not a disappointment. Nor was its therapeutic effect. Once he got to Paris the traffic and the lights dwindled, and he made it to Berryville in time to grab a quick burger at a diner along Route 340. The Appalachian Mountains rolled like heavy hills over a low ridge in the near distance, carpeted in a brilliant and heavy green lush with vegetation and hints of wildlife. It was an impressive backdrop, the path before them broken by the open fields and fence posts that marked Virginia's horse country. He could understand why Sergei Chernov had chosen this area to settle in after he had been exfiltrated from Europe less than a year ago. Despite the impressive scenery, the real estate prices were low enough to offer a real bargain to a newcomer living off a reward and a stipend from Uncle Sam. His information on KGB and GRU activities and personnel in Europe had certainly been worth it, even if it had been like pulling teeth to get it past James Jesus Angleton. Now Baier wanted to see if there was anything else he could glean from Chernov's extensive experience and insight that might help Baier meet this new challenge.

This was Baier's first visit to the reclusive expatriate, and he was surprised by the modest bungalow Chernov had purchased, one that sat on the outskirts of town, presumably to keep curious eyes and inquisitive neighbors to a minimum. Chernov's location—he was living here under an assumed name, of course—was still a strictly guarded secret, given the Soviet habit of trying to knock off those whom the Kremlin believed had betrayed the Revolution, such as it was. Even Baier had been denied information on the Russian's location until he could come up with a plausible reason to know it. Apparently, the loss of three Soviet assets in the space of six weeks provided reason enough.

The modest, two-story structure looked inviting and comfortable, and it was probably more than enough room for a bachelor like Chernov. Baier suspected that he still harbored dreams of bringing any surviving siblings he might find to the United States, plus their families, which would probably require a move to something larger. Until then, this would certainly do. The half-acre that belonged to the property also gave Chernov plenty of room for the gardening Russians were so fond of. He just hoped this Russian did not present him with jars of cucumbers and tomatoes and the like, pickled for use through a long Russian winter.

"Herr Baier, to what do I owe this distinct pleasure?"

Chernov stood in the open door behind a porch that stretched along the entire front of the house. A porch ceiling of white plywood under a set of dark grey shingles that lined the roof kept the sun at a distance. Baier left his car in the driveway that ran beside the house to a two-car garage at the back. He assumed the Russian must have seen him drive up.

"Not out gardening or taking care of your lawn today? Or have you hired a landscaper, like a good American capitalist?"

Chernov laughed. "No, no. Yard work is about the only exercise I get these days. That and the gardening. And I should be able to send you home with some fresh tomatoes, which I am sure your lovely wife will appreciate. I still have a few."

Baier climbed the stairs and extended his hand. "Thank you. I like them, too."

"They are the last of my crop…"

"Perhaps you should keep them in that case," Baier interrupted.

No, no." Chernov shook his head while still shaking Baier's hand. "They will be perfect for your country's famous BLTs."

Chernov led the way indoors and pointed to a sofa set along a back wall in a living room that looked out on the street in front of the house. A brick fireplace to the left was already set for a fire. Baier nodded in its direction.

"You'll find it's kind of early for that sort of thing in Virginia. Remember, Sergei, you are not in Russia now."

"Yes, yes, of course. But old habits die hard, Herr Baier. Besides, it makes the home look more welcoming, I believe." He started toward the kitchen. "It's too late for coffee, but can I get you something else to drink? A vodka, perhaps?"

Baier shook his head and waved his hands. "Gosh, no, Sergei. I have a long drive home. A beer will do."

Chernov returned with two bottles of Pabst and two glasses. The two men took their seats at either end of the sofa. Chernov poured Baier's beer, before taking care of his own.

Baier surveyed the room, noticing the absence of any wall hangings. "Still getting settled, Sergei? Or are you waiting until some of your family are found and able to join you?" Chernov had never married, and he had no children. But he had left a brother and sister behind in Europe, both of whom had fled the Revolution in 1917. Baier had discovered that the brother had been shot by a Soviet assassin, which touched off Chernov's own betrayal and flight. Neither Baier nor Chernov had been able to locate the sister before Baier was forced to smuggle Chernov to freedom after fifteen years of on-again-and-off-again competition and cooperation in the world of Cold War espionage.

"Alas, Herr Baier, that reunion remains a dream for me."

"Have you met any of your neighbors yet?"

Chernov laughed briefly. "Yes, sort of. Several have stopped by to say hello, and the lady across the street brought over a hideous casserole to welcome me to the town. Something with a pasta she called macaroni and tuna fish. There was also some bland soup mixed along with green peas to cover the vegetable part of the recipe, I guess." He shrugged. "But as you can imagine, I have avoided becoming too friendly and close with anyone here. You never know…"

"True, Sergei, true. I'm glad to see that you remain a real professional. You will live longer that way."

Chernov leaned back against the cushions of the sofa. "But I am sure you did not come here for a social conversation. I am assuming you are here primarily for professional purposes. What can I do for you?"

Baier raised his glass and pointed it at his host. "Cheers, Sergei. And, yes, you are correct. I am here to see you professionally, although I am glad to see that you appear to be reasonably happy." Baier paused to consider how best to phrase his next question but then decided to plunge in. "What might you know about KGB operations in Turkey?"

Chernov sipped his beer, then set the glass back on the coffee table to their front. "That is a big and very open question, Herr Baier. What specifically would you like to know? I'll see what I can remember, although I am not sure any of it is still relevant."

"Can you give me some idea of how large a presence your old organization might have there and what sorts of things your former colleagues would concentrate on?"

"I seem to recall us having a fairly large group there, something like thirty to forty officers in various cover positions. Not all were posing as diplomats, of course."

"That's pretty damn big."

"Yes, of course. And that is actually a conservative estimate. But Turkey is an important strategic target. And naturally we would try to infiltrate the Turkish government. They are, after all, a member of NATO. We would target the military especially, since they practically run the country and provide the foundation for its standing and the basis for its power in the region."

"Okay, that certainly makes sense. What about us?"

"Us? You mean the Americans in general?"

"Sure. Who would your former service be most interested in?"

"Herr Baier, surely you realize that any American would be viewed as a great prize. If someone could recruit one your countrymen, it would guarantee that officer's future. American diplomats, but even more, members of the American military in Turkey would be special targets, if only because of your close relationship with the Turkish hosts."

"What things besides the military capabilities and intentions of the Turks would you be interested in?"

"The government's policies, of course. But especially relations with your country and other members of NATO. And then there would be interest in views and policies on the Soviet Union." Chernov sipped his beer. "But that should be obvious, Herr Baier."

"Have your old colleagues had any success there? Either against the Turks or us?"

Chernov shook his head and reached for his beer glass. "Not that I am aware of. But then you surely know that a recruitment like that—I mean the Americans, of course--would be closely guarded. Only a handful of people would be aware of an operation like that."

"And the Turks? How valuable would that be?"

"Oh, very much so, I would estimate. But not as much as one of your own, Herr Baier." He paused. "Unless, of course, it provided an opening to an American recruitment."

"How serious would your counter-intelligence efforts be in Turkey?"

Chernov chuckled. "Surely, you are aware, Herr Baier, that our CI programs are intense wherever we work. Such a thing is unavoidable when you have so little trust in those who work for you."

Baier drank some more of his beer. Chernov had learned the American practice of serving his beer cold, which made it especially tasty on a hot and humid day like this one. Chernov pointed at Baier's glass with a questioning look in his eyes. Baier waved him off.

"No thanks. One will be enough. But what about my colleagues there?"

"Oh, that would be an even bigger prize. Your people sit at the top of the list. Surely you have guessed as much as that." Chernov smiled. "And I do not say that out of flattery, Herr Baier. I already have my house and stipend."

"Did you ever hear of any hint that one of us—my people, I mean—had been recruited?"

"No. But as I said, if such a thing did happen, that would be a very closely guarded secret."

"And a Turk?"

"I am afraid that is a negative as well. Again, it would be heavily guarded. Not as much as an American, of course, but still protected all the same."

"Well, that's good to hear, I guess. But if the KGB was to discover that Soviet officers from whatever organization had betrayed their country, what is the most likely way for them to find out?"

"Ah, that is difficult to say. It would, of course, depend on the specific case. Someone on your side could have gotten careless with his security or tradecraft. Or perhaps the recruited source did. The temptation to spend new money is great after a life in the Soviet Union."

"And if it is none of that?"

Chernov frowned. "Then the most likely way to learn of something like that is through a penetration of your government. Or dare I say it, of your organization." He paused. "There is always the possibility of a penetration of the host government or its security service, but that would probably provide little benefit against your activities. If you had recruited one of ours, for example, I doubt you would share this sort of information with the Turks. Or any host service, for that matter. So, in such a case a penetration of the host, or Turkish service would not help much. No, it would have to be a source in your organization."

Chernov drained his beer and studied the face of his guest. Baier kept his own eyes focused on the small chip in the glass top on the coffee table next to the coaster that held his beer glass. He glanced over at Chernov's glass when the Russian returned it to the table empty. He then looked up at his host, but he stayed silent.

"Have you lost an asset in Turkey, Herr Baier?" He paused, then raised a hand. "No wait. I do not expect you to answer that."

Baier did not respond for several seconds. "How long, Sergei, would your old organization let a case run once they knew that one of your people—I mean, any Soviet officer, not just someone in intelligence—had turned before taking action to close it out?"

Chernov shrugged again and looked out his front picture window before turning his attention to Baier. "That depends, of course. They would let things continue for some while, in all probability, in order to learn more about your own officers and their tradecraft. It is always an objective to learn how the other side operates in order to negate their activities. In my experience, once we had learned as much as we thought we could, then we would, shall we say, terminate the case."

"But wouldn't you try to turn our asset? You know, run him as a double agent?"

"Again, that depends."

"On what?"

"On the individual and his motivation, what sort of leverage we would have."

"Leverage?"

Chernov nodded. "Yes, leverage. Over the man, his family, his motives for the betrayal. You know, many officers must leave their families at home when they serve abroad to prevent defections."

"You wouldn't try to run a disinformation campaign?"

Chernov glanced out his window again, then stood and paced the room. He stopped in front of Baier, who remained seated. "Herr Baier, you must understand something about my former service. Indeed, about the Soviet mentality. We were—and still are, I am sure—essentially defensive in our outlook and planning. We have been since the Revolution. Everything we do, especially as a service, stems from this perspective. You, of all people, should know that counterintelligence is our primary objective. It happens when you have so little trust, as I have said, in your people and how they are asked to live."

"You are not going to try to tell me that your services never initiate offensive operations, are you? Your people have had some very active operations in that field. They are even called 'active measures,' I believe."

"But you must realize the shell we have lived in ever since the expected world revolution failed to materialize. Berlin was supposed to be the center of the proletarian revolt, not Russia. When that failed, we essentially fell back into that shell. Even the move of our capital from St. Petersburg to Moscow reflected that changed outlook. In some ways it was the victory of the Slavophiles over the Europeanists because we basically turned our backs on Europe and retreated into our own medieval past. We have always seen ourselves as under attack from the West, a West that is in many ways superior. So, our purpose has largely been to protect ourselves. We have taken that to an extreme, in my view, but it usually precludes an offensive operation, such as the one you mentioned. Besides, those are extremely difficult and risky."

"You know, we have a saying here, Sergei. 'The best defense is a good offense.' Have you heard it?"

Chernov shook his head and smiled. "No, I have not. But for us that would almost certainly apply in military or diplomatic affairs. Not in intelligence matters. And if there was a rare situation in which we wanted to run an 'active measure,' as you say, we would never use someone we had turned. Rather, it would probably be someone we planted on your side and for that very purpose."

"Why is that?"

"Because you would almost certainly recognize the change in the individual's reporting. And then your suspicions would prevent you from accepting the new, tainted information. It might even give you an advantage of your own in the operation."

"But is there always this kind of risk in your eyes?"

"Yes, I believe so. And that has always been my sense of how our superiors viewed such an operation as well. The risk is that disinformation is often exposed almost immediately because it contradicts other, related information. And that exposes your own agent as someone who is being manipulated with this false information. And besides, it is nearly impossible to prevent leaks of what is going on to broader circles. The risk in losing our source is very high, and the prospect that your side will just accept our information is very small."

"So, you would count it out."

"Such a thing is conceivable only in very special cases. The potential reward would have to be very high to consider such a plan. And the broader purpose it supports would have to be very important, critically important."

"I see," Baier said. Thank you, Sergei."

Chernov studied Baier for a moment. "May I give you a word of warning?"

"What is it?"

"If indeed you have lost someone in Turkey—or anywhere, for that matter--they will try to convince you that the loss of your source has come about through a fault of your own. They are likely to try to blame it on a lapse in tradecraft by one of your officers. That serves two purposes, Herr Baier."

"And those are?"

"It protects their own source inside your government, assuming they have one. And it gives them an opportunity to thumb their noses at you. I believe that is the saying you use. They would take whatever opportunity they have to undermine your confidence."

"Yes, that is the phrase." Baier stood to go. "Thank you for the beer, Sergei."

"Yes, of course. I hope your visit helped with whatever problem you have right now."

Baier extended his hand. "Yes, as always. But you know, here in America you no longer need to call me 'Herr Baier.' It sounds unusual and too formal."

Chernov took Baier's hand and shook it. "Ah, but I like to use that title. It sounds good to my ears. It reminds me of our time together in Berlin and afterwards, times I like to remember." He smiled again. "Godspeed, Herr Baier. And good luck, Karl."

# CHAPTER FOUR

The morning sun broke over the mountains that ringed the Turkish capital with an orange glow tinged by streaks of yellow. It was a sky that looked as though it had broken from a furnace in the heavens, brighter even than Apollo's chariot and lit by centuries of history. Baier peeked through his half-closed eyelids at the Anatolian dawn that seemed to hold the promise of bright new revelations. He sat up, stiff from a night of uneven and uncomfortable sleep in unyielding airline seats. But then drifting clouds cast shadows thick with lines the color of charcoal that rolled down the sides of the rock covered mountains. Just moments earlier they had reflected a warming glow of morning sunlight.

Baier closed the shade over his window and shut his eyes again. His thoughts drifted back to Sabine. Their last night together before his departure had certainly been blissful, if such a mild word could accurately describe a night of lovemaking that had surprised Baier by its intensity. It was as though she had feared losing him and sought to strengthen their bond by a physical connection that had weakened with the years of marriage and familiarity. Baier shifted his weight to turn his head away from the commotion as the flight attendants began serving breakfast. He was not really hungry. He did ask for some water to quench the thirst that inevitably followed the free drinks he had been served much of the night before. And he certainly missed Sabine.

He really had no idea what awaited him below. It was October 12, and he already felt well behind the curve in his investigation. It had not taken long to set this trip in motion, which in Baier's mind demonstrated how seriously his superiors in Headquarters saw the recent losses in Ankara. They had even moved quickly to address what would normally have been a big problem, the cover for his visit. Delgrecchio's office had arranged, with the approval of the minions on the seventh floor, that he would continue his role as a trainer to avert suspicions from his Turkish hosts, State Department officers working in the Embassy in Ankara, and any overly curious members of the foreign intelligence community resident in the Turkish capital. Temporary training assignments abroad were not that unusual, and it was hoped that others in the American community in Ankara—if they took any notice of Baier's presence in the first place— would see him as just another Washington bureaucrat.

Many of the spies at least were aware of the recent deaths of the Soviet officers, of course, since something like that was all but impossible to hide. Rumors flew immediately. Baier was sure the local service—as well as some of the foreign ones—would be aware of his presence within hours of his arrival. But hopefully, none were aware of the double lives these three individuals had led, and the last thing Baier or any of his colleagues wanted was for someone to concentrate on his presence and its real purpose. That would seriously jeopardize whatever chances of success he might have. A crowded field in this line of work virtually guaranteed failure. So, Baier would pretend that he was there to provide additional training for Americans working at the Embassy should anyone, especially the foreign intelligence services and Turkish security, ask. Hopefully, he could leave it at that. If the Turks bought it, that might even help to spread the impression that his mission was an innocuous one. It would certainly help reduce any obstacles or adversaries he might encounter.

Breckenridge met Baier with a smile and an outstretched hand as soon as he walked through customs. After an overnight PAN AM flight to Paris, and the extension to Ankara on the Turkish national airlines, Baier was ready for a friendly face. His mouth was dry—the two cups of water had not helped much--his hair was matted in a sleepy hairdo that produced some odd angles, and his shirt and jacket looked as wrinkled as he felt. The sight of the transportation certainly helped, though. Breckenridge took Baier to a black Chrysler sitting comfortably at the curb just beyond the entrance to the terminal with its motor running and a driver standing at attention by the back door on the passenger side. The driver's crisp black suit matched the one Breckenridge was wearing, and Baier immediately felt a tinge of concern. He just hoped the symbolism of the color was unintended.

"Nice ride, Jim." Baier settled into the plush leather seat in the back as the Station Chief dropped in next to him on the driver's side. "You must have a nice budget. I'll have to see what I can do to follow in your footsteps out here."

"Well, I hope that won't be for another year or so. You haven't come to send me home, have you?"

Baier smiled and waved his hand in dismissal. "I'm not sure yet what I've come out here to do. At least not yet. But I am certainly not expecting any unpleasant surprises on your end."

Breckenridge relaxed back into the seat and made a half-turn in Baier's direction. "That's good to hear. But tell me, how was your flight? I assume you'll want to check in to your hotel first to freshen up after your journey."

Baier nodded. "Absolutely. Those transatlantic flights are getting tougher on me with every passing year. I got maybe an hour or two of sleep last night, and maybe another hour on the flight from Paris. So you can imagine how much use I'll be today."

"Understood. I was able to push your courtesy call on Ambassador Hare off until tomorrow afternoon. I realize you might still be fighting jet lag at that point, but your condition and attention span couldn't be worse tomorrow than it will be today."

"Thanks for that." Baier nodded in the direction of the driver and arched his eyebrows in question.

Breckenridge nodded in turn. "Yes, he's Turkish, and his English is patchy but good enough to get by as a member of the Embassy community. He's been driving me and my predecessors for about a decade now. It's really helpful to have someone who knows the city and its surrounding area, and who is used to driving in this country. As you can imagine, the rules of the road are considerably different here, and an American driver, especially one newly arrived, would probably cause about an accident a week on these streets. And that's if he was careful."

"Understood." What Baier really understood was that he would keep the conversation to generalities about Turkish history, culture, and the scenery. "And my accommodations?"

"We've put you in the Elit Palace. It's a nice place, quite classy actually, and it's just a couple blocs off Ataturk Boulevard, a major street in Ankara and the one our Embassy is on. It's about a fifteen-minute walk to our office."

Baier held up an index finger. "Ah, but, Jim, I am a fast walker."

Breckenridge smiled. "Okay then, make that a fourteen-minute walk."

"That's better. Tell me, though, what the heck happened here with the military coup two years ago? Just how stable is Turkey these days? They've been struggling with a patch of pretty shaky coalition governments, from what I understand."

"Who did you hear that from. Our analysts?"

Baier nodded. "That's right. I found them to be pretty helpful before I left. Getting the lay of the land, so to speak."

Breckenridge looked into the distance from the window behind Baier and pointed at the mountains several miles off. "I'm sure they were. I don't know what all they may have told you, of course, but maybe I can pass along some impressions of my own, impressions that point to some of the underlying currents here."

"Sure, go ahead. I got some of that back home as well, but I'd certainly like to hear what you have to say after living and working here for over a year."

"Well, you see those hills? And the shacks that run up and down the mountainsides?"

Baier turned and looked in the direction the station chief was pointing. The sight of sprawling shacks of corrugated metal rising from the ground toward the sky like new and wild vegetation along the sides of mountains that ran into the horizon lay off to the car's left as it sped down the highway towards the city proper.

"Sure. I noticed those when we approached Ankara for our landing. And?"

"Well, they symbolize a lot about modern Turkey. Or I should say the Turkey that is still trying to leave its Ottoman legacy behind and modernize itself into the twentieth century."

"How so?"

"Those are called 'gecekondos.' It's means 'without a permit.' Those shacks you see—mostly walls and roofs of corrugated tin with no modern conveniences like plumbing or electricity—are settled by people coming in from the countryside looking for work and a future. They throw those things up without any kind of building permit because they're quick and cheap."

"What's that got to do with the coup and the coalition governments?"

"A lot of the political turmoil here has to do with the economy. Menderes and his Democratic Party thought they could modernize Turkey's economy and society by simply opening everything up as an instant transition to the liberal, capitalist economy on the Western model, as we and other countries urged him to do. But the DP never laid the basic groundwork to bring it off. The ones who benefited were the large landowners who were able to exploit the new system and the cheap government credit to expand their property and wealth, forcing a lot of the peasants either into indentured labor or off the land altogether. But there's little industry here, at least not enough to absorb all the excess labor. There were other problems as well, like lack of foreign investments and hard currency, which cut back on imports and industrial production while fueling inflation..."

"So, it was all about the economy?"

"No, not quite. The DP emerged as the most popular party by complaining about the one-party dictatorship of the Republican People's Party that preceded them for about thirty years..."

"Ataturk's party, right?"

"Yeah, and they ruled pretty much as a one-party dictatorship, just like many complained after Ataturk's death in 1938. But once Turkey opened up to a multiparty system and Menderes became prime minister he evolved into more of a dictator than the RPP ever was, both regarding Turkey and his own party. Plus, the fool dabbled with the whole religious-secular issue, which is probably the biggest hot-button in Turkish politics and society."

"How so?"

"The analysts explained the importance of secularism for the Ataturk Revolution, right?"

"Yeah, of course. He abolished not only the Sultanate but the Caliphate as well and mandated strict restrictions on Islam's public role," Baier explained. "I understand he wanted to remove not only the Ottoman's role as the hereditary leaders of Turkey, but also their position as the religious leaders of Islam. He even forbade the use of Arabic script, substituting the Latin alphabet, and the use of Arabic in the call to prayer."

"It's true that the RPP established religious education in the schools in the late 40s, but that was basically to control it," Breckenridge continued. "Well, Menderes re-allowed Arabic for the prayer call and returned religious channels to the radio. He didn't do a whole lot more than that officially, but he created the impression of a more permissive attitude, which in turn generated a lot of religious activity in opposition to the secular government. And secularism is mandated here by the Constitution."

"One of the more useful conversations I had with the analysts before I left Washington was about that very issue," Baier said. "I get where Ataturk was coming from in terms of wanting to restrict the role of religion in Turkish society because he saw it as hindering the country's transformation. But the analysts noted that it wasn't all that easy. You know, the old adage about things being easier said than done. There are actually two Turkeys, they claim. One is the secular part of society that is all in on Ataturk's goal. Those are the people in the military and the civil servants, as well as the liberal intelligentsia and commercial classes, especially in the western part of the country."

"And you will find that many of those people have family connections back to the European parts of the old Ottoman Empire in the Balkans," Breckenridge interrupted. "Many of those families returned to the Anatolian heartland after the collapse of the Empire in 1919, and even in the years before right before the war when the Ottomans lost control of much of their Balkan holdings."

Baier continued. "The other group is mostly the rural peasants in the countryside, who remain very suspicious of all this modernizing and secularism, not to mention very conservative socially. In fact, there were even some revolts against Ataturk's reforms in the 1920s."

Breckenridge nodded enthusiastically. "That's right. Our guys in Langley know what they're talking about. And I doubt from what I have seen and heard in this country that those conservative and rural elements have bought in to the Revolution, as Ataturk and his cohort like to label the changes."

"Then why aren't they out there rebelling now?"

"Because they still follow the lead of their local strong men. You know the heads of the clans or tribes. Those guys have found it very lucrative to be a part of the system, and they all have arrangements with the parties to deliver the votes of their followers. Which pays them and the regions they control handsomely." He sighed. "Besides, there's always the Army."

"What do you mean?"

"Those guys see themselves as the guardians of Ataturk's Revolution, and they will not let anyone—and I mean anyone—endanger the progress they believe the changes installed by Ataturk have brought to Turkey. You know what 'Ataturk' means, don't you?"

"'Father of the Turks, right? And the tarikats, the religious orders that were supposedly driven underground after the rebellions in the 1920s? Are they still strong? Do they have many followers?"

Breckenridge sat back, and his eyes went wide, as though in surprise. "Oh, hell yes. I get the impression here that just about everyone—whether secular or openly Islamic—has some kind of connection to the tarikats, either through himself or a family member or a friend. It points to something else you might want to keep in mind as you pursue your mission here."

"And that would be?"

"The Turks have a very ambivalent view of their relationship with the West. Sure, they admire us and want to follow our lead, especially that of the U.S. That's actually been one of the major complaints against the government, regardless of the party in power, over the past few years: that Turkey is too dependent on us. But then there is also the deep-seated hatred of communism here, or anything that smacks of it. And believe me, there is no love lost here when it comes to the Soviet Union, especially after Stalin started pressuring Turkey for land concessions around the Straits and in the eastern part of the country as soon as the last war was over. He treated the Turks just as Catherine the Great and other Tsars did. And the Russians did make a lot of headway into eastern Anatolia in the First World War. It was in the Caucasus and along the Black Sea, territory the Russians have long coveted."

"And they have long had designs on Constantinople, if I remember my history lessons."

Breckenridge nodded. "Oh, hell yeah."

"But how did Stalin justify his push? Turkey was neutral in the second one."

"You think Papa Joe gave a damn? He was just following the dictates of the tsars' old foreign policy with its aims on Turkish territory. As you said, seizure of Constantinople was always a Tsarist dream, and Stalin was demanding a role in defense of the Straits. Guess where that would have led."

"It almost sounds like a love-hate thing with us?"

"Exactly. They do want to become more like the West and be accepted as such. And they do like to have our security guarantee. But there is a residual resentment and distrust that stems from the long history here."

"How far back does that go?"

"Way back. Memories are very, very long in this part of the world. They still think of and often refer openly to all Westerners as 'Franks.' That is a derisive term that harks back to the days of the Crusades, which they view from a completely different perspective. As you might imagine."

"The analysts also pointed to the lingering resentment over the Treaty of Sevres that would have broken Turkey apart after World War I."

"That's right. And I swear, most Turks believe that we Westerners continue to hold on to that Treaty as a guide to what we would like to do with Turkey at some point in the future."

Baier shook his head and rubbed his face to push the sleep and exhaustion away from him a little while longer. "Thanks, Jim. This is all very helpful. Like I said earlier, it is always nice to get the lay of the land for any area you'll be working in. I do wonder, though, what it will have to do with my investigation."

"That's one thing about Turkey you need to keep in mind, Karl. There are a lot of currents at work in the country, many of them contradictory. I wouldn't be surprised if the things you discover—assuming there is anything to discover here—fall into the middle of those. It all has a tendency to multiply the challenges and obscure the trend lines. Not to mention the threats."

"Well, in that case, thanks again. And I'm glad we had such a good discussion during the long drive in from the airport. Just how far out is the damn thing? I mean, how long have we been driving here? And it looks like we still have a ways to go. We are still in Turkey, right?"

Breckenridge laughed. "It is quite far out. I've never asked or measured it myself. But it has to be at least ten to fifteen miles. Maybe more, even twenty. And as you no doubt noticed, there isn't much in the way of development on the way in." His arm swept the view outside their windows. "And you'll see that Ankara reflects the polar-like divisions I mentioned in Turkey. Pretty soon we'll be passing through the older part of town that stretches back to ancient times when this place was a trading outpost for the Greeks and Romans. You will see how narrow the streets are and how full of pedestrians, who seem to just spill over from the aged and crowded buildings around them. The old structures are more like remnants of packed dust than stone and brick. There's even a citadel on a hilltop you should visit. It's surrounded by a wonderful market where you can find some great bargains on carpets, copper, and spices, all of it surrounding this ancient stone fortress. Unfortunately, that is in pretty bad shape, although the government is making noises about restoring it."

"I'll keep that in mind. Sabine, I'm sure, is expecting me to bring something nice and useful back with me."

"After that we'll enter the more modern part of town. There you can see all the government buildings in their neo-classical style with these large and impressive stone and concrete presences that look like testaments to the endurance of Ataturk's dream. And the residential sections aren't bad either. You'll find some really modern and spacious properties there."

"Like your house, I'm guessing."

Breckenridge smiled. "Well, yes. I've been living pretty well on this assignment. I'm guessing you'll spend most of your time in this part of the city. Unless, of course, you decide to visit some of the sites in the older part of town. They've got an excellent archeological museum, with a nice café where you can sit and take in the view of old Ankara. If you're so inclined."

"In addition to the citadel?"

"Oh sure. The historical museum covers the Hittite and other ancient periods really well. Didn't you have a background in history from your days at Notre Dame?"

"Yes, I took a minor in that. It has always been my great love, even though my parents insisted I study something more practical."

"Like chemistry?"

Baier smiled again and nodded. "That's right. But it was that chemistry degree that eventually led me to our employer. In a roundabout way."

"Which was?"

"I started my career as part of Operation Paper Clip in Berlin. Since I had been a science major, the Army had the bright idea of sending me to the German capital to report on Germany's scientific capabilities and maybe even round up a few of those famous German scientists along the way."

"Have you done much work on chemistry or other fields since then?"

"Nope. None whatsoever."

Breckenridge punched Baier's shoulder. "Well I guess that's how most of us get wherever we end up. Via a roundabout way." Breckenridge's hand shot up in the air between them. "One other thought, though. And it's important. Be careful with the food. Remember the axiom: 'if you can't peel it, don't eat it.' And stick to bottled water. I doubt you've had to worry too much about that sort of thing during your European tours."

Baier shook his head, then turned toward his window. He watched the old and modern sides of Turkey's capital pass by their car as the driver sped through the city as though he was in a hurry to get somewhere. It was probably that haste that kept Baier from falling asleep in the back seat of the car. For the most part. When he glanced up their car was pulling up to the curb in front of his hotel.

"Thanks for the warning. About the food and water, I mean. As for my schedule and plans, Jim, we shall see. I'll be dependent on you and your officers, of course, but hopefully I will be pursuing leads of my own at some point."

Baier climbed from the car and waited for the driver to drop off his luggage. A porter was at Baier's side almost immediately. He nodded in greeting, then carried Baier's suitcases inside.

Breckenridge leaned toward the open door on Baier's side. "Why don't you take it easy today, Karl. Like I said, you don't have to see the Ambassador until tomorrow. We have an office set up for you to use while you're here, but you'd probably just fall asleep if you came in today."

"That sounds like a reasonable plan, Jim. Hopefully, I'll also be able to speak with the officers involved in this. Have you set anything up with their schedules?"

"Not yet, but I'll see what I can do. That shouldn't be a problem."

It had better not be, Baier thought. It bothered Baier that the station chief hadn't thought of that. As he took in the hotel entrance through eyes fighting to hold their focus through a sleepy daze, Baier hoped that there were not other things the chief had overlooked. But he'd find out tomorrow.

Then Baier checked himself. There was no reason his sleepiness should make him so grumpy and suspicious his first day there. First some lunch. Food always helped. Then he would check his room for listening devices and any other unwelcome surprises. If he stayed awake long enough he might even try to call Sabine to let her know he had arrived in one piece.

# CHAPTER FIVE

The station chief was true to his word to provide an office for Baier to use while he was in town. To a degree. It was a very generous use of the term 'office.' True, Baier did have his own space, but it was more of a cubicle than an outright office. In fact, it was actually part of a larger office space, separated by a large temporary wall that did provide some degree of privacy. To be honest, though, that resembled a chalkboard more than a wall, resting as it did on a set of wheels. But at least no one was writing on it. There was also a desk, over which Baier could spread any files he was reading or notes he was taking. The working space was also set in the back corner of the larger office, where Baier had to make due with several pictures of Turkish landscapes and tourist spots from the previous year's calendar taped to the wall at his back for decoration. There was no window, and his chair provided the only coat rack of any sort. His dark blue suit jacket hung there now.

That was just what he was doing—plodding through a file—when Fred Badger knocked on the edge of his partition, as though it was a real office door. Badger made a weak attempt at a smile as he glanced at the ersatz wall.

"Sorry about the cramped working conditions, but we're pretty starved for working spaces right now. Hopefully, something will open up over the next few days."

Baier sat back and tossed his pen on top of the notebook he had set next to the file. Badger surprised Baier by the solid lines of his shoulders and chest, outlined against his white dress shirt. The blue tie made a nice match with the blue slacks. Badger actually gave off the impression of a college athlete waiting for his body to turn soft, something that looked to be a few years off yet. It was not what Baier had expected from reading the man's file.

"Oh, that's alright," Baier continued. "I don't plan on being here all that long anyway. Unless something really interesting and disturbing turns up. I suspect the real answer to our problem lies up in Moscow, anyway."

'Yeah, well, that remains to be seen. I have some suspicions of my own I'd like to pass along. Whenever you're ready, that is." Badger paused to take in the rest of the room, where two officers sat at their desks. Three more workspaces remained unoccupied, their occupants presumably off on field work of their own. "I don't want to prejudice your own efforts so early in the project, but..."

Baier raised his hand. "Not to worry. I'm a big boy. I think I can handle it." He waited but Badger did not offer anything more. "Is this a good time?"

Badger looked around the room once more and shrugged. "Sure. I suppose so. But let's go to my space."

The deputy chief led Baier about twenty yards down the hallway to an office on the left. Badger used his body to shield the numbers he selected as he spun the dial lock on his office door from Baier's view, then swung the door open and motioned for Baier to enter before him. Baier smiled, thinking the blocking maneuver was unnecessary, but that it was still nice to see that the officers here routinely practiced good security. At least from what he had seen so far. Baier took a seat on the sofa facing the desk and the window behind it, while Badger assumed his own place in the chair behind the desk.

"Before I start I wanted to ask if the Ambassador had anything interesting to say. As you no doubted expected, we had to reveal the real reason for your visit to him."

Baier sat back against the dark leather cushions and crossed his legs. The woolen fabric in his dark blue suit made a slight scratching sound as he did so. Badger followed suit, but his cotton slacks stayed silent. Baier noticed that they were dark blue, almost the same hue as his own. He guessed they both must have gotten the same fashion memo, as his colleagues at Langley liked to joke.

"Oh, and by the way," Badger continued, "I'm sorry we had to move your appointment with the Ambassador up to this morning. He had a change in his schedule with a call from the Foreign Ministry for later today. Rumor has it that the Turks are not too happy about the stories in the press that we may try to negotiate our way out of this missile crisis in Cuba by trading off the Jupiters we have stationed here and in Italy."

"Well, don't worry about the shift in my schedule. I may have had to come in earlier than planned, but, I mean, the Ambassador's the boss here. I'm working on his patch, so I'm always happy to accommodate his schedule."

"How did that meeting go?"

"Well, as far as I could tell. He was mostly interested in any scuttlebutt I could bring from Washington."

"About our missiles here?"

"Not that so much. More about when we might get some results from the U-2 overflights over Cuba that resumed a couple days ago, back on the 10th. It is still October, right?"

Badger laughed and nodded. "Jet lag still playing tricks with your head?"

"Yeah, probably," Baier conceded. "But I guess the Ambo figures there's no point in interfering in our efforts to understand what happened with the Soviet assets. He knows we have to investigate this kind of thing." Baier nodded more to himself than his colleague. "After all, he's the kind of customer who benefits as much as anyone from our reporting."

Badger leaned forward, his arms coming to rest on his desktop. "What did you tell him? About the overflights, I mean."

Baier picked at some lint on his slacks, then rolled his sleeves up just past the wrists. "I told him the truth. That I had no idea, especially since it wasn't information that would be broadcast around town. But if we did find anything, it would probably go right to the President. Not only are we in the midst of a major crisis with all sorts of implications for the future of our planet, but it was Secretary Rusk and National Security Advisor Bundy who decided to call them off in the first place. I also made so bold as to tell him that I did not think it was a very wise decision simply because there had been some problems from flights elsewhere, mostly over the Soviet Union. Sometimes the need for information outweighs the risks involved." Baier blew out his breath. "I did not add that it was a good thing those guys over at the Defense Intelligence Agency…"

"You mean DIA?"

Baier nodded. "Yeah, they helped pull our proverbial chestnuts out of the fire when they noticed back in September that the airbase and defensive missile layouts corresponded to those protecting ballistic missile sites back home in the USSR and started a drum beat to get the U-2 flights going again."

Badger almost laughed. "Well, even mentioning what you did to the Ambo took balls. We usually avoid commenting on policy. Did he have anything to say about that?"

"But in this case it touches directly on our work and our mission to keep the policymakers informed." Baier sighed. "In any case, the Ambo was a true diplomat. He took my protest in stride, even nodding in acknowledgement--if not in agreement—before continuing."

"Did he say anything about his appointment this afternoon?"

Baier shook his head. "Not really. He just said that he expected more difficult conversations as the crisis wears on."

"Did he say anything about the situation and mood in Turkey these days?"

Baier shook his head again and uncrossed his legs to lean forward. "Not a whole lot. He did say he thinks our analysts are a little too critical of Turkey nowadays."

"More so than the intel analysts at INR, I gather," Badger added. "I get the sense they've got a real case of clientitis over there."

"You mean the intel analysts in State's own shop?" Baier asked. Badger nodded.

"Well, he didn't belabor the point," Baier continued. "I assume that's because he didn't think it was all that appropriate or relevant to my mission here. I take it you think differently about Turkey these days than INR. Or am I wrong?"

Badger sighed and sat back against his chair. He ran his hand through the thick red hair along the top of his scalp and down the back while he studied the parking lot outside his window. The back end of the lot was bordered by a narrow brick building that housed the cafeteria and community store, where you could purchase liquor, soft drinks, snacks, and even some canned or boxed food. Baier considered grabbing a bottle of bourbon or single malt Scotch before he returned to his room at the hotel. It might help him sleep, at least until he got over his jet lag.

"No," Badger replied, "you are not wrong. I think the political situation in this country may have a part, even a big part, to play in this whole thing."

"You mean the Cuban missile crisis, or the loss of our assets?"

"Well, both, actually. But mostly the latter."

"How so?"

"Look, I gather Jim gave you an earful on the long ride in from Esenboga Airport yesterday about the basics of Turkish political life, especially the importance of Ataturk's reforms and the guy's godlike stature here."

"Yes, he did. I also had several extensive conversations with the analysts back in Langley before I left."

Badger nodded. Several times. "Good, good. But there's something going on here that you need to be aware of. I can't say that it definitely applies to your work here, but it could at least provide an important backdrop."

"And that would be?"

"Well, let's call it the many faces of Turkish nationalism. Look, they've been solid allies for us, and their army makes up a sizeable component of NATO's forces. They're probably the second largest military force after us. And the Turks definitely do not want to jeopardize their standing in Washington."

"So, what's the problem?"

"The problem is that attitudes are shifting here. I don't mean that the Turks are about to bolt from the Alliance or turn to Moscow any time soon, if ever. Good lord, if anyone tried to implement Communism in this country—no matter how it might look or what label you applied—there would be bodies swinging from every lamp post in the country. Washington is still the lodestar for politics and economic policy in Turkey."

"Again, so what's the problem?"

"The problem is that popular attitudes are changing, especially among the academic crowds and the intelligentsia."

"Do those matter all that much here?"

"Oh, for sure. It's kind of like Europe in that regard. And again, it isn't a 180-degree turn that I see coming. It's more of a feeling that they've been too dependent on us and for too little in return. It's more like grumblings of how some people are thinking that Turkey should be more open to pursuing its own way with regards to Africa, the Middle East, and even Europe. The latter is their most important trading partner, you know."

"What has set all this off and where do you think it's heading?"

"It has to do with that sense of too little payback from Washington. There has been some resentment at the lack of investment and what many here consider paltry economic aid. But the big deal right now is Cyprus."

"Oh, Jesus, the analysts mentioned how emotional that is," Baier remarked.

"I'll say. The Greeks and Turks were able to put the lid back on that bottle for a little while, but if you ask me, the genie could sneak out again anytime. It's a very emotional issue in Greece as well. The Turks basically distrust our Cyprus policy."

"Why is that?"

"Because they don't think we have their backs on what is a truly critical issue here. And the Brits are not handling it well at all. Those guys are still stuck in their old imperial mindset and think they can just muddle through, as they like to say. I mean, look at that total fuck-up over the Suez. They seem to be incapable of looking ahead. Their orientation is just so backward."

"Okay, but how does this fit with what I'm doing here?" Baier asked.

"Well, part of that greater self-reliance has to do with the Soviet Union."

"Go on."

"There are plenty here who want to see a less hostile policy toward the big neighbor to the north, especially now that Stalin has gone. The Soviets have been making all kinds of nice noises toward the Turks. Again, I don't see any big shift in policy here, but you need to remember that the Turks will always want to see themselves as their own bosses. Their ideas of Turkish history and the nation's importance will not always square with ours, especially regarding their present role in the world, or even the region. And there is a sense that the new developments in nuclear strategy—you know, like with the Polaris submarines and the more independent means of a nuclear response that they provide—have undermined Turkey's geostrategic importance. That is making them nervous. And nervous people react in unpredictable ways."

"Do you think we could encounter difficulties with the Turks as we investigate these three cases?" Baier pressed.

Badger sat forward again and shook his head. "I have a lot of trouble going that far. But you do need to remember that the Turks are not really our friends. They are certainly not our enemies. But they define their needs and interests differently, especially now. And that can lead to problems for how we—and I mean our Agency in particular—do business here."

"But you have nothing specific at this point."

Badger shook his head. "No, not really. But I would urge you to keep your mind open about a Turkish role in this business." Badger held his hand up as though to ward off a protest. "I'm not saying that they are solely responsible. But they could have been involved in some way. Just keep your mind open on this." Badger pushed himself away from his desk and stood. "I'll let you get back to the files. I just wanted to get all this off my chest. Besides, you must be getting pretty tired by now. Would a cup of coffee help?"

Baier stood and brushed the wrinkles out of his slacks. "Thanks, Fred. I do appreciate this. And, yes, coffee would most certainly help."

● ● ●

Baier--and Badger, for that matter--had been only partly right. The coffee helped, but only a little. Part of it was the files themselves. There was little in them that Baier had not seen already back in Langley. The newest pieces were the long, elaborate cables detailing the counter-surveillance routes the three case officers had taken before their meetings with the three Soviet assets and afterwards throughout their time in Ankara and Istanbul. Those ran on for pages as they described in intimate and boring detail the routes taken, block by city block, and everything the officers had registered about their surroundings and whatever suspicions might have been raised. But according to these accounts, all had gone smoothly. Nothing pointed to lapses in tradecraft, at least not on this front, that would have betrayed the nature and purpose of the engagements. Nor was there any reference to problems with the discretion and tradecraft of the three Russian assets. The cases all read like textbook examples of how to run an operation.

But Baier persevered. He wanted to get this background reading out of the way before he visited the sites of the kidnapping and murders in person to get a better feel for what might have gone wrong. And he almost made it through the entire program. It was only when he found his head nodding off and falling to pages on the desk that Baier decided to call it a day. He was actually quite proud of himself for having made it to late afternoon.

He decided to swing by the Embassy store to pick up a bottle of Jack Daniels before heading back to his hotel, along with several bottles of water for drinking and brushing his teeth. Baier recalled the station chief's warning about getting careless with his food here, and he figured that that must go double for the drinking water.

He also decided to walk back to his room, thinking that the fresh air would help rejuvenate him. Besides, it wasn't all that far. There were certainly plenty of taxis available, had he wanted one. The entire length of Ataturk Boulevard, one of the city's main arteries, was awash in little yellow cabs that flowed up and down the street like a small yellow tsunami. There were so many of the damn things that Baier wondered how there could be any pedestrians left to use them. He guessed that if a Turk wanted to start his own business, all he had to do was purchase a small vehicle, paint it yellow, and then head out on the streets.

After a few minutes, even that image began to fade as exhaustion threatened to overcome Baier. Fortunately, he was just blocks from his hotel. But later on, Baier would tell himself it was probably why he missed the tail that followed him all the way home.

# CHAPTER SIX

It was a little before lunch, around eleven o'clock on the following day, when Fred Badger strolled by Baier's cubicle.

"I gather you slept in this morning. I hope you feel better and more rested."

"Yeah, I think I do," Baier replied. "Hopefully, I've gotten my body clock over to Ankara time today."

"Good. Then let's go for a ride. I want to show you something that should give you a better picture of what went down when my guy was grabbed by the KGB swipe team."

"You mean over by the citadel in the older part of town?"

Badger nodded, then motioned with his head toward the door. "That's right. It will help you get a physical sense of what happened. Not that there's much I can tell or show you. It all went down pretty fast. It looked pretty damn professional."

"Do you think the team had any help? From the locals, I mean?"

Badger shook his head. "I know you're probably asking that because of my comments yesterday. But, no, I don't think these guys needed it. They had clearly scouted the area thoroughly and knew what they were doing. Besides, I can't see the Turks helping a Soviet operation. Not that way, not directly. And not against us." He paused, shaking his head some more. "I doubt the Turks even knew about our source. I really do."

Baier studied the deputy chief for a moment. "I'm guessing you planned this before coming into work today," Baier said.

"How so?"

"Well, your wardrobe. You guys don't wear blue jeans and sweaters to work every day, do you?"

Badger shook his head.

"Then I just wish you had phoned to tell me before I threw on this official looking charcoal grey suit and solid red tie," Baier added. "From what I hear about the Citadel, I'll stand out like some kind of rich American tourist. You'll be the only one blending in."

"Don't worry about it. We won't be there that long. Besides, I'd rather not discuss anything about your visit here on the phone. You never know who may be listening." Badger smiled as he paused for thought. "No, check that. I know exactly who is listening."

"Our Turkish friends?"

Badger nodded. "Well, them for sure."

Once outside on Ataturk Boulevard they grabbed one of the ubiquitous yellow taxis, and Badger gave the driver instructions in halting but competent Turkish. At least the driver understood where he was supposed to go.

"These taxis can be a godsend if you want to cover your tracks."

"How does that work? I've always found cabs to be helpful but hardly foolproof."

"Well, there everywhere for one thing. You never have to wait for one, so you can always get moving quickly. And these guys," Badger nodded in the direction of the driver, "can play as dumb as you like. As long as you tip them enough."

"I imagine they're also hard to follow." Baier waved his hand at the traffic outside. "I mean, talk about blending in."

"Yeah, how would you like to pick the one cab you need to follow out of this kind of crowd? I won't say it's impossible, but believe me, it's tough. Very tough."

The driver dropped them off at the edge of Hisar Cadesi, what looked to be a main drag through the neighborhood surrounding the Citadel to the fortress at its heart. The two Americans strolled up the brick pathway that led them past a host of shops selling rugs, spices and dried fruits, copperware, and just about anything you might need to set up a house or shop in town. Turkish men in sweaters that looked remarkably similar to the one Badger was wearing, albeit more patchy and dirty, lounged in front of the shops, nearly and all of them working sets of prayer beads through the fingers on one hand, and beckoning to passersby to come inspect their wares and produce with the other. Dressed as he was, Baier attracted more than the usual attention from the shopkeepers.

"I told you so," Baier admonished.

"That's okay," Badger assured him. "They won't bother you once you've passed."

"But they'll remember me."

Badger stopped and gave Baier an incredulous stare. "Remember you? For what? We're not coming here to rob a bank. We'll wander around a bit, maybe grab some lunch, and even take a look at some rugs. Just like a tourist. If you really want to take Sabine something special, purchase some saffron. It's incredibly cheap here."

Assuming the role of tourist director, Badger led Baier along the walls of the fortress, where they looked out across the city and the sprawling waves of red tiled roofs on ramshackle homes that looked to be little more than stone huts. The newer section of Ankara rose in the distance, gleaming structures of steel, stone, and glass that looked as out of place as a thatched hut in Manhattan. The extent of construction underway suggested the disparity would soon favor the new over the old, however.

"You can see why the Byzantines took over the original fortress here and built it up into a major point of defense. Just check out the views. You can see for miles around in every direction. Imagine an army trying to march in here unnoticed."

"When did they fortify this spot?" Baier asked.

"I believe the inner walls went up in the seventh century. But it was the Emperor Michael II who really built the place up in the ninth century. The Seljuck Turks took it over, of course, when they conquered the region, but as you can see," Badger did a full 360-degree turn, "their heirs have let it run down somewhat."

"Yeah, no shit," Baier agreed, surveying the worn and crumbling brown brick walls. "How big is Ankara anyway?"

"Oh, it only had about 30,000 inhabitants when Ataturk moved the capital here in the 1920s. But it's got to be pushing a million or just under that by now." His arm swept the horizon. "As you can see, the growth has been phenomenal."

They moved away from the edge of the walls and started down the steps that led to a large courtyard.

"I don't know about you, Sir, but I've had enough of playing the tourist for one day. As you have no doubt guessed already, this is not my first visit." Badger pointed toward the main gate at the front of the fortress. "Let's grab something to eat. There's a nice café just inside the fortress walls. The food's only so-so, but you can get a great feel for the old Ankara in there."

A waitress led the two men to a table by the window, as Badger had requested. Badger ordered a glass of the local white wine grown in the Ankara region, but Baier stuck to tea. He did not think his body could handle alcohol this early in the day, not with the uncertainty of where it stood with regard to his changing body clock.

"Try the kebobs. They're the best thing here. You can go with either chicken or lamb. They'll come with a nice pita bread you use to roll the meat in if you're looking for something that approximates a sandwich."

"Thanks for the advice. You actually sound like you come here often."

"Not often. But this is where I was sitting when the Russian snatch team took Levkovsky. I liked to use this café because of the view it afforded of the street and the courtyard. I didn't realize at the time that the two hulks in dark suits checking out some dried prunes and pistachios were actually here for a different purpose."

"You thought they were tourists like me?"

Badger nodded as the waitress brought their drinks. When she had left Badger resumed his tale. "That's right. They were not dressed like you; more like me, actually. It was only later that I realized they stood out from the usual customers around these stalls, because they never seemed interested in actually buying anything. With hindsight I can say that they were just killing time, maybe doing their final counter-surveillance check. I had grown too confident about our tradecraft. I had never picked up any kind of surveillance, so why should I worry about strangers on the street?" He drank half his wine in a single gulp. "Goddammit, but I can still kick myself over that."

"Well, if it's any consolation, it doesn't sound as though you're alone there."

Badger shook his head. "There is no consolation. They guy's dead, from what we've heard. And I can't help but feel responsible in some way."

"What sort of reporting were you getting from him?"

"Oh, it was great stuff. He kept us up to speed on KGB activities here, and in pretty good detail. We were able to spot and identify practically their whole residence here. And we know that it was complete, because the Soviets swapped out the entire group a few weeks after he was gone."

"What sort of targeting did they do? What were they interested in?"

"No real surprise there. The Russkies were really trying to get inside the Turkish military, since they're the guys who basically call the shots here. Some of us at the Station have a pool going on when the next military intervention with the government will come." Badger smiled and finished his wine. "Some of us think we'll only have to wait a year or two. I'm holding out for later in the decade, maybe even the early 70s. The military likes to bide its time and not interfere too often or too blatantly. I think they actually dislike having to step in. They only waited a year before handing things back to the civilians this time."

"How generous. Did the Soviets have any luck in their targeting?"

Badger shook his head as the waitress dropped their plates in front of them. Baier studied his chicken, while Badger began to dissect his lamb and sperate it from the metal rods that also held an assortment of peppers and onions. Baier followed suit.

"Not that Levkovsky knew. They were a bit more successful with some of the political parties, mostly on the left, but also some among those that we would label the conservatives. It sounded like the Soviets paid well."

"How do you explain that? The conservatives, I mean."

"Well there is the money, of course. But I think for some it's because they're nationalists. They resent their country's dependence on us—at least, that's how they describe the relationship—and they want to level the playing field, as it were."

"Do you think that played a role in this case? Maybe gave the Soviets the upper hand in getting their guy out?"

Badger studied his lamb for about half a minute. "No, I don't think so. I doubt the Soviets would have asked for any help. That's not how they play. At least not here." Badger glanced up. "But you probably know that already, given your past work."

"I see. So, what happened after the guy was grabbed?"

"That's what I found so interesting later on. They must have had everything planned out well in advance. Rehearsed, too. That's how I figured it for a very professional operation. They disappeared down these alleys in minutes, seconds really. It was like they had been doing practice runs for weeks. I tried to follow to get a sense of where they had gone, but I lost them almost immediately. When I came back here to settle my bill, the owner was squawking like one of the chickens about to end up on the menu. I guess he thought I had bolted to avoid paying my tab."

"Can we get back to a Turkish angle? You mentioned some suspicions about the Turks yesterday. If I recall from my haze of exhaustion and sleepiness, you claimed that despite our best wishes, they are not our friends. Not always, anyway. And now you mention some ill will on the part of conservatives, as well as the left."

Badger shook his head vigorously. "I believe those sentiments are real enough, but I'm still not sure how they play out in a practical sense, especially in the work we do. It's more a matter of being part of the political landscape here. I don't want to sound naive, and I do harbor some suspicions about the Turks. But as I keep replaying this case in my head, I have real trouble seeing how it might fit in this case. They hate the Russians a lot. A lot more than they might be unhappy with us. Besides, it didn't look as though this team needed anyone's help. I mean, you've seen what this neighborhood is like. All you need is a couple safehouses and no one is going to follow or find you." Badger blew out a breath spiced with cumin and yogurt. "It's fucking impossible to figure out. At least for me. I have this nagging suspicion about some kind of Turkish role, but I can't make it fit."

Baier hesitated before he posed the next question, knowing that it could be sensitive. He did not want to lose Badger as a possible ally in the investigation.

"Fred, let me ask you this, do you have any ideas as to what might have gone wrong with the other two cases?"

Badger stared at Baier for what felt like a full minute, chewing his food slowly and thoughtfully. When he did speak the words came in brief, crisp sounds that gave Baier the impression that Badger did not want there to be any misunderstanding of their meaning and finality.

"You should know well, Mister Baier, that cases like ours are strictly compartmented. I knew vaguely that Steve and Bob each had a sensitive asset they were running, and I suspected they were Soviets. But I never knew any of the details or particulars of their cases. Just like they never knew any of mine."

"Even though you were the deputy chief of station?"

"Jim kept a tight hold on all the information regarding our cases. It's what he's supposed to do. At least, that's what I've always heard and believed."

"Okay, good enough. And you're right about how one needs to manage cases like this. But I had to ask. I need to consider all the possibilities."

They finished their lunch in silence. Baier found the chicken and peppers to be roasted just right: done but still moist. He noticed that Badger ate no more than half his dish, the discussion of recent events and the unhappiness of it all probably having ruined his appetite. Afterwards, they stopped at a few of the stalls, Baier promising to return at some point to have a closer look at some of the rugs in one shop and picking up several packets of saffron across the street.

"You can always mail stuff home through the Embassy's postal office," Badger said. His mood appeared to have improved with the walk. "We get to use the military's postal system."

"You mean the APO? I remember it well from my tours in Vienna, Berlin, and London."

Yeah, it comes in pretty handy here. We have the added advantage in being able to run out quickly to the air base outside town for basic groceries and stuff."

"By the way, where's your boss today? I was surprised not to see him in the office this morning. When we spoke yesterday he didn't say anything about taking today off?"

Badger shook his head and shrugged, his hands deep in his pants pockets. "He said he had to drive down to Adana. It's just outside the big base at Incirlik. We have a consulate there as well."

"But no base, as I recall. Did he say why?"

Badger shrugged and shook his head. "Nope. And I have learned not to ask. He came down pretty hard on me for losing the KGB asset, which as you can imagine is like gold these days with all the crap going down in Cuba." He stopped and slapped his forehead in anger. "That reminds me. I almost forgot. The Ambassador wanted me to tell you that the U-2 flights have taken some very useful shots over Cuba. I guess the imagery analysts at our place are pouring over them right now."

"Wow, today's October 14th. So it only took them what, four days? Any word yet on what they've found?"

"No, not yet. It will take a day or two to process and study the film. I guess the big decision is to whom they show the stuff if they've found anything."

"Well, I am pretty damn sure that if they do find something, those photographs will go straight to the President. But thanks for letting me know."

"Oh, sure. But the Ambo said Washington was also thinking of sharing them more broadly, like maybe even at the U.N."

Baier stopped abruptly, a smile spreading across his face. "Now, that would be interesting."

When he got back to the hotel later that evening after a dinner of yogurtlu kabob at a restaurant around the corner from the Embassy that specialized in the dish—it was actually all they served, but it was delicious—Baier knew that he had other problems beside the chief of station's absence or the disappearing act of the KGB's snatch squad in the rough brick and cobblestone warrens surrounding the old Citadel. Someone had searched his room. A quick check of his luggage and belongings did not point to anything missing, but the suitcases and clothes in the armoire had been rearranged. It was clear that whoever did this was not interested in finding anything valuable or incriminating. They probably knew even before they entered the room that the search would not turn anything up. They just wanted to send Baier a message. They were telling him they knew he was there…and why.

# CHAPTER SEVEN

Baier's first thought as he took a seat on the sofa behind the coffee table just inside the door to Jim Breckenridge's office was that October seemed to be similar to those early fall days in the Washington area. And this one was sunny as well.

"Don't get too used to the bright and open skies around here," Breckenridge said. "If you stick around long enough, you'll see what I mean."

"What constitutes 'long enough'?"

"When they turn the heat on."

"What he means," Fred Badger chipped in, "is that they burn that soft brown coal for heat, which puts one helluva lot of pollution in the air. It will be perpetually overcast."

"Yeah, and when it rains your feet will crunch all the particulate matter that collects on the sidewalks," Breckenridge added.

"Wonderful," Baier replied. "That should inspire me to get through this case as quickly as possible."

Everyone appeared to have read the same instructions on the proper dress this morning. It almost looked like they were all back at Headquarters. For the first time since he arrived, Baier was not the only one to show up for work in a suit. His light grey number was actually the most casual one in the group, as both Breckenridge and Badger were wearing navy blue suits with white shirts and regimental striped ties. Different regiments, though. Robert Hughes, one of the case officers who lost a Soviet Foreign Ministry asset, had joined them and was sitting in a narrow wooden chair by the office door. He, too, had on a suit, but it was more of a tan or beige one fit for summer. Baier had always had trouble distinguishing between anything beyond the basic colors, like red, green or blue. Brown was one of those, but this was definitely not brown.

"So, how have your first few days been, Karl? Any clues popping out? Are you ready to solve the riddle?" Breckenridge asked.

Baier laughed. "Hardly. In fact, I've barely gotten started. I did have an interesting tour of the Citadel and the surrounding area yesterday, though, thanks to Fred here." Baier nodded in Badger's direction.

"So Fred tells me. Did it help?"

"Oh, sure. It always helps to have a tangible feel for what actually went down, and seeing the area gives me a better sense of the possibilities."

"What sort of possibilities?" Breckenridge continued.

Baier leaned forward and clasped his hands together between his legs. "Well, for example, how the snatch team could have operated so quickly, how professional their operation must have been, and if they had needed any assistance."

"Assistance? From whom?" Hughes asked.

Baier turned and stared for a moment at the case officer. Few were so bold as to speak up when senior management was carrying the conversation. Baier wondered how deeply this one felt about what had transpired on his watch, how deep an impression the killing of his asset must have left. The young man's face did not betray any emotion, however. Baier wondered at that as well. Was he really this calm and collected, or even cold-hearted? Baier doubted it. Otherwise he would not have spoken up so quickly. In fact, the more Baier considered it, the more he thought of how this Hughes fellow looked more nervous than confident. Baier acknowledged to himself that he would have felt the same.

"Assistance from any number of angles," Baier continued. "For example, how big a team was required? How close were the hiding places or the transportation? And, I hate to raise this, could they have had help from the locals?"

"The Turks?" Hughes pressed.

"Sure. Why not? They may well have an interest here. You know, my room was searched yesterday. I'm assuming our Turkish friends were behind that."

"Oh, that's pretty standard stuff," Breckenridge said. He tried to sound reassuring and dismissive at the same time. "When they didn't find anything—and I'm guessing they did not, Karl—they'll leave you alone. They can be a suspicious lot, but they are not likely to disrupt you or obstruct your efforts."

"I guess that's good to know. But if you don't mind, I'd like to keep my options open on that front for now," Baier replied.

Breckenridge shrugged. "Whatever you say."

"It also suggests they know why I'm here. Would they pay this much attention to someone here on a training mission?"

Breckenridge waved Baier's words away, while Badger and Hughes displayed wide smiles. "Oh, hell, Karl, the Turks don't believe anything we tell them about who's here and why. They are always going to try to find out everything they can for themselves. Who knows what sort of thing they've concluded from yesterday's search. I would recommend that we do a sweep of your room, though. What's your room number?"

"341. Why?"

Breckenridge tossed an inquisitive glance at both Badger and Hughes. He was smiling when he looked back at Baier. "That figures. You're not the first visitor we put there, and the management—I'm sure at the local service's direction—selects from a small group of rooms. 341 is from that bunch."

Baier settled back against the cushions again. "Okay, then. Sure. One thing I meant to ask you yesterday, Fred, was if you had ever had any suspicions that the Soviets were running this KGB man against us. If they had doubled him back."

Badger's answer was immediate. He sat forward on the other corner of the sofa from Baier as though he wanted to make sure his point got all the way to Baier's end without any interference. "No way. I never got any sense of that whatsoever. His stuff was always good, and it checked out with the desk back home. I'm not sure what purpose it would have served to give us so much good information. And what would they have gotten out of it all if they had doubled him back on us?"

"Well, that depends on what they would have wanted to know. I take it you never passed along anything of value beyond the requirements. That alone could be valuable stuff. You know, giving them a sense of where our interests lie, where the gaps in our understanding of certain issues are."

Badger nodded and held out his hand, as though to ward off any additional requests or suggestions. "Yeah, yeah, I get all that. I guess much of it was stuff they could have guessed we were interested in anyway. They're not idiots."

"Oh, I am aware of that. Believe me." Baier thought back for a moment of all the tangos he had danced with Chernov and other Soviet and Warsaw Bloc antagonists over the course of his career.

"But he never used the panic sign we had agreed on to warn me that the material was tainted or that he was under suspicion."

"Okay. But do you have any sense of how long the KGB might have been on to their errant officer?" Baier asked.

Badger sat back and shook his head. "No, I'm sorry, but I never discerned any change in my guy's behavior, or anything else that would have suggested he was acting under some kind of duress or that he was concerned for his safety. At every meeting up until the end he had followed the security protocols we had agreed on."

"You know this how?" Baier asked.

"I know this because I always made it a point to get there early to check on his approach. The guy was clean every single time."

"Okay, thanks. Please, go on."

"He never hesitated when I gave him a new set of requirements. We always had pleasant conversations about his personal life—his wife was here with him, as well as their two kids—and he was actually looking forward to taking them to America someday."

"Was that his motive for coming over? Was it ideological?"

Badger nodded slowly, thinking for a moment. "Pretty much, yeah. He said he had been disillusioned after the Khrushchev speech in '56, you know the one that exposed Stalin's abuses. And he got tired of the crappy lifestyle at home. He claimed he and many of his colleagues doubted they or their children would ever see the fruits of the Revolution. He would say in an aside that the party bosses were already enjoying their shares of those fruits, though."

"And he reported entirely on KGB operational matters? Nothing in the way of policies or plans from Moscow?"

"Oh, yeah. KGB operations were his bailiwick. He wouldn't have known or had access to the other stuff." Badger paused before his eyes widened. They also brightened with the light of new idea. "Now that you mention it, though, he did claim to have something really interesting that he wanted to share at our last meeting. He claimed he had heard of a report that our bosses in Washington would find very interesting." Badger looked down at the floor. "But he never got the chance to pass that along."

Baier leaned over and patted Badger on the shoulder. "Now that is interesting. Really. Thanks, Fred. And it could be very important. But you say he did not have any of the specifics on this extra bit of information?"

Badger shook his head. "No, he didn't have anything definite yet. That's what he claimed. He told me to wait for our next meeting."

"And that was the one where he was taken?"

Badger nodded but stayed silent, his eyes searching the floor at his feet.

"Gentlemen, I think it's time we break for lunch," Breckenridge interrupted. "I also have a question for you, Karl. Although it's really more of a suggestion."

"Sure. Go ahead, Jim."

"Would you like to go to Istanbul? You said it helped to put your feet on the ground where these incidents took place. Do you think it would help to view the scenes of the crimes up there, as it were?"

Baier stood and nodded vigorously. "Absolutely. That would be great. How soon could I get there?"

"Oh, hell, you can be there by this evening. I'll have Clara, my secretary, make the flight reservations—I recommend that over a train trip; much quicker and definitely more comfortable—and we'll try to get you a room in the Pera Palace."

"Isn't that where the one asset was poisoned." Baier smiled and looked around the room. "You wouldn't be trying to get rid of me, would you?"

Breckenridge stood and laughed. "Hardly. From what I hear, you're too tough for that. Anyway, I really would recommend lingering in the Orient Bar over a glass of raki. Have you ever had ouzo? It's pretty much the same thing. But it's almost de rigeur for that place. Ataturk enjoyed his share while he lived there shortly after the war. The first one, that is."

"In the bar?" Baier exclaimed.

Breckenridge waved his hands in the air over his desk. "No, no, up in his room there. I'm afraid we won't be able to reserve that one for you, though. You can get a tour of the suite, however. Like just about everywhere else he stayed, the room is now a shrine of sorts. Or a mausoleum."

"Well, I'll be sure to ask."

"It's also right next door to our Consulate there in case you need to get ahold of us. That is also an interesting building. It's an old baroque mansion I believe we purchased from some Italian businessman."

"Italian?"

"Oh, yes. That part of town is across the strait from the old heart of Constantinople. It's where the European businessmen and traders had their various colonies and communities. I believe some Byzantine emperor back in the thirteenth century, or whenever, gave the Genoese the area as their own to set themselves up in. Other European traders and many of the civil servants that ran the Ottoman Empire settled there as well."

"The Ottoman bureaucrats?"

Breckenridge nodded. "That's right. Most, or at least many, were Greeks. Probably a lot of Armenians and Jews mixed in there as well. If you get the chance to wander around you'll get an impression of what it might have been like when there were more of them living in the old capital, especially all the Greeks. Some

Turks will tell you Istanbul only became truly Turkish recently, since the war. The second one."

"Well, thanks for the introduction, Jim. I'll be sure to try to get around some."

The Station Chief motioned toward Hughes, who was now standing in the doorway. "I'll send Bob along, too. He could be a useful guide and keep you out of trouble. He could also give you some pointers in the bar. That's where his asset, Alexander Kosrov, had his fatal last drink. I don't know if it was raki, though."

"Nope. Claimed he hated the stuff," Hughes said. His words sounded heavy, burdened by sorrow and disappointment.

• • •

The bar in the Pera Palace was a bit run down, like the rest of the hotel, but it certainly had that old world ambiance. Baier had read in the tour guide back in the Station that the hotel had been built in the 1890s as the end station for the Orient Express. That had allegedly inspired Agatha Christie to write her mystery set aboard that famous train while she stayed at this very hotel. "I wouldn't try to stay in her room," Hughes had warned Baier. "They say it's haunted by her ghost. Something about her spirit fleeing back there after her many years stuck in either a miserable marriage or just being generally unlucky at love."

"Not to worry," Baier had assured him, sipping his raki with a wince and adding some more ice to thin the drink. "I've got enough challenges here without taking on the supernatural as well."

"You mean the case?"

"Sure, there's that. But even this glorious old hotel is a challenge. My pipes banged whenever I ran the water, and I'll be interested to see if anything hot comes out when I try to take a bath."

"They put you in the Leon Trotsky room right? This was his first stop when Stalin had him expelled from the Soviet Union. How's the noise?"

"Not too bad. I'm in the front of the hotel, thankfully, so I shouldn't have to deal with the sounds of traffic running along the road at the back."

Hughes nodded and sipped at his own raki. He seemed to have become accustomed to the taste, which made sense since he was on his second year in Turkey. "Yeah, I can appreciate that. They have me in the Viktor Emmanuel room, which is also near the front. I forget which famous person stayed in the room I once had at the back. It might have been Hemingway. But I was up most of night listening to the lorries rolling past."

Baier studied the bartender for a few minutes while he worked on his raki. The man sat back behind the bar, his gaze focused on the street outside as the smoke from his cigarette curled up towards the pressed tin ceiling and slowly rotating fans. There were only four other tables occupied by a smattering of guests, none of them seated close enough to eavesdrop on the Americans' conversation.

"Bob," Baier finally said, "I'd like to put the same questions to you that I asked Fred earlier today. "Had you noticed any change in your asset's behavior before he came here that night?"

Hughes seemed to ponder the question for almost a minute before answering. "No, I can't say that I did. It's pretty much as Fred explained with his guy. His mood never shifted from one of cheerful cooperation. He was always receptive, in fact, almost eager, to get the requirements. He understood why we asked what we did. He was pretty sharp."

"And what did we ask? For this particular asset, I mean."

"Mostly Russian, or excuse me, Soviet policy for the Middle East. It's what he had access to during this assignment. He knew we were still reeling from the rise of Nassar and the British and French fiasco over Suez. Plus, how much the deterioration in the Israeli-Palestinian dispute has been bothering Washington…"

"And quite a few others as well."

"For sure. And the changes in Syria and Iraq have not been very helpful either. He had served in Baghdad during the military coup in '58, and he had a pretty good handle on what the Soviets hoped to get out of the rising instability in the area. You know, with the end of the ruling houses the British and French imposed here after World War One. So, we were interested in whatever he could get us on Soviet policy in this part of the world."

"I see. Anything else?"

Hughes thought for a moment more. "No, not really."

"Did he ever volunteer anything else?"

The answer was more immediate this time. "Nope. Never. He just responded to our taskings."

"And did you have any sense of how long the Soviets might have been on to him?"

"As our source, you mean?" Baier nodded. "No. Like Fred, I followed the standard procedure on countersurveillance and never picked anything up. This guy also followed all my instructions, and I never had any of the unpleasant surprises some of my colleagues have had to deal with because of an asset's laziness or carelessness. This guy was a model of good behavior."

"No use of the panic signal? You had one, of course."

More raki went down. Hughes signaled the bartender for another. "Yes, of course."

"And his information?"

"Always got top grades back at Headquarters and positive comments around town. I have to say that I was actually a little surprised at how much he had access to," Hughes added. "He was only their equivalent of a second secretary."

"That didn't give you any suspicions?" Baier pressed. "About the quality of the information and his access?"

"No. He always explained it as the result of poor security practices in their embassy here. And this is not the first time I've heard that story, and not just about this country. It sounds like the Russians are a careless lot."

Baier was reminded again of his many encounters with Soviet antagonists, and he had to concede that Hughes had a point. He surveyed the room. A thin cloud of smoke hovered near the ceiling, obviously unbothered by the slowly circulating fan blades at either end. Given how much people smoked in Turkey--Baier had been struck by this almost the minute he arrived in the country—he knew the fans were little more than a cosmetic effort at the smoke's dispersal. The lighting was also sparse, about what one would expect in a hotel bar just about anywhere in the world. But here it did help hide the smoke some.

"Where exactly did the murder take place? Can you point out the spot discretely?"

Hughes raised his left hand, then let it settle across his right arm a with a finger stretched out toward the middle of the bar.

"That table in the front?" Baier asked.

"Yes." Hughes had grown suddenly quiet, sullen almost.

"And where were you seated?"

"At this very table. I was waiting for him to have a drink or two, and then the plan was to meet up outside for a stroll separately down toward the Galata Tower. It's a pretty common tourist spot, so we would have had plausible cover."

"I see. How did it happen?"

"He was about halfway through his first glass of Scotch—he always refused to drink raki. Said the stuff made him nauseous. It was about fifteen or twenty minutes into it when he seemed to get sick, violently ill really. Then he fell out of chair and onto the floor. The barkeep rushed around to his aid, as did the waitress. A manager ran in and yelled about calling an ambulance at the front desk. One came eventually, after about half an hour, but the poor guy was already gone."

Baier stared at the spot for a little while. He wasn't sure for how long as he tried to picture the man's final agonies and the crowd that must have built around him. Poisoning, he thought, must be a horrible and painful way to die.

"Any idea, Bob, how the poison got in his glass? I'm assuming that's how he got it."

Hughes shook his head slowly. "No. I've though back on that night plenty of times, but I just don't see how it could have happened. No one got near his drink that I could see…"

"The bartender or waitress?"

"Well, he had to pour the drink, sure, and she had to carry it over," Hughes explained. "But I'd been in here, as had he, several times, and obviously, nothing like this had happened before."

"Of course, whoever did it could have been waiting for the

order to proceed with the operation. The same work crew?" Baier asked.

"Yeah. I was sure to check that sort of thing. You know, being aware of your surroundings and all that. But I had also gotten used to the routine here, and I don't remember seeing anything unusual or different that night."

"Can you absolutely rule out that one of those two, the bartender or waitress, might have slipped whatever it was into his Scotch?"

"No, I can't rule it out completely," Hughes admitted. "But when I think back I just don't see how they could have done it. It wasn't crowded that night, and I was able to keep my eye on everyone in here. Then again, I guess there could have been a moment when I might have missed something. I still don't see why they would do it, though. The risk would have been too great for them. And where's the motive?"

"What about a reward? Money can be a powerful motivator."

Hughes shrugged. "Yeah, I suppose."

"Was there ever a police investigation, a report or something?"

"I suppose so. I do recall a couple of articles in the press. But the whole thing seemed to blow over pretty quickly."

"Did you find that kind of suspicious?"

"Not really. I mean, the Turks would not have wanted to dwell on it. It's pretty embarrassing to have something like that happen in your country. For a number of reasons. You'd like to be able to claim that foreign diplomats are safe on your turf."

"But no one suggested that the KGB or GRU might be behind this?"

Hughes shook his head. "Not that I saw. Not in the press anyway. And we were not about to go to the cops. That would only raise suspicions about our possible involvement."

"Okay. Thanks, Bob. I know this has been tough on you and your colleagues. If anything else pops up, please let me know."

"Sure thing," Hughes said. "Steve Garner will be joining us tomorrow for our trip to the Bazaar. Maybe our discussion then will remind me of some useful details or touch off some other thoughts."

"Great. Until then. This has been very helpful."

• • •

He caught sight of her as she approached from his right. She moved with an effortless grace that allowed her to float through the space between them. Or so it seemed. She was hard to miss, and not just because they were standing alone in the hallway in front of his room. Baier had just unlocked his door, but it was still closed. That probably helped. He had seen this woman in the bar, and at times he had trouble keeping his eyes off her. Even through a light haze of smoke and darkness, she stood out in the room like a beacon. At least to Baier.

"Can I bother you for a light?" she asked.

Baier smiled and shook his head. "I'm sorry. I don't carry matches."

He had never seen a raven in person, but now he could understand the meaning of the phrase 'raven-haired.' Hers was long, reaching past her shoulders in a wave of smooth silk that reflected the light from the ceiling lamps above. In the front, it fell across her forehead in small bow-like tresses that covered the top half of her forehead, the better to draw someone, anyone who was near, into the round eyes that beckoned like an altar. Her white cotton shirt was unbuttoned down to the v in her black sweater, framing her cleavage like it was a relic, or an invitation. Baier gulped a breath of dry air that seemed to lodge itself in his throat.

"Perhaps a cigarette then. I can always find a match in your room."

"No, I'm sorry, but I don't smoke."

Her skin was smooth, and it carried just what Baier imagined the olive-like coloring would be in a Mediterranean beauty. The slacks hugged her rear end and thighs like a second skin. Baier could see why her handlers had chosen her for the approach. She was nearly irresistible. He wondered if Leon Trotsky had ever been approached like this when he stayed in this room. If he had, he probably hadn't appreciated it. Too focused on the global revolution probably.

"You can still invite me in. Do you have something to drink inside?'

She leaned against the door frame close enough for Baier to smell her breath. It smelled as though she had been eating honey. Maybe some lemon, too.

He held up his hand. "I am very flattered, but as you can see, I am married."

"Then where is your wife? I do not see her here. And she was not with you in the bar."

"Ah, but she is here with me in spirit. She is waiting for me at home."

"How can you be so sure?"

Baier thought back to the night he had told her of his assignment and upcoming journey. That had not been the last time they made love before he left, and he remembered every occasion as though it had just occurred. Almost as in a dream.

"Oh, I'm pretty sure she is." He gripped the handle and was surprised how moist his palm had become. Then he paused and let out a deep and profound sigh. "But thank you. If I was single, I would most assuredly take you up on your offer."

And if he was single, Baier was pretty sure the offer would never have been made. But one thing was sure. It didn't really matter if Baier had any hot water for a bath tonight. A cold one would probably be better.

# CHAPTER EIGHT

"So, this is the café you were sitting in when the hit on your asset took place? Is that right, Steve?"

Baier and Robert Hughes sat at opposite corners of the table inside the café—more of a restaurant than one of the traditional Turkish teahouses—where Steve Garner had joined them in the early hours of the afternoon after he took the train down from Bursa in Turkey's northeast. He had been scouting for a safe house in the city in case, Baier guessed, he should need someplace other than Istanbul to meet future sources. The Soviet diplomat Viktor Topokov had been the single source he had handled since his arrival earlier that summer, but he claimed to have two more developmentals underway. These, however, were unlikely to be Soviet targets. Probably members of the other eastern European diplomatic corps and security services. Baier understood that there was a standdown on activities regarding the Soviets in Turkey, an obvious requirement in view of recent events. Baier was a little surprised that the station was still operational at all, at least until they got to the bottom of the three lost assets. But that was not his decision. Garner did not explain the nationalities or assignments of these new targets to Baier, as he should not have. Like a good case officer. Protecting his potential sources.

As he studied the man, Baier asked himself whether Garner had it in him to go out and recruit someone else, having witnessed what he did with his last asset. His skin looked pale and his eyes, rimmed with a thin line of red, were supported by bags the size of small coins. He glanced nervously around him as he sat between Baier and Hughes, clearly uncomfortable revisiting the scene of the crime. He had offered to take Baier and Hughes to a famous teahouse in the heart of the bazaar, but Baier had wanted to see the exact spot Garner had occupied on that fateful day. And he was glad he had done so. It gave Baier not only a chance to get a better picture of where and how the hit had gone down. It also gave him a better chance to assess the impact on the Soviet's handler.

"That's right." Garner's head moved slightly, which Baier took for a nod in agreement. "I was sitting where you are now," he explained to Baier. Hughes remained silent. He had not said a word since their arrival.

"And you never saw the whole thing coming, correct?" Garner nodded again, almost imperceptibly. "In fact, according to the cable reporting the incident, you had looked away momentarily and responded only when you heard the sound of the gunshot."

"Yeah, that's how it happened," Garner answered. "They must have had a silencer on the weapon because you could hardly hear it. More of a small pop than a real gunshot. I figured that's why nobody else around here at the time seemed to hear it or recognize it for what it was. No one else responded until they saw Viktor slumped over the table, his blood and brains all over the tabletop and the chair opposite. It was pretty damn gross, I can tell you."

"I believe you," Baier said. "I've been there and hope I never am again." He paused to study the heavy flow of human traffic moving along the streets. Stalls packed tightly together spilled light and products out onto the alleys, as the owners beckoned customers to stop long enough to inspect their wares, which ranged from dried fruit to rugs to leather and clothes of all sorts and sizes. The avenues were labelled 'streets', but they were more like walkways, actually. "Why do you think they chose to knock Viktor off here?"

Garner looked around and spread his arms wide before dropping them back in his lap. "Look around, man." His eyes dropped before focusing on Baier again. "I'm sorry. I mean, sir. It's virtually impossible to run anyone down here. This place has something like over sixty streets, and it gets over 250,000 visitors a day. At least. It's so easy to lose someone, especially if you have alternate escape routes plotted out beforehand."

"Do you think they did?"

"Oh hell, yes," Garner exclaimed. "I mean, they disappeared in seconds."

"Did you try to follow them?"

Garner shook his head. "No, not really. I ran up to the corner over there where I saw them disappear in the crowd. Then I came back to see if there was anything I could do for Viktor. It was silly, really. I guess I just acted on instinct. But there was no way he could have survived a shot like that."

"And there was more than one?" Baier asked. "Assassins, I mean. Just the one shot, though?"

Garner nodded. This time more vigorously. "That's right. One bullet was all they needed. The shooter met some guy at the corner over there." Garner pointed down the street to a spot about twenty yards away.

"How did you know they were together?" Baier asked.

"Because the shooter slipped his gun to the other one, who sped off in another direction. It all looked pretty professional."

"I don't doubt it. Can you describe these guys?"

Garner shrugged. "Not very well, I'm afraid. They were both tall. I'd say about six feet. And they both looked like they had muscular bodies, at least as much as I could tell with their raincoats on. Their shoulders looked pretty broad, and they didn't have much in the way of necks, as far as I could see. And both men had fedoras pulled low to hide their faces as much as possible."

"Did you learn anything more from the police?"

Garner smiled and shook his head. He almost laughed. "Are you kidding? They were a real stone wall. They said they would handle it and they were waiting for a formal request from the Soviet Embassy before they could begin their investigation."

"So, they knew the victim was a Soviet diplomat right away?"

"Sure. Viktor still had his identification with him, including the dip passport. The police also informed me that it was none of my business, even though I offered to provide eyewitness testimony. They were pretty frank about it."

"Do you know if the Soviets ever filed such a request?" Baier pressed.

Garner shook his head again and sighed. "I haven't heard anything about that."

Baier looked over at Hughes. "Does anything here strike you as familiar? Any similarities?"

Hughes shifted his weight. "Actually, this is the first I'm hearing about Steve's experience. We haven't discussed this among ourselves."

"Seriously?"

"That's right. Breckenridge told us to keep the cases separate and not to talk about it with each other."

"Why was that?"

Hughes looked over at Garner, and then back at Baier. He shrugged. "I guess it has to do with security and protecting methods and sources. Like Fred told you, the chief kept these cases pretty strictly compartmented."

"Although the sources happen to be already dead?"

"True, but we do need to protect our penetrations, or the fact that we had some" Hughes reminded him.

"From whom?" Baier wondered. "The Soviets apparently knew all about them."

"So, you're pretty sure it was them?" Garner asked.

"Who else? Especially since there were three of them, and whose killings were grouped pretty damn close together." Baier looked at his companions. "That should also tell us something."

"Which is?" Garner asked.

"It's the question we need to ask. Why all three and why so close together? Given what's going on in the Caribbean, I would think the answer would come from that. I mean, why not let these things run on for a while and control the information they provide. You know, keep it simple and non-damaging. That way the Soviets get to observe us and our methods a little longer."

"That would depend on how long they knew about our assets," Hughes said.

"True," Baier replied. "But you guys claim there had been no signs of stress on the part of your people, and no indications of an unwanted presence throughout your handling of these assets. Your tradecraft was solid, or so it would appear. So, the revelations must have been pretty recent for Moscow." Baier paused for a moment. "You do have to wonder how solid their information was, though."

"What do you mean?" Garner asked.

"Well, if they were going to arrest or kill these guys, they must have been pretty certain of their guilt. But what had they done to accumulate the necessary evidence? None of you saw any indication that these men were under suspicion until the very end. So, that suggests to me that Moscow Center got the damning evidence near the end. And it must have been pretty convincing."

"Have you considered the Turks?" Garner asked.

"Yes, I have, and I've discussed it with your bosses in Ankara. But you have to ask yourself why they would do something like this? Wouldn't it make more sense that if the Turks found out they would protest to us and demand access to the reporting?"

Garner looked at Hughes this time. The latter answered. "That makes sense, but it's really above our pay grade."

"But tell me," Bier asked again, "why suspect the Turks? I mean, they're our allies, right? Is the relationship that difficult? I mean in your experience so far?" Baier continued.

The two American officers looked at each other, as though waiting for the other one to speak. Finally, Hughes spoke up. "No, they're our allies alright. But they would be pretty pissed to learn we were running these Soviet assets without telling them."

"To the point of murder? Or betrayal to the KGB?"

Garner leaned in. "That does sound pretty extreme. But the Turks are really, really sensitive about what goes down on their turf." He leaned back against his chair. "Everybody is, of course. But I think it goes to their sense of inferiority toward the West." He grimaced, as though he had just swallowed a glassful of raki. "Maybe that's a bit strong. But most Turks think they don't get the respect they deserve from us Westerners. And that can play out in surprising ways."

"But still? Murder?" Baier added. "Or even exposure? And three times?"

Hughes pitched in. "You're probably right. I doubt they'd go that far. The worst thing they'd probably do would be to betray these guys to the Soviets and wait for some kind of payback. But even that's a stretch."

Baier looked over at Garner. The third American sat in silence, studying the ground around their table. Baier signaled to the waiter for their check. The three teas and baklava—Baier could not resist the opportunity to taste some authentic Turkish pastries—cost less than ten dollars once he worked out the exchange rate in his head. After he paid, all three Americans stood.

"We've still got some time to play at being tourists, don't we?" Baier asked. "I think we could use the opportunity to unwind a bit after our talk and the memories this trip must have stirred for you two."

"Sure," Hughes and Garner echoed. "Why not?" Hughes added.

"The Hagia Sophia and Topkapi Palace are not that far away. I would love to have a chance to see the Seraglio, a real live harem. According to the tourist map I checked at the hotel those sites should be pretty close. If they're further away, I'm sure we won't have any trouble finding a cab in this town. It looks about as easy as in Ankara."

"Come on, then," Garner said. "I know the way. And it's easily walkable. We just have to head down Kalpakcilar Caddesi. It's just a block or so over. That will take us right there."

"You know the area pretty well, do you?" Baier asked.

Garner nodded with a smile. It was the most relaxed Baier had seen him all day. "Sure, I do. This part of town is called Fatih and was the heart of old Constantinople. It's a great place to do your countersurveillance runs. Which, by the way, always went smoothly for me, as you noted. I never picked up a tail before my meetings, all of which were in this town. Every single time the proverbial coast was clear. And Viktor was an old pro. He had been reporting for us for several years, almost a decade. They guy knew what he was doing. And so did I."

"Like I noted before, Steve, I believe you. Both of you. It's one of the reasons I've come up with the explanation for the timing about the Soviets action here."

"One?" Hughes asked.

"Yep. One of them," Baier replied. "More later. When I know more."

As they made their way down the street, or 'caddesi,' as the Turks called it, Baier noted how familiar the refrain of solid tradecraft and counter-surveillance had become during his stay in Turkey. His investigation always turned up that response whenever the question of tradecraft by the Agency officers and their assets came up. He had seen no reason to doubt the claims. But if it was so true, then what the hell had happened?

• • •

He was really looking forward to a final raki, or two, maybe even three, before getting up early tomorrow morning to catch the flight back to Ankara. But no sooner had Robert Hughes joined him and Baier had settled into his chair, than he discovered the siren from the night before at a table in the back corner of the bar. If he hadn't met her last night, he might not have noticed her there. But her beauty—hell, her sex appeal—seemed to call for his attention. She was dressed more conservatively tonight, a loose flower print dress with tones of blue and yellow that made her look almost matronly. If such a thing were possible. No, on second thought, Baier decided, it was more like a secretary who had just gotten off work, or a university coed taking a break from her studies. Whatever it was, she still looked pretty damn inviting. Almost like a Venus fly trap, but without the threatening edges. He guessed that was a part of her appeal.

She smiled in Baier's direction and raised her drink in a toast of recognition. Baier nodded and raised his own glass in response.

"My God, who is that wonderful woman?" Hughes asked.

"She's just someone I ran into in the hallway last night. We had a pleasant conversation."

"That's all? You just talked?"

"That's right. We came to an understanding, of sorts."

"So, is this going to be your lucky night? Or was that yesterday?"

Baier smiled and looked over at his companion. "Not lucky in the way you think. Remember, I am a married man. And happily at that."

Hughes raised his glass in a salute to Baier. "Well, good for you. Here's to your health then."

Baier sipped his raki but could not keep his lips from wincing at the taste. "Thanks, Comrade."

"Still getting used to the taste?" Hughes continued.

"Yeah, I gather it's an acquired one."

"You got that right."

At that moment Baier felt a hand come to rest on his shoulder. It felt heavy, and when Baier looked up, he could see why. The hand was a thick and hard extension of an arm that looked to be just as strong, even though it was mostly hidden in the sleeve of a black suit jacket. The knuckles on the five fingers were scarred and ragged. A face marked by a curtain of short black whiskers that looked to be about three days old bent low enough to whisper in Baier's ear. The breath stank of day-old cigarette smoke.

"We hope you enjoyed your visit to former imperial and Ottoman capital, Mr. Baier. We also hope your work here is done."

"Who are you, and why should you care?"

The whiskered face broke into a rough and unpleasant smile as the new visitor straightened himself. Baier could see that this man, accompanied by a stranger at his back, was a solid, six-foot man, chiseled like a piece of stone. His partner did not look much different. Even the smoke and darkness that pervaded the room failed to hide the implied menace in their presence.

"Let us just say we are not friends. But we do have interest in your presence here." Baier struggled to pick out the man's accent as he spoke slowly and haltingly in English. It was as though he wanted to make sure that he chose precisely the right words from a foreign vocabulary.

Baier turned in his chair to face the men. "Could you be a little more explicit?" The face of the nearest man, the one who had spoken, displayed no recognition of what Baier had said. "Just who the fuck are you, and who do you think you are to confront me like this?"

The only thing that moved in the man's face were his lips. "There is nothing here for you to do. Everything is being taken care of."

"Just what do you think I have been doing here then?"

"Have pleasant flight back to Ankara tomorrow, Mr. Baier. You have been warned."

With that, the two men turned and marched from the room.

Baier watched them leave, incredulous. "What the hell was that?" Baier asked no one in particular.

"Whatever it was," Hughes said, "the threat was pretty damn obvious."

"Not too subtle, eh? It would be nice to know what it was all about, though."

"Well," Hughes continued, "my guess is that those two creeps were Soviets."

"Not Turks?"

Hughes shook his head and reached for his glass of raki. "Nope. I'd put the accent as Russian. But then my mastery of that particular language is not very good. My meetings with Kosrov were all in English. And it did sound a lot like that of Kosrov's struggling English. And I'd say they wanted to make sure you dig no farther."

"But how did they even know what I was doing here? If that's what it is?"

Hughes shrugged. "Beats me. Did you see them here in the bar when we arrived?"

It was Baier's turn to shake his head. "No, I'm sorry to say that I did not. You?"

"They did look a bit familiar from our walk to Topkapi this afternoon. I picked them up after we left the Hagia Sophia."

"Good for you, Bob. But how did they even know to follow us?"

"Maybe we've got a leak somewhere. Or else their side is all over the recent deaths here. They may have picked us up at the

Bazaar. And they clearly do not want any interference. Of any sort, and from any side."

"Yeah, especially us, since the Soviets somehow figured out that we were running those guys."

Baier glanced toward the back of the bar to see if the woman was still there. He could have used a pretty face to remove the memory of the two thugs who had just called on his table. But the damsel was gone, disappearing like the fabled lady of the lake.

# CHAPTER NINE

"Well, did you find what you were looking for in Istanbul?" Breckenridge asked. "Any closer to an answer of what happened to our three Soviets?"

Baier was back in the same spot on the sofa across from Breckenridge's desk. He had attended the morning staff meeting at nine o'clock, and when the group broke up at nine forty-five, Baier had followed the chief to his office. Breckenridge appeared almost surprised to see Baier at his back when he turned around behind his desk.

"We know what happened. At least to two of them. The third—our KGB buddy—is a little less certain, but his ending is pretty predictable. It's the why that I'm after."

"Okay. Then are you any closer to the 'why'?" Breckenridge continued. "And as far as our KGB friend, Moscow Station feels confident that they know what happened. And, yes, it is predictable."

"In any case, I have to say that I am still a long way off. But a number of interesting things occurred that I'd like to run by you."

"Sure. Such as?"

"First of all, what's your impression of the three officers involved?" Baier asked. "How have they been handling the loss?"

Breckenridge sat back in his chair and swung himself around to look out the window before turning to face Baier again. He ruffled his hair and stroked his blue and yellow flowered print tie before replying.

"I'd say they've handled it pretty well. Of course, something like this can be very tough. As you well know, Karl, case officers are taught not to get too close to their assets, not to get too emotionally involved. But that is often easier said than done. In fact, it can be damn tough."

Baier did not respond at first, thinking instead of his own interest and involvement in the personal lives of some of those he had handled over the years. There was the Russian Chernov, of course, but also the Hungarian asset he tried to rescue during the revolt and Soviet invasion of that country six years ago. Hell, you could classify his wife Sabine in that category. If you stretched the definition.

"Were these three officers?" Baier asked. "Emotionally involved, I mean?"

"It was always my impression that they remained professionals in every sense of the word. But I suppose it was inevitable that they would develop some kind of friendship with the three men. I had the impression that all three Russians were genuinely nice guys, two of them with families. And they all looked forward to a future life with their loved ones in the U.S. I don't mean to say that things got overly sentimental, but they were sincere in their opposition to the Soviet Union. The relationship was definitely not mercenary."

"I haven't seen any of their reporting yet. Just how valuable were they?"

"Very," Breckenridge claimed. "And they were taking great risks to provide us with critical information, some of which, I might add, helped inform us about Soviet plans and intentions in Latin America."

"Did that include Cuba?"

Breckenridge leaned forward, his elbows coming to rest on his desktop. "Yes, it did, principally from Topokov. One of the Foreign Ministry guys. That was his background, you know."

"Yes, I remember reading as much."

"That was not his major area of responsibility, of course, at least not since his arrival here last spring. But he occasionally reported on material he had seen or on inquiries along those lines from Moscow. Because of his expertise, you see. That's how he got wind of them. He was often consulted on those matters."

"I can see that," Baier conceded.

"But those few reports were graded very high, largely, I think, because we've had so little else. They were also very closely held, which is probably why you haven't seen them yet."

"Have you been reading any other intel on Cuba?" Baier asked. Breckenridge nodded. "If that stuff was so restricted how did you pull off getting your own access?"

Breckenridge smiled. "Well, it's a big damn deal to the Turks, you know. They're playing host to our Jupiter missiles here, right on the Soviets' doorstep, as it were. The only other place where those things sit in range of the USSR is Italy. So, I argued that I needed to be kept abreast of reporting on just what the hell the Russkies are up to during this crisis. You can see how Russian intentions regarding our own missile deployments right now would be intense, to say the least. I've already had several very uncomfortable meetings with my counterparts in NSS."

"Turkish intelligence?"

Breckenridge nodded. "That's right. The National Security Service. And they're pretty good at letting you know when they're unhappy."

"And what has our reporting from the Caribbean been telling us?"

"Unfortunately, most of it is junk. That is, the stuff off the island. You know, rumors picked up at a friend's house from someone who works in the government or is in the army. Or mysterious sightings of trucks with tubes and shit like that. And almost always by people who don't know a missile from sewer pipe." The station chief paused and smiled. "There was one report, however, that pricked everyone's ears a bit."

"And?"

"It said that some villagers claimed that they saw Soviet trucks moving through a village where they had to keep backing up to make some turns. Most trucks, they claimed, don't have those sorts of problems, not in their village anyway," Breckenridge explained. "And that got the analysts to thinking that they might be medium-range ballistic missile tubes, because they would have been long enough to create those kinds of transportation problems on an island like Cuba."

"But all of it was still pretty sketchy, right?"

"Yeah, but the Ambo told me this morning that our hopes are up back in Washington that we'll be able to find out more. And soon." Breckenridge smiled. "In fact, they already have."

"How so?"

"The U-2s have gotten some pictures of missile sights and construction work."

"So the analysts have been able to determine what they're up to in Cuba?"

Breckenridge nodded while sitting back again. He started petting his tie again. "That's right. The imagery analysts believe they've now found at least four missile sites. The Ambassador told me the President has already been briefed."

That's pretty damn quick," Baier said. "Today's the 17th right?"

Breckenridge nodded. "Getting confused by all the travel and excitement, Karl?"

"Yeah, I guess so. But that's pretty damn quick. I mean, the U-2s have been in the air for about a week, right? And now they've gotten the photographic evidence, the analysis, and given the President what he needed."

"I guess that shows how fortunate it was to get those planes back in the air," Breckenridge added, "especially because of all the bad weather. There have apparently been a whole lot of goddamn clouds over the island. The satellites haven't been much use."

"Even the infrared ones?" Baier asked.

Breckenridge shook his head and finally let his tie fall back into place at the center of his white dress shirt. "I guess not. Apparently, the resolution has also been pretty shitty. Too much so for the imagery guys to make out anything definite."

"And the Soviets? What have they had to say?"

Breckenridge waved his right hand in the air. "Oh, more of the same nonsense. You know 'we would never put offensive weapons in Cuba. Anything we deliver will be defensive only.' And so on and so forth."

Baier thought about what the next steps were likely to be if the Agency and the White House were so confident about the new information. The Joint Chiefs and Congress would probably start demanding an immediate military—or some kind of 'tough'—response. Given his hesitation and indecision during the Berlin Wall crisis, Baier wondered how Kennedy would handle that sort of pressure. More information from human sources would certainly help.

"So, what has your reporting, especially Topokov's, done to help?"

Breckenridge took this opportunity to stand and move over to the sofa, where he took the seat at the opposite end from Baier. He leaned in close with both hands dangling between his knees, as though this might help prevent anyone from overhearing what he was about to say.

"Well, for one, thing, the guy knew the people involved in making recommendations to Khrushchev and who the real decisionmakers are on Cuba. I guess it's because he served there before coming here."

Baier leaned in close as well, hoping to prod Breckenridge to be more forthcoming.

"I can see where that might help," he said. "But it sounds like he was one step removed. He wasn't actually contributing to the policy discussions, but he knew the people who were?"

"That's sounds about like it," Breckenridge responded. "But he could still give Washington a sense of what those advisers are like and what sort of perspectives they might have."

"Anything concrete on the missiles themselves? You know, deliveries, construction, locations, command and control?"

The station chief leaned back. "No, not yet. He complained that he had to be very cautious in terms what he tried to see. He did not want to raise any suspicions, which is good tradecraft, of course."

"Of course. But did you give him requirements for that sort of thing? Like specifics on Soviet decisions? Given the tensions in both capitals that sort of knowledge would be invaluable. People are talking about a possible nuclear war here."

"Oh, hell yes. You don't think the Soviet Division in Headquarters was pressing us on that? And we were happy to oblige. But Garner said Topokov would get very uncomfortable whenever he brought the issue up. It was almost as though he was already under suspicion or pressure of some sort. He did give us some good background stuff on the Big K, though."

"Like what?" Baier pressed.

"He claimed that Khrushchev was the instigator of the policy on the missiles in Cuba. He claimed that the Soviet leader thought he could manipulate Kennedy again, like he did in Vienna and Berlin. That the Big K believed our President would not be able to stand up to the pressure."

Baier thought back to his own experience in Berlin as the Wall went up and of the general confusion and hesitation that reigned in Washington. He was not surprised to hear that the Soviet leadership, especially a street tough like Khrushchev, had drawn that sort of a conclusion.

"So, did he say that there were ballistic missiles in Cuba?"

Breckenridge nodded. "In so many words, yeah."

"And how did that report go down back home?"

The hair ruffling and tie stroking resumed. "Well, you see, we did not send that in," Breckenridge confessed.

Baier stood, running his own hand through his hair, then massaging his cheeks before speaking. "You what? What the fuck, Jim?"

"It was too vague. The sourcing was more like speculation. Can you imagine what sort of impact that might have created? Given the importance of the issue, I wanted more clarity. More certainty."

"But surely you sent it back in an operations cable, something that would have stayed in our building. It did not have to be disseminated intelligence if you had those kinds of concerns."

Breckenridge stood and faced off with Baier. "Oh, come off it, Karl. You know damn well someone would have run downtown with that or shot their mouth off at some White House meeting."

"That's not your decision, Jim. Surely, you followed up, though. Did Topokov have anything to add?"

"We never got the chance to follow up. He's dead, Karl. Or have you missed that?"

The silence that hung between the two men was heavy and hard. Baier noticed that his heart was beating at a pace like he had just climbed two or three flights of stairs. Breckenridge's chest heaved like his was doing the same. The Americans stared at each other for about a minute. Finally, the station chief broke the silence.

"Perhaps we should continue this discussion after we've had a chance to calm down and reflect a little more."

Baier looked at the floor and nodded. "Fair enough."

"Is there anything else before we do, though?" Breckenridge added.

"Just that you should know I was approached twice at the Pera Palace. You might want to keep our people away from there for now."

"Why what happened?"

"The first was a mild sort of pitch. More of a honey trap, actually."

"Oh really? Interesting. Who did it come from?"

"I think it was the Turks. At least she looked and sounded Turkish. Really beautiful and one hell of a body. She approached me outside my room."

"You sure it was a trap?"

Baier nodded.

"Too bad," Breckenridge consoled.

"Yeah. She was back in the bar the next night, but only waved at me from across the room."

"What scared her off?"

"The two Soviet goons who came to my table to warn me off this case. Or cases."

"Say what? The Russkies are trying to scare you away? What the hell…?"

"That's what I thought. At least Bob Hughes thought they were Soviets. And the accent did remind me of what I heard working with Soviets in Europe over the years. I suppose they could have been Turks, but I would bet against it."

Breckenridge shook his head. "Naw, not likely. They wouldn't have stuck around the bar. Unless they wanted to get some drinking in as well. Our friends here would be more likely to pull you in, throw you in a chair, and then sweat you for a couple hours. After which, they would set you loose with heartfelt apologies about their terrible 'mistake.'"

"And the woman?"

Breckenridge's smile returned. "Now, that is a mystery. That's actually pretty subtle for our Turkish hosts. If it is them, then they have upped their game considerably. But I'm skeptical there as well."

"Why is that?"

"They don't need to go that route with us. They could always press me or one of the other officers to find out whether their suspicions about you are correct."

"Suspicions?"

Breckenridge's smile widened. "Hell, Karl, they're suspicious of everything we do here." The chief laughed and shook his head. "Karl, you need to break away from that training division and get away from your desk. You obviously miss being in the field."

Baier turned to go. "I am away from my desk. I'm in Turkey," he said and let the words drift over his shoulder as he left the office.

• • •

This time, Baier did catch his tail.

Breckenridge had agreed to let Baier have a look at the reporting from the three Soviet assets over the last six months, which Baier had requested. He had asked for anything from the three sources that would take him back before the beginnings of the Cuban missile crisis that started during the summer. He had found little there in the way of revelations, at least until the week before the assassinations had occurred in early September. And it was not in the intelligence reporting shared more broadly in Washington, but in the operational cables that explained the background and discussions of the meetings themselves.

It was in the last week of August that both Topokov and Levkovsky, the Foreign Ministry and KGB officers, respectively, had mentioned some information that had arrived in their residence about a Soviet measure that would be aimed at both the Turks and the Americans. Nothing more specific had been noted in the operational traffic. Both men had claimed that they wanted to check on the documentation itself, the reporting of which had not come by their desks. They did not have the "need to know," apparently. Instead, they had picked up the information from loose office gossip, of which they claimed there was always way too much around the Soviet Embassy.

To give himself some added time to consider the various angles of this revelation and its many possible implications, Baier had decided to return to his hotel later that afternoon in a leisurely stroll along Ataturk Boulevard. More conscious now of the potential for hidden danger in his surroundings after the run-ins in Istanbul, Baier had also kept an eye out for any surveillance the Turks—or other strangers—might put on him.

And sure enough, just about halfway to the hotel and five or six blocks from the Embassy, Baier had noticed the consistent presence of two heavyset men in long black raincoats who had accompanied him along the way. They took turns shadowing him, a maneuver intended to present alternating looks and confuse Baier as to whether he was being followed. But Baier had seen both men more than once in the short distance he had walked, so the unwanted company had naturally gotten his attention.

Baier decided to make sure by taking a detour through a residential neighborhood off to the right, which was also in the direction of his hotel. In addition to houses and apartment blocks there were several restaurants and shops, enough to give Baier the opportunity to stop and window shop while checking for the tails, but not enough to give his newfound friends much to hide in. He sighted both men at once, after which they disappeared, almost certainly spooked by their failure to remain unnoticed.

Back in his hotel room, Baier had another surprise. More unwanted company. A short, thin individual sat on the edge of his bed, while two more men—both of whom had body frames well over six feet tall—stood to the side. They also appeared to carry broad shoulders and muscular arms underneath their dark blue suits. Their cropped black hair was matched on each face by thick black mustaches that fell over their upper lips. Baier did not bother to look any further. The man on the bed wore a grey suit with a pale blue dress shirt and dark red tie that had some kind of checkered pattern in black. Paris fashion it was not. Neither were his manners.

"It is about time you returned, Mister Baier. You've kept us waiting too long," the smaller one of the group on the bed complained.

"My apologies," Baier answered. "I was delayed trying to get rid of two of your colleagues who insisted on following me back here."

The man on the bed look puzzled. "Our colleagues? Following you? Why would anyone do that? We already know where you are staying." He waved his right arm around the room. "You see, don't you, that we are already here. Waiting for you to return. Why would we need to follow you when we already know what you are doing here?"

"Then just who," Baier continued, "where those clowns out there tripping over themselves?"

The man shrugged. "Perhaps they are your real enemies."

"Real enemies?"

"Yes, the Russians. Those are the ones you need to concern yourself with. Not us. We are your allies." He glanced at his companions, who both nodded in agreement. "Yes, they were Russians."

"Fine. But then what the hell are doing in my room? Uninvited, I might add."

The man rose from the bed and approached Baier, his hand extended. "Allow me to introduce myself," he said. "My name is Mucip Sadak, and I work for Turkish intelligence, the National Security Service. I am sorry we have gotten off to the wrong start, as I believe we will be seeing more of each other while you are here."

"And why would that be?"

Sadak smiled and glanced at his companions. "Come now, Mister Baier. We know why you are here. I mean, do you really expect us to believe that you are here on a training mission for your American colleagues in the Embassy? A man with your background?"

"That is not really up to me to determine what you believe or do not believe. I do not care. If you have any questions you can direct them to the Embassy, and Counselor James Breckenridge."

"Ah yes, your station chief. We are already aware of him and his presence. In fact, we have developed quite a good working relationship with him. As I noted earlier, we are allies, and our liaison relationship is an important one."

"Then why are you here?" Baier pressed. "And again, uninvited? I assume the hotel management let you in. I will have to file a complaint and let the Embassy know how official visitors are treated here."

"Oh, you can complain all you like. If it makes you feel better. We are hoping that you can keep us informed of what you find out about the deaths and disappearance of the three Soviet officers. We would like to offer our assistance and ask for some of yours in return."

Baier smiled and shook his head. "I am afraid the only assistance I can offer is in some training on management and intra-service cooperation. Does your service need that? I am sure my organization would be happy to provide it. I cannot guarantee that I will be the one to teach those classes, but I can guarantee that whomever we send will certainly be qualified."

Sadak's face took on a frown and deep color as he stepped in close enough for Baier to smell the tobacco on his breath. He also appeared to have eaten fish for lunch.

"If you continue to insult my intelligence with this cock and bull story, Mister Baier, I will be forced to ask my colleagues to intervene. They are not nearly as diplomatic as me."

Baier looked over at the two muscle men and shrugged.

"They would also not be nearly as sweet and pleasant as the woman who visited you at the hotel, Mister Baier."

Baier could not hide his surprise. "So that was you guys? Imagine that. Do all the women in your service look like her?"

Sadak's smile returned. "Perhaps you will see for yourself someday. But for now, you should know that we have photographs."

"Of what?"

"Of the two of you together."

"Nothing happened."

Sadak shrugged and displayed a smile that reminded Baier of a snake. "We can always let others be the judge of that."

"And you guys are asking for my cooperation? Is that how you want to play this?"

"Remember, Mister Baier, you are on our playing field now." He stepped back and slapped himself on the cheek. "But what am I thinking? You are correct. This is no way to begin our friendship. You must have made me lose my temper."

Sadak stepped away further, moving toward the door. He retrieved his overcoat, which Baier noticed just now one of goons was holding. Baier assumed it had been draped over the chair at his back, as it seemed to have appeared from nowhere. Sadak held the coat out to his colleague, who spread it open behind Sadak's back. Sadak then ran his arms through the sleeves of the coat and pulled it up to fit over his shoulders. He shook his head again and gave Baier a look as though to say that the next move was up to him.

"As I said before, Mister Sadak, I have nothing I can give you beyond pointers at the challenges of personnel management and perhaps drafting reports to send back home. And even for that you will have to speak with Mister Breckenridge."

The three Turks moved toward the door. Just shy of the entrance, however, Sadak stopped and turned to Baier. His lips were pursed, as though they were troubled by a deep thought, while his eyes studied the floor. When he looked up there was no smile, only a look of recognition, that he was about to reveal something of great moment to Baier.

"We will be seeing more of each other, Mister Baier. We have been with you all along, and that will not change."

"You are welcome to waste as much time as you like."

Sadak paused and stared for a moment at the floor. When he looked up again, his smile had returned. "Perhaps it would help you to know something about this Levkovsky fellow, Mister Baier. Something that will help you make the right decision."

Baier stared at his guest. He said nothing.

"This KGB officer was also working for us."

Baier remained silent as the three men left his room.

# CHAPTER TEN

"Mucip Sadak, you say?" Breckenridge asked.

Baier nodded. "That's right. And he seemed to know a lot about why I'm here."

Baier found himself in what was becoming his usual spot on the sofa in the station chief's office: the corner closest to the door. He hadn't chosen it for a quick escape or anything that dramatic. It was just the most convenient place to drop whenever Breckenridge told him to grab a seat. Both men had shown up at work that morning in dark grey suits, although Baier's blue dress shirt offered a modest contrast to Breckenridge's white one. Their ties were also different. Breckenridge had on the striped one Baier remembered from his first full day in Ankara, while Baier wore a light blue number with small yellow polka dots. If Delgrecchio had been there he would have accused Baier of reverting to the fashion tastes of the Eisenhower Administration once again. For this session both had left their suit jackets either hanging on the peg by the door in his office—or in Baier's case, the chair in his cubicle. Somehow, their respective uniforms and the considered absence of their jackets reflected a combination of seriousness and relaxation. It was the working environment that Baier preferred.

"Like what?" Breckenridge pressed.

"Like that I am not here on any sort of training mission. He knows I'm here to investigate the deaths of the three Soviet assets. I don't suppose there's been a leak of some sort."

Breckenridge frowned, then shook his head. "Naw, I seriously doubt that."

"You should know if there is."

"Yeah, of course. They probably put two and two together and surprisingly came up with four. It isn't that hard to figure out, if you think about it. They know about the Soviet officers' deaths."

"But how do they know our connection to the three men?"

Breckenridge shrugged. "Good question. You should probably be looking into that as well."

"Fine. But what impact could that have on my assignment here? Will they interfere? Will they try to steer us away from what really happened?"

"What did really happen? Isn't that why you're here?"

"Dammit, Jim, I still feel like I am just getting started on this thing. No one seems to know anything about how these assets could have been blown and why the Soviets—assuming that's who's behind the three deaths—acted how and when they did."

Breckenridge thought for a moment and slowly wheeled his chair in a full circle. "Well, the Levkovsky case was certainly the Soviets. I mean, the guy was hustled back to Moscow, so I don't see who else it could be. It is interesting, though, that the Turks have approached you as they did. First a honey trap..." Baier started to speak. "... or an attempted honey trap. And now Sadak himself puts in an appearance in your hotel room. Waiting for you, as you say."

"Yes, that's what I say, and that's what happened. Just what is his position?"

"Well, that does make some sense. He's the head of the American desk over at NSS."

"That would explain his good English. But what's he like? Does he like us, or does he consider it his life's mission to put us in our place and send us back across the Atlantic?"

Breckenridge smiled as he shook his head. "No, no, it's nothing like that. I've always had the impression that he rather likes us Americans. And that he believes in our alliance and working together."

"Why is that?"

"I think it comes, first of all, from his family's background. His father's family came to Turkey from the Crimea back during the reign of Catherine the Great, when Russia was busy gobbling up land to the south and in Ottoman territories around the Black Sea. Or so he told me. And his mother's family came from Bulgaria when the Ottoman Empire was imploding back at the beginning of this century. He even said at one point that he still has relatives living among the Turkish minority in Bulgaria. And they are not too happy, apparently. But it's those people with the European heritage that support Turkey's western orientation. And we, of course, are a big part of that now."

"Small wonder there. So, it's safe to say that he's anti-Soviet and anti-Warsaw Pact. And that he sees us as a good antidote in this rough neighborhood Turkey lives in."

"Even if you're going to mix your metaphors, Karl, I think that's right. It has certainly been my impression."

"So, his approach—and I'm assuming he's behind the honey trap thing—has just been a bit ham-handed?" Baier asked.

"That would be my guess. Of course, the inspiration for that awkward move could have come from another office, and Mucip was just pressured into it. In any case, I doubt you have much to worry about."

"Then how would you recommend I play his approach?" Baier raised his hand. "And do not suggest that I invite the beautiful young woman into my room if she approaches me again."

Breckenridge laughed. "Heaven forbid, Karl. Sabine would have me castrated if I made any such proposal. Even if it would be in the interests of national security." His face turned serious. "I think you'll need to keep him at arm's length, though. You obviously do not want to get too serious with him, and by extension, the NSS. We cannot afford to make him aware of our unilateral efforts here, even if they are against a common target and enemy." Breckenridge held up his hand to ward off a possible protest from Baier. "Yes, I realize they appear to know enough already, but plausible deniability remains our objective on matters like these. Can you imagine what they would be demanding in return if we fessed up? We would lose control of those operations, as well as lose all kinds of tradecraft that we do not want to share. You might want to discuss this with Fred

Badger, though. He's usually the one who meets with Sadak and people from his office."

"Why Fred? I would have thought that you would have taken the lead on this relationship."

"Fred has much better Turkish than me. I think he's more of a linguist than I am. He's really taken to the language, and frankly, I've struggled with it. It's pretty damn complicated."

"Sadak seemed to speak pretty good English yesterday."

"But it's like a lot of these countries, Karl. I'm sure you experienced the same in Germany. The natives appreciate it so much more if you can converse in their tongue, especially when you've obviously made the effort to master one as tough as Turkish."

"Okay, then fine, I'll reach out to Fred. But I agree with your recommendation, Jim. I will find a way to keep our Turkish friend at arm's length. I should be able to manage that."

"Good. I know you are not exactly a novice at this game, Karl. I trust you."

That is good, Baier thought as he rose to leave. But he plodded out of the chief's office with a distinctly uncomfortable feeling deep in his gut. It looked like the Turks had already penetrated at least some of our operations in their country, Baier thought, if this Sadak fellow knew as much as he let on yesterday. And was that all he knew?

More significant in Baier's eyes was the claim that they had also been running the KGB asset. Baier certainly expected them to go after that target, especially on their home turf, given the country's history and international alignments, especially its membership in NATO. But why and how did they chance upon our one asset from that service in this town? Coincidence was a difficult concept to accept in this business, and Baier seriously doubted he could blow this double-sided recruitment off to that. Maybe this Levkovsky was too open to approaches from a hostile service, and that may explain how the Soviets stumbled upon his work for the Americans. Or perhaps they hadn't even been aware of the American angle, and they grabbed him because he had been working for the Turks. The possibilities and explanations were multiplying just when they should have been narrowing. An even bigger explanation that Baier could not provide was why he had failed to inform Breckenridge about Levkovsky's triple play. Another gut feeling? If so, then about what?

• • •

Baier and Fred Badger agreed to take a stroll after sharing a lunch of white rice and chicken cutlets in the cafeteria at work. That plate was the special for the day, and Badger assured Baier that those two ingredients were usually pretty safe in Turkey. Baier noticed that Badger passed on the salad, though, so he did the same. They crossed Ataturk Boulevard and headed up a hill through a small park that led to a series of shops and to a couple new hotels rising on the horizon. It was close to the neighborhood where Baier had lost his surveillance team the day before. He liked the area, as it reminded him of the sort of neighborhood one found in many European cities. Perhaps this was what Ataturk and his acolytes had had in mind when he decided to turn Turkey's face to the West. At least commercially and socially. The contrast with Ankara's eastern neighborhoods was remarkable. It was like the presence of two different worlds in the same city, a gulf that was coming to fascinate and intrigue Baier at the same time.

"Jim tells me that you've been handling a major part of the liaison work with the Turks. Is that true?" Baier asked.

Badger shrugged and nodded. "I suppose so."

"Why is that? Has your boss set any kind of limits or boundaries?"

Badger shook his head. "Not really. He says he trusts me. There haven't been any problems that I'm aware of." He glanced over at Baier. "Or am I wrong?"

Baier looked back at the deputy chief. "Not necessarily."

"I was hoping for a more-ringing endorsement."

"What would you say your boss's relationship with the Turks is like? He seems pretty relaxed."

Badger was silent for a moment before responding. "I don't think he likes them. He just doesn't trust them as much as he would one of our European allies. At least, that's my impression. I think that's why he would rather have me deal with them."

"And you? How do you feel about them? Do you trust them?"

Badger shrugged again and stopped. He surveyed the park and then looked back at the heavy traffic along Ataturk Boulevard. It was a sunny day and warm enough for many of the locals to be taking their post-lunch stroll in shirt sleeves. "I like them," he answered. "I also think I understand them and where they're coming from."

"And where is that?"

"It's where they find themselves at the moment. That's why they want to be close to us. They're surrounded by historical enemies and historical instability. We offer them a way out."

"Do you think they're sincere in their commitment to NATO and the alliance with us?"

"Oh, hell yes. That part is real enough and unlikely to change for the foreseeable future. I really doubt they would do anything to undermine their relationship with us."

"And yet, I sense there's something else there," Baier continued.

"Yes, I'd say there is. This place is different from any of our other allies. At least the ones I've known, mostly in Europe."

"How so?"

"It's because there are so many other historical currents at work here. And they all flow in different directions. The biggest one is their history as an Islamic country and Turkey's role as the Caliphate during the Ottoman Empire. Sort of like Islam's Vatican."

Baier thought back to his own use of the phrase when explaining Turkey's religious importance under the Ottomans. "And what is that impact on Turkey today?"

"It's hidden mostly. But every once in a while it starts to rear its head. I think that's what was happening under the Menderes government, and it's why the military stepped in. Those guys are not going to let anything upset the secular apple cart. But the religious question will not go away. Not in my view, anyway."

"And where could that lead? Surely not towards the Soviet Union, godless as that is."

"No, I seriously doubt that. Although there are a lot of Muslims in the USSR as well."

"So?"

"So, that's where you might see some impact. Not that Turkey would become more aligned with the Russkies. Even if the religious atmosphere did become more open in the Soviet Union, it would be dominated by the Russian Orthodox Church. And the Muslims up there would get the short end of that social and historical stick. But that religious issue could become a more important factor in policy here. Maybe even make Turkey less of a western country and more of a Middle Eastern one." Badger laughed. "But that is a long way off yet. The military and other secularists have a pretty good handle on things. So, I think our alliance is secure for now."

The two men resumed their walk, but this time they headed back down the hill and a return to their desks. It was well past the lunch hour by now, and Baier was looking forward to his afternoon coffee. Try as he might, he could not completely shake his jet lag.

"Where would you put Mucip Sadak in all this?" Baier asked.

This brought Badger to a halt. "Mucip? Why do you ask?"

Baier looked his lunch partner in the eye. "Because he paid me a visit at my hotel room yesterday evening. In fact, he was waiting in my room when I got back."

"Holy shit! Why would he do that?"

"I was hoping you could help me figure that out," Baier replied. "How well do you know the man? Is he the one you've dealt with over at NSS?"

"Well, he's one of them. And, yeah, I have seen him a lot. He has always impressed me as pretty pro-American. Not because he likes our movies or music, mind you, but because of what I said before."

"Remind me."

"Because he sees us as good for Turkey and where it needs to go. We provide support in this troubled area they live in. By 'we' I mean our country and our service. And we can help steer Turkey's future toward the West and a modern economy and society, and away from what the Kemalists see as Turkey's dark past."

"Kemalists?"

"That's the label for the secularists. Ataturk's original name was Mustafa Kemal."

"I see," Baier said. He thought for a moment as the two Americans resumed their stroll. "So, you don't see anything threatening or ominous in his visit."

Badger shook his head. "No, I can't see it that way. What did he want? Did he say?"

"Yes, he did. He wants to work with me on investigating the loss of our three assets. Either that or have me keep him informed."

Badger whistled. "Shit, Sir, you can't very well do that. I'm surprised they even knew about all that." Badger was silent again, but then he shrugged. "Those guys are not stupid, though, especially Sadak. I can't say as I'm surprised that they eventually put it all together. I mean, they had to suspect something was up when those three guys suddenly disappeared. And then you arrive." He smiled. "I wondered how long your cover story would hold."

"What about Levkovsky? Did you ever discuss the Turks with him?"

"No, why should I? He did make some comments that he enjoyed living here. He said it was much nicer than back home. But then I thought he could say that about anywhere. Or just about anywhere."

"And you're pretty sure that Levkovsky was not aware of the other two sources we had here from his country?"

Badger nodded and looked around the park before returning Baier's gaze. "Yeah. Why? I mean, he never said anything to let on that he knew more was up."

"It's just that the Soviets are notorious for loose talk and gossip. Someone could easily have said something that your asset might have picked up."

"I suppose that's true. But my guy never said a word if he did hear anything."

"Fair enough. I'm just trying to explore all the possible angles. I'm sure you understand." There was a moment of silence before Baier continued. Their walk had slowed, as both seemed to enjoy the warm sunshine and the absence of humidity. It was very un-Washington-like.

"Did he say something about a Soviet plan regarding Cuba and its objectives there?" Baier asked.

"He mentioned something about that. He said that a new directive had arrived from Moscow, but that he had not had the chance to see it yet. He was going to try to get a look at it before our next meet."

"And when was this?"

"It was back in early September. The 10th, if I remember correctly. He said it could be very important, but he wanted to make sure whatever he told me was accurate."

"How frequently did you meet with him?"

"Once a month, usually near the middle. But with things in Cuba heating up, I wanted to meet again sooner. We had our next meeting set for the first week in October." Badger eyes found the ground, where his gaze stayed for several seconds before he looked up at Baier again. "I keep wondering if my pressure to meet again so soon is what did him in."

Baier laid a hand on his shoulder. "No, that wasn't it. I'm pretty sure your tradecraft was not the issue."

"Then what was?"

Baier ignored the question. "And the Turks never let on or gave any hint that they knew about your relationship with Levkovsky?"

"No, nothing that I would interpret as such. Why? What are you driving at?"

Baier sighed and looked around. When he turned back to Badger, there was a different look to the man's face. The eyes had narrowed to slits of suspicion, and the lips were tight together, as though he wanted to make sure that no words, no thoughts escaped.

"The Turks were running him as well," Baier said. "That's why you never picked up any surveillance, at least from our local hosts.

They already knew all about your meetings with him. He probably passed along whatever you two discussed. I'm just wondering who else might have known."

# CHAPTER ELEVEN

Once again, Baier had company waiting for him when he returned to his hotel. This time, though, his visitor knocked at the door to his room. To his surprise, it was the beautiful maiden from Istanbul.

"What, you don't have your own key? The rest of your organization seems to."

She smiled and leaned against the door frame, a movement that in itself seemed packed with mystery and innuendo. "No, I am afraid I am not that important." She paused, as though waiting for something to happen. Her eyes broke from Baier's face just long enough to look into his room. "May I come in?"

Baier stepped back and held the door. "Of course. Others in your service have no trouble coming in, so why not you as well?" He studied his new visitor as she walked toward the middle of the room, where she stopped and looked back at him over her shoulder. "I thought you worked out of Istanbul," he said. "Don't tell me you followed me here."

She resumed her march, sliding her hips, aware that Baier's eyes had not moved from her. She got as far as the bed, stood for a moment pondering the pillows, then wheeled in Baier's direction with a move that was quick, light, almost soundless, as though she could walk on a cloud. "No, I am based here in Ankara. I was sent to Istanbul to follow you."

"Then you are very good. I never noticed you until you appeared before my room at the Pera Palace."

She smiled and fixed Baier with her eyes. "They told me that is what would happen."

"So, to what do I owe this dubious pleasure? And would you please tell me your name?"

"My name is Dafne. And I am here to invite you to visit Mister Sadak at our service's headquarters."

"Dafne does not sound like a Turkish name."

"Oh, but it is. Or it can be. It is the Turkish spelling for the Greek name Daphne." She spelled both for Baier. "I am sure you have heard that before. We Turks are very open about those sorts of things."

"Did not the founder of modern Turkey, Ataturk…"

"I know who he is."

"…Say something like, 'Happy is he who is a Turk'? That does not sound very open. In fact, it sounds overly nationalistic. Xenophobic even."

"What he actually said was, 'Happy is he who calls himself a Turk.' It means there should be no limits placed on a citizen because of his or her ethnic or racial background. This land has been crossed and occupied by many nations and tribes."

"I see," Baier said. "But couldn't it also mean that he was creating a new identity for this country, one no longer associated with a multinational empire like the Ottoman one? An identity that is, in fact, dependent on a particular ethnic or religious group?"

She smiled and shrugged. "That is what some say."

"And you? What is your background?"

Dafne took a seat on the edge of the bed. She let her skirt slide above her knees like an invitation. She crossed her legs to make sure Baier got an even better view. "My family comes from the Black Sea region, in the town of Trabzon. My people come from the Pontic Greeks who had settled the region centuries ago. Do you know the country there?"

Baier shook his head. "No, not really. Or not at all, actually."

"It is quite beautiful. The Pontic Mountains run almost to the sea, where Trabzon sits between the two like a beautiful nest. Among many here of Greek backgrounds there is a pride that the town and surrounding region did not surrender to the Ottomans until eight years after the fall of Constantinople. After the fall of the Empire in 1919 and the Revolution many left for Greece."

"You mean expelled, don't you?"

Again, the smile. "Some see it that way."

"I would say most see it that way."

"My family were rather prosperous and decided to adopt the new nation as its own. After all, Turkey had been our home for generations, whatever its name or its government."

"And where did you learn your excellent English? You sound almost British."

"My father sent me to school in London. The educational opportunities for women are still rather limited in Turkey, despite Mustafa Kemal's efforts to modernize our country in that way, too."

Dafne recrossed her legs, and the skirt rode inches higher above her knee. After a few seconds Baier realized he was staring. He shook his head in an effort to clear it. He needed to think straight.

"And now you are employed to follow and seduce an American visitor."

Dafne's smile widened. It had never disappeared almost from the moment she entered the room. Her straight, white teeth sparkled. "Oh, I have other tasks as well. Which is a good thing, because I do not believe you are willing to be seduced."

Baier nodded. "That is correct. For a number of reasons."

"And those would be?"

"Well first of all, I am married, as I mentioned in Istanbul."

"Yes, I remember."

"I also do not think it is right for you to be used in this way. You appear to be a very intelligent and talented woman. But regardless, it is wrong. Although I know it is common. In many places."

Dafne stood. "Thank you for that. But that is also not why I came to see you this evening. I have no intention of seducing you."

"And in Istanbul."

She smiled. "No, not there either."

"Oh? And why are you here tonight?"

"As I said when I entered your room, I am here because Mister Sadak would like to meet you to continue your discussion from the other evening."

"I was not aware that we had more to say to each other."

She approached Baier and came close enough to touch him. "He believes you do. He thinks he can help you with your work here. He thinks you will need his help to overcome certain hurdles."

"What hurdles would those be?"

She walked toward the telephone next to the bed and wrote something on a slip of note paper. Then she moved toward the door. "I will let Mister Sadak explain those to you. But he believes there are people who want to prevent you from succeeding here."

"I see. And what exactly is in it for Mr. Sadak?"

"That is up to him to say." Dafne walked to the door, then paused with her hand on the doorknob. "I hope you will accept Mister Sadak's invitation. I am supposed to be the notetaker. That is, if you want there to be notes. He also thinks that I should serve as your liaison to our service." Her smile slid away slowly. "Because of my excellent English."

Baier watched the door close behind this remarkable and alluring woman. He turned back into his room, struck suddenly by the shabby atmosphere he found there for the first time since he had arrived. The red carpet, the scarlet curtains, the plump bedding, and even the white and silver wallpaper in the bathroom, all seemed suddenly so worn and tired. Almost like a cliché from decades past. He had not paid much attention to the décor when he first arrived and only noticed these things now. He had not expected something akin to the Ritz or the Waldorf, of course, and at most moments this hotel would qualify like any other four-star accommodation. But now it all seemed cheap, like a setup he could not escape.

He decided to go down to the bar and maybe take a walk through the neighborhood. Anything to get out of the room. When he got back, he would make sure it wasn't bugged once more. He realized he should have done that every night, as soon as he returned. But he had been far too complacent, confident that he had little to fear from the locals or any other service in town. This was, after all, friendly territory. He had been foolish to the point of acting like an amateur. He realized now the only friend he could fully trust was himself. But he would still see what this Sadak fellow had to offer.

• • •

The last thing Baier was going to do at this point would be to pay a call at Sadak's office in NSS headquarters. He might as well save himself the time and simply paint a target on his back for everyone to see, including his colleagues in the station. Instead, he called Dafne the next morning to ask her to arrange a meeting—after checking the phone for a bug—in a restaurant where they could have some privacy for a candid discussion. She claimed that would be no problem and gave him directions to a restaurant on a back street behind the main shopping district downtown at the end of Ataturk Boulevard where the government offices faded into a commercial district.

Baier spent the rest of that day reading through the reporting from the three Soviet sources. He was interrupted only once when Jim Breckenridge came by his cubicle around the middle of the morning.

"Hey, Karl, I just left the Ambassador's morning staff meeting, and he wanted me to be sure to pass something along for you."

"Sure. What is it?"

"Well, my man, it looks as though the U-2s have picked up something very interesting."

"And that would be?"

"Construction for additional missile batteries, and the folks in Washington are pretty sure that they are all designed to house medium range ballistic missiles. And nuclear-capable ones at that."

Baier shot up from his chair. "Jesus Christ! How do they know that?"

"For one thing, there are the launch pads. Far too big for short range defensive things. You know, the kind that would be used to repel shipping in support of another Bay of Pigs operation. Like we'd be stupid enough to try that again."

"Well, let's hope not. But was there anything else?"

"Oh, sure. They did have defensive surface-to-air missiles in place, presumably to protect the installation from an air attack. And then there were the missiles themselves."

"They actually identified the missiles?"

"Not exactly. They were still in their casings. But the size suggests they couldn't be anything else. People in Washington are shitting bricks, as you can imagine."

"I'll bet. Any word on our response?"

"Not yet. There's a White House meeting today, chaired by the president himself. He's convened something called the Executive Committee of the National Security Council, or EXCOMM for short."

"Let's use that term instead of the full title," Baier suggested.

"Yeah, no shit. Anyway, I guess they'll review the photos and then discuss options. There are already a couple on the table, from continuing the diplomatic efforts to a full-scale invasion. I wouldn't be surprised if they sent out some briefing teams to the Allies. Things are going to get hairy, and it would be a good idea to have them on board if it comes to shooting. Any interest in joining that club? The briefing teams, I mean. You still have plenty of friends, from what I hear, in Bonn and London."

"Things must be getting serious back home," Baier said. "It's only the 19th, and we've gone from the initial photographs to a discussion of possible military responses."

Baier studied the papers on his desk as he thought about the importance of bringing our allies, especially those in NATO, up to speed on what we had found in Cuba. "That would be interesting. But I think I'll stick with my work here."

Breckenridge shrugged. "Suit yourself. I would have thought that you'd jump at the chance for a trip to see your Kraut friends, or the Brits."

"Any chance our briefers will come to talk to the Turks?"

"Not sure. But I'll be sure to let you know if they do. If not, the Turks will be plenty pissed. They are convinced we're going to sell them down the proverbial river with those Jupiters, using them as leverage to bring the Soviets to a bargain. That is, if we don't go to war first."

• • •

As he entered the restaurant Sonja had directed him to, Baier understood why the Turks had chosen this place. The outside looked modest enough, with a string of lights that would have made for a nice show on a Christmas tree back home. They were stretched over the poles that lined the garden area in front, and grapevines ran up the sides and along the patio covering to provide a modicum of privacy for the visitors. Underneath those there were about a dozen tables for diners when the weather was nice. Like tonight, although only three tables were occupied. And those could well have been patrons from the National Security Service on this particular evening.

Inside, there was a large dining area with about another twenty tables, and only about a quarter of those were in service. Baier doubted that every customer tonight worked for the NSS, but given the apparent reach of the service in Turkey, he would not have bet against it. At the back there were three private dining rooms, and Sadak waited at the entrance to the one on the far left. Sonja, to Baier's pleasure, stood right behind him. Inside another gentleman waited at the table.

"Ah, Mister Baier, welcome to this restaurant. I am so glad you decided to come. And I hope you are hungry for some real Turkish food."

Baier took the hand that was offered as they strolled to the table. "Dafne made it sound as though it might be helpful. I thought the least I could do would be to sound you out." He surveyed the restaurant. "And, yes, I am looking forward to a true Turkish dinner tonight."

They sat, and waiters immediately brought in a tray of meze, the array of Turkish appetizers that included such delicacies as stuffed grape leaves, small bowls of hummus with a variety of spices, meat pastries, and other dishes that Baier did not recognize.

"We could make a meal of this alone," Baier said.

"Yes," Sadak, replied, "many do. But you will want to eat carefully because there will be plates of kebobs after this, of course."

"Yes, of course. Then perhaps we should get down to business before I become too groggy from all the food and wine." Baier pointed to the glasses of red and white wine that sat next to his cutlery.

Sadak smiled and nodded. "Of course. Perhaps I may begin with a question."

"Of course," Baier answered.

"What do you know of the Soviet presence here? Its size, and its composition?"

Baier thought for a moment while he finished one of the stuffed grape leaves. "Oh, I'd say it's probably about 50 intelligence officers, or so. Some working out of the Embassy here and the Consulate in Istanbul. Others from the TASS offices and the trading organization, Amtorg."

"Mister Baier, if you doubled your number you would be closer to the truth, but probably still short. Have you tried to see what they were up to when your agents disappeared?"

Baier spooned some hummus onto his plate and only looked at his host without answering right away. When he did speak, Baier shook his head and smiled briefly.

"I'm not admitting to anything Mr. Sadak. Although I do have an interest in the Soviet presence here. As do my colleagues. But you already know that."

"Of course, I do," the Turk continued. "And I suppose I cannot expect any admissions from you, at least not yet. But in terms of the Soviet presence here, it would be an impossible task for you take that on alone. Besides, we know you have not tried anything so ambitious. And your office here does not have the manpower to take on such a task either. I am sure they have compiled a list of their own, but it probably includes only some of those working out of the Soviets' official presence here. You know, the Embassy and Consulate."

"So, do you have something to tell me on this subject?"

Sadak looked over at his companions who sat across the table from Baier. Dafne, he noticed, was not writing anything down. "I am sure you know as well as I do that the Soviets would not use locally-based officers for something like this."

"Like what?"

"The killings and kidnapping. They would send in a team from outside. That has been their practice elsewhere."

"Yes, I saw as much in Europe."

"Good, then at least we are both on the same track."

"Are you telling me that your investigation into these cases is ongoing? In addition to the police?" Baier chewed some more. "That's very interesting. Hypothetically, of course. Have they found anything?"

Sadak, whose plate remained empty, nodded to his male colleague.

"We do not have anything to report from the police," the companion said. "Their investigation was perfunctory, little more than a formality. And the bodies of the two diplomats killed in this country have been returned to the Soviet Union."

"So, the police in Istanbul were not able to conduct a thorough investigation? Or were they not interested?" Baier asked.

The man shook his head. "Please, Mister Baier, let us not raise doubts about the professionalism of our police. Their hands were tied. There were only preliminary inspections done at the scenes of the crimes. We were not able to conduct an autopsy on either victim. The Soviets insisted on their immediate return."

"Tied by whom?"

"By people with the authority to do so."

"Still, there was little doubt as to the cause of death, right?"

The Turkish officer nodded. "That is correct. Death by poisoning—it was apparently cyanide—and death from a gunshot wound to the head."

"Well thanks for that much anyway. But it does point a finger directly at the Soviets, does it not? Any indication of who exactly might be involved and where and when they might have come in? That is, if they were not here in the first place."

"Mister Baier," Sadak resumed, "what have you learned?"

Baier chewed slowly. "These meat pastries are wonderful. You are not eating, Mister Sadak?"

Sadak sighed. "I had hoped we would be able to avoid these games, Mister Baier. This exchange is not intended to be a one-way street, as you say in your country."

"Well, I am afraid I have not gotten very far, in that respect. As you well know, I am here on a training mission."

The Turks around the table scoffed.

Baier paused before continuing. "Although I do find the cases interesting. But I have little I can say. My interest has been focused elsewhere."

"And where is that?" Sadak pressed.

Baier simply shook his head.

"Then perhaps I can give you this much," Sadak continued. "You are aware, no doubt, that the Soviets have numerous allies in the services of their East European partners."

"Yes, I am aware of that." Baier noticed that his glass of white wine was empty. So, he began on the red since no one had come through to refill his other glass.

Sadak raised an arm and snapped his fingers to catch a waiter's attention. When one approached the table, Sadak pointed to Baier's empty wine glass.

"Thank, you," Baier said.

"Have you thought to look there?" Sadak asked.

"Have you?"

"Of course, we have."

"And which ones have you chosen?"

"There is one service in particular that we know well, "Sadak said. "They are a neighbor of ours. We have checked our entry and exit data, and we discovered that they had two small groups enter our country shortly before the deaths of the two Russian diplomats. And each one left Turkey the day after the deaths."

"And the kidnapping?"

"The same."

"And which neighbor was this?" Baier asked.

"That, Mister Baier, you will have to determine on your own. I believe I have given you enough assistance this evening to help point you in the right direction. Your service does require you to know how to read a map, I assume."

"I see. Well, I must admit this does help. To a point."

"And what point would that be?"

"What exactly have you learned about the disappearance and likely death of your KGB asset? Surely, you made your own inquiries regarding that case." He paused while the waiter refilled his glass with white wine. "I mean, more than that he was simply grabbed by some Soviet lackies."

Sadak paused while the waiters removed the appetizers and set a platter of chicken and lamb kebobs on the table. When they had left he reached for his first food of the evening, a twin set of chicken kebobs, and several spoonfuls of white rice. The other Turks did likewise, except for Dafne, who took just one of the lamb offerings to go with the leftover appetizers on her plate. She appeared to like hummus and the pita bread that went with it. Baier gave the food another glance, then he also opted for one of the lamb kebobs. It was a meat he rarely found at home.

"Unfortunately, we know little of that one. We were hoping you could help us there. We were present at that least meeting, waiting for your officer to show up. But it all happened so quickly, we could do nothing to stop it. It was a very professional operation."

"Would you have stopped it?"

Sadak nodded. "Yes, we would have. Or we would at least have interfered, if only to learn more. We would have liked to rescue the poor man, and probably offer him to you in exchange for any information you would have learned."

"Why us? I am sure you could have handled him well enough."

"Ah, but you would have been able to do more in getting him safely resettled."

"I see. I am afraid I have little to offer you there as well. Again, my efforts have been focused elsewhere."

"And which you unwilling to speak to us about. Is that correct?"

Baier remained silent. He concentrated instead on his lamb.

"Mister Baier," Sadak continued, "I must admit that this has been a rather disappointing meeting for us. You do not appear to be very interested in an even and honest exchange of information." He paused, as though weighing his next words very carefully. "Perhaps you do not realize that not everyone you may meet from my service would be as helpful and cooperative as me." Sadak paused again and sighed. "But I will need something in return."

"I am sorry, but there is almost nothing I can tell you at this point. I mean, surely you know that since this all happened on your turf, as it were, you are the ones with the information to share."

"And where have you focused your efforts? They may be merely personal and academic, but that alone would help us a great deal."

Baier shook his head. "I am truly sorry, but I cannot tell you that."

"I see. So, you are looking into your own people. That is very interesting."

Baier sat back and studied his Turkish host. "I never said that."

Sadak smiled. "You did not need to, Mister Baier. But let me ask a more general question. One about American policy more broadly. Are you free to discuss possible responses to the Soviet missiles in Cuba. That is, if there are any there with an offensive capability, as you seem to fear?"

"What in particular are you interested in?"

"Just what have you found?" Sadak pressed.

Baier decided right off that that information was something he could share. If briefing teams were heading for European capitals, then surely the material could be passed in some form to the Turks. They were, after all, a NATO ally.

"We have evidence, very solid evidence, that the Soviets have constructed bases for their intermediate range missiles and that those missiles are already in Cuba. That is all I know."

"What of the Jupiters?. Are those now your bargaining chips with the Soviets?"

"Why do you worry about them so much? Aren't you afraid that they make Turkey a target for Soviet retaliation, or a pre-emptive strike?"

Sadak smiled at the American's apparent ignorance of regional affairs. "Mister Baier, are you unaware of our centuries-old conflict with Greece? It is a hostility that now brings us together in competition for your nation's favor."

"Yes, I am aware of that. It's hard to avoid that subject if you spend more than two minutes in the region."

"Well, what purpose do you think those Jupiter missiles serve?"

"To act as a deterrent to Soviet aggression. It is something you Turks have experienced many times over the centuries."

Sadak's smiled widened, then disappeared. "For the moment it helps make us more important to you than the Greeks. It does not matter how old or accurate they are. Only that they are here."

"Yes, I can see that."

"So, can you tell us what your government plans to do with them?'

Baier leaned forward and took another lamb kebob, forgetting his chicken. "There again, I am afraid that you are asking the wrong person. I am not privy to those discussions. You had best ask the Ambassador about that."

"And once again, you have disappointed me, Mister Baier. I truly wonder if it is worth continuing this discussion."

Baier looked at the Turkish officer in silence, then he shook his head. "I am sorry if you feel that way."

Sadak sat back and sighed again. His face wore a look of disappointment bordering on disgust. The rest of the dinner occurred in silence. Baier noticed, though, that Dafne, who had not written a word that he could see, did not take her eyes off him for the rest of the meal.

# CHAPTER TWELVE

If this keeps up, Baier thought, I'm going to have to switch hotels. The pickup occurred about a block from his hotel the very next morning as Baier made his way toward Ataturk Boulevard and the straight walk from there to his cubicle. It was a Soviet Zil sedan, whose black exterior gave off an air of evil depression. It was almost as though it carried a sign in the rear window, warning all who entered to give up hope. It was a nice and effective touch, Baier conceded, especially when you had an idea of what was coming. The two escorts who jumped out of the back seat bore a remarkable resemblance to the thugs that had braced him in the Orient Bar of the Pera Palace his last night there. They must produce these clowns from the same factory in some military-industrial complex located somewhere in the Ural Mountains, or further east, he surmised. How else could they all look so much alike? They were tall—easily over six feet—broad shouldered and minus their necks. The black suit jackets barely held their biceps, as the fabric threatened to burst at the seams. And forget buttoning the jackets. Much the same problem seemed to confront the pants legs around their thighs. Baier even wondered if they ordered their suits a size too small to emphasize their physical attributes. They had still forgotten to add any in the brain department, though, for their line of work. Maybe the hat factory was out of the extra material it would have needed.

Each one took an arm and tossed Baier into the back seat. One jumped in the back with him, while the other dropped into the passenger seat up front. As the doors were closing, the driver stomped on the gas petal, and away they flew. Baier tried to sit up and glance out the window, but a heavy hand that felt like iron pushed his face back into the leather where butts usually rested.

"What the hell is going on?" Baier tried to shout. The sound came out muffled by the upholstery.

"Quiet," the driver responded in heavily accented English. Clearly Russian even if it was only one word. "Soon." Same accent.

Whatever the hell that meant, Baier thought.

He continued to think that for about another ten minutes while the car weaved through the dense Ankara traffic before rolling to a stop at the park surrounding the Ataturk Mausoleum. They did not actually go inside the museum and the tomb that housed the remains and memory of modern Turkey's father. They did not even go through the gate at the top of the hill to enter the grounds. That all would have been foolish, because of the heavy and steady stream of Turkish schoolchildren that were led obediently through the displays that featured pictures from Ataturk's life, his limousine and other belongings, and finally, his tomb. There was also a heavy military presence, with armed guards every few yards or so. An incident in this holy place would bring immediate arrest and expulsion, if his kidnappers were who Baier thought they were.

Once the car had stopped, Baier was allowed to sit up. The heavy hand remained on his shoulder but did not attempt to push his head in any direction. A smaller sedan—it looked like one of the Fords the Turks produced locally, sort of an overweight Fairlane; production had resumed around the end of the previous decade— pulled up and parked right behind their own. A thin individual well under six feet, Baier guessed, walked to the car. He, too, was dressed in a black business suit, but one that fit him much better. Baier guessed that this one must be a diplomat. He was too small and comfortably dressed to be KGB or GRU. Or maybe he was someone very superior and high-ranking in the Soviet's service.

The window by Baier slid into the door, and the man leaned into the opening, his hands resting on the ledge. He smiled at Baier, while the creep from the front passenger seat took a position directly behind him.

"I thought we had warned you about the need to stay away from the disappearance of our officers, Mister Baier."

"Oh, you mean that wonderful evening in Istanbul?"

He nodded. "Yes, that one." The man's English was excellent but with an American touch this time. He must have served on more than one assignment in the States, Baier figured. "Unfortunately, you are still here."

"Nobody said anything about me leaving."

"Do you not think that would be the best option?"

Baier smiled in turn. "Not really. I am not finished."

"Oh, but I think you are."

He nodded to the thug sitting behind Baier. The hand of steel moved swiftly to the back of Baier's head and slammed his face into edge of the door. The pain shot through Baier's head and down his neck. Anger flooded his mind, and he wanted to hurt someone badly. Sadly, he realized, the numbers were not in his favor. Nor were the pounds. Instead, he looked up through eyes blurred with tears that he wiped away with the sleeve of his own suit jacket. This one, however, was not black but navy blue. Baier looked to see if there was any blood, but thankfully there were only signs of moisture clotting the material along his sleeve.

"You see, Mister Baier, my friend here can be very persuasive."

"Friend? You need to hang around in a different circle, asshole."

The guy's fingers gripped the edge of the door tightly enough to turn white around the fingernails.

"What is it you Americans say, 'sticks and stones may break my bones, but words will never hurt me'? Well, it looks like all you have are words, Mister Baier. We seem to have the sticks and stones. So, you should be more careful in how you speak. Also in how you act." He nodded at the man behind him. "As you can see, it is very easy for us to get to you."

"Your parents would be so proud."

"I do not know how they would feel, since they both died in the war at the hands of your brethren."

"I am an American, you creep. Born and bred."

"No matter. But my superiors in Moscow certainly are. Proud,

I mean." He then looked around the grounds surrounding the tomb. When his face returned to Baier, it wore an expression of extreme seriousness. He also spoke slowly, pronouncing each syllable with care. It was almost as though he wanted to be sure that Baier took in every word and their implication. That there would no mistaking their meaning. And the threat behind them.

"You should be aware that we have friends in this city who can make things very uncomfortable for you. They, too, would like you to cease and desist, again as you Americans like to say." He finally smiled. "I have watched many of your police shows on television. You live in a violent land, Mister Baier."

"And just who are these friends?"

The smile stayed. It looked like it was made of paste. "Stay in Turkey and you will find out. Much to your disadvantage, I am afraid."

The individual stood up straight and turned to his companion and spoke in Russian. The creep outside the car nodded and answered 'Da.' The man in charge returned his attention to Baier but stepped back several feet away from the door.

"My colleagues will drop you off at your Embassy. I hope you remember our conversation this morning." He pointed at Baier's face. "I think you will need some ice for that. It is already starting to bruise."

"Thanks for the advice. But is that wise? I mean do you really want to advertise what you've done this morning?"

The chief looked at his companions and then back at Baier, nodding all the while. "That does not matter to me. But I do want your colleagues to see us deliver you. That is an important objective today."

• • •

"Jesus Christ," Breckenridge yelled. "You look like you ran into one helluva wall, Karl. The Marine guards are just bubbling with excitement. They want to go out and find that car and pound the crap out of whoever happens to be in it."

Baier waved off the suggestion. "I'm touched, Jim. Really, I am. But I'm afraid it would only make matters worse. I am quite sure it was the Soviet rezidentura who ordered it, if he wasn't there in person."

Breckenridge's face set hard, and his jaw muscles worked themselves back and forth as he thought. "What did he look like?"

Baier described his interlocutor.

Breckenridge nodded. "Yeah, it sounds like him. That motherfucker. I've met him at a few receptions, and I really dislike the prick. He likes to play hardball, and he can be arrogant as hell."

Baier turned and fell into the usual spot on the sofa in the chief's office. "Well, that does sound like the guy I met this morning. He seemed pretty damn sure of himself. But before we do anything else, could I get a couple aspirin?"

"Oh, yeah. Sure thing." The station chief punched the intercom button on his desk. "Marjorie, can you bring in a glass of water and a couple aspirin for Mister Baier. No, make that four aspirin. He'll need them all."

"Thanks, Jim. Any idea why they pulled this stunt?"

Breckenridge shook his head. "I was about to ask you the same question. I take it this was a follow up to your conversation in Istanbul."

"Oh, for sure. But it wasn't much of a conversation. More like an order being issued."

"Well, I can see why they may think we're encroaching on their turf. Those three were their people, after all."

Baier leaned back against the cushions and rested his head on the back of the couch.

"But how do they know what I'm here for?" he asked. "We haven't had any contact with them about this subject or anyone else, for that matter. And why would they care so much? They'd achieve a lot more by simply stonewalling us. I take it that's what they've done with the Turks. I mean, this only heightens our interest because it emphasizes the importance of it all."

The station chief sat down and pulled his chair in close to the desk. "Speaking of which, I understand you've been meeting with our hosts on this. Just what the hell did you think you were doing, Karl? And when were you going to tell me?"

Baier blew out his breath in a long, slow sigh. "Yeah, I am sorry about that, Jim. It came up pretty suddenly. It only happened last night. They know where I'm staying and have been putting some pressure on me to hold forth on my visit here. I've had regular companions on my way to and from work. Plus, they must have a pass key or someone to let them in to my room whenever they need it."

"Probably the latter. All the hotels in this town realize it's in their best interests to cooperate with the service." The chief shook his head, then continued. "What kind of pressure?"

"Well, it's primarily been nice pressure."

"Nice? I didn't think the Turks would be capable of that."

"I think it's nice anyway. Mostly in the person of the woman I mentioned from Istanbul…"

"The pretty lady from the Pera Palace?"

Baier nodded, but then held his head when it began to hurt. "Yeah, that one. Apparently she's been assigned as my liaison officer."

"Worse things could happen." Breckenridge pressed a button on his intercom again. "Marjorie, see if you can find a cold damp washcloth as well." He nodded. "Yes, thanks."

"I'd say you got that much right," Baier continued. "About the femme fatale, I mean. But I guess she's the carrot. The stick has been to insist that I keep them informed if I don't want to get tossed out. The imply that they have some useful information on the three disappearances." Baier paused to consider how much he should reveal at this stage. "Did you know they were also running the KGB guy?"

Breckenridge's reaction was not what Baier had expected. Instead of shock or anger at this revelation, Breckenridge turned his frustration and disappointment not at the Turks but at Baier.

"Just what the hell are you insinuating, Karl? I suppose the Turks told you this. And what proof do you have that they are telling the truth?"

"Jesus, Jim, don't shoot the messenger. Perhaps you should have someone like Fred run through the files with this in mind to see if there were ever any indications that it might be the case."

"Ah, so now you're telling me how to do my job?"

"No, goddamit, Jim, I'm just passing along what I've learned. How you handle it is your business. I know it's your station."

"Well, thank you for that. I'll try to keep it in mind." Breckenridge leaned back and glanced at the ceiling. Then he stood and paced back and forth, his eyes on the window. Baier doubted he saw anything of importance out there, but when his attention returned to Baier his face looked as though he had come to an important decision. He studied Baier for a few seconds before speaking.

"Karl, in view of what happened this morning I think it would be best if you returned to Headquarters."

Baier stood. It was a little too quickly, and he felt dizzy for about ten or fifteen seconds. But the pause also helped him check his temper.

"Okay, Jim, I can see how you might think caution is the new watchword here, but look, we can't let the Soviets run us off this case, or cases."

"And we can't give them an excuse to interfere in the business of this station either."

"They don't need an excuse. We need to stay firm in the face of their pressure campaign."

"There is also the matter of the Turks. You should never have gone to see them without running it by me first. Dammit, Karl, you said it yourself. This my patch, and I can't do my job here if you are going to be running your own liaison operation. That is inexcusable."

"What's inexcusable, Jim, is blocking my attempts to gain additional information on one the most serious counterintelligence cases in recent memory. And it comes at a time of incredible tension in our relationship with the Soviets. Shit, man, we're about to go to war. Corridor gossip says that Kennedy is now studying options for a response, and that the Joint Chiefs are pushing for an invasion. Do we know more yet of what the U-2s turned up?"

"Yes, as a matter of fact we do. And there are definitely intermediate range missiles being deployed in Cuba. And nuclear capable ones at that. That makes me even more determined to get a firmer grip on what we're doing here. There is too much riding on this for you to be running around in a free-lance operation. I'm sending off a cable to headquarters today. You might as well head back to your hotel and pack your bags." He nodded at Baier's face. "With that kind of bruising I doubt you'd get much accomplished today anyway."

"May I ask how you found out? About the Turks, I mean."

"Sure. The chief of the service told me himself. He also pressed for cooperation. But fuck him. We're not discussing these cases with anyone else. Not even the Brits. In fact, they'd be the last people to talk to about a CI issue."

"You know I was sent out here expressly at the wish of the seventh floor. What makes you think they'll agree?"

"I guess we'll just have to see," Breckenridge said.

"Yeah, I guess we will."

Baier passed the secretary on his way out, taking the aspirins, the glass of water, and the cold compress with a murmur of thanks and appreciation. It was only then that he noticed the presence of Richard Spronk, the chief of operations in the Agency's Soviet Division. The man stood behind the secretary's desk, stirring his cup of coffee with a small silver spoon and measuring Baier with the same cold stare he had used back in Langley. Spronk looked even thinner that he did at his desk back home, as though he had stretched his elastic body to its full height, spreading his flesh to cover the entire frame. His face held the same steely visage it had the last time Baier had seen him, only colder and paler this time. Maybe it was jet lag. But more likely it was a distaste that had strengthened since Baier had last seen him.

Odd, Baier thought, that Breckenridge had not seen it fit to mention Spronk's presence, much less invite him into his office to discuss the case. Baier left wondering what the visitor may have had to do with the station chief's shifting mood and effort to send him home. And just what else the man wanted to do while he was here.

• • •

The knock on the hotel door was soft, very soft. But it was loud enough to wake Baier as he rolled his head from the middle of the pillow to the side by the door and away from the window. He had fallen asleep and forgotten to pull the curtains closed. The sunlight burned his eyes when he opened them.

"Yes, who is it?" he asked.

There was a moment's pause. "Mister Baier. May I come in?"

Dafne. There was no question as to who was waiting on the other side of Baier's hotel door. He almost pinched himself to see if he was dreaming. But the pain throbbing in his temples told him that he was well awake.

"Mister Baier? Karl? Are you there?"

Baier slid his feet to the floor. "Yes, just a minute."

He stepped slowly to the door and pulled it open even more slowly. Yes, it was Dafne alright, and Baier's dream-like consciousness gave way to confusion. Just what the hell was she doing here again? And at this time of day? Shouldn't she be in her office? Or perhaps they had sent her here. That would certainly make sense.

"May I come in?"

Dafne didn't bother to wait for an answer. She slid inside the door, her back tight against the doorframe, and walked to the middle of the room before stopping to turn around. Her face grew alarmed, and her right hand rose to her cheek.

"Oh my God, I had heard that you had been taken by the Soviets, and I wanted to see if you were alright or if there was anything you wanted to tell us. But I did not know that you had been assaulted. Did they do this to you? Are you okay? Do you need anything?"

Baier shook his head and returned to the bed, where he fell against the mattress and the pillows. "No, no, that's okay. I think I just need to rest. I've already called room service, and they brought up some more aspirin and a bottle of water. I think sleep will do the most good, though."

Dafne stood in the middle of the room, her hands ringing each other while her teeth chewed at her lower lip. If Baier's vision had not been blurred by the sunlight he would have sworn there were tears in her eyes. But he also realized that was almost certainly wishful thinking.

"What can I do for you, Dafne?"

"I...I wanted to ask about this morning's incident. I also wanted to follow up on the meeting at dinner last night."

"What do you mean by following up? I am not sure what else there is to say. I cannot give your people what they want. It is that simple."

She glided toward the bed and sat on the edge. Baier was surprised by her boldness. Pleased, but surprised.

"Please, you do not realize how important this is. Mister Sadak needs something from you."

"What would that be? And why?"

"Anything. He is under great pressure from our superiors. They do not trust him in this operation. He is pressing forward in the face of resistance in certain quarters. Some suspicion even."

"Then why is he being allowed to run it?" Baier pressed. "And why do they not trust him? And who are these people? Where do they work?"

"Perhaps I misspoke. I am not at liberty to say where these other people sit. And perhaps it is not so much a question of trust, as it is one of faith."

"I'm afraid I do not understand."

"They think his confidence in you is misplaced. They are afraid that he will give too much away with next to nothing in return. You see, our service realizes how much we need your organization right now. But there are also many who do not trust you. Mister Sadak is not one of those."

"And why is that? What have we ever done to you? Your service, I mean."

"It's not what you have done, although America has a way of hurting others. Unintentionally, I believe. But it happens all the same."

Baier sat up. "When have we hurt you?"

"It happens all the time. You like to give orders or act without thinking of the impact on others, including those who are your friends." She paused and studied Baier's face. "It is not about you personally. It is because of where you come from."

"Where is that?"

"The West. Europe." She raised her hand when Baier began to protest. "It is all the same. At least to us."

"But what does that have to do with anything here and now? It sounds like you people carry a large burden from the past."

"Be that as it may, there are things we need to know. But for your purposes, I also believe there are things you need to know. And Mister Sadak is prepared to tell you those things to help you. He thinks it is important that you succeed in your mission, but that at the moment you are lost."

"I see."

"But he needs something from you."

"What?"

"Anything. He needs to prove to others in our service that his plan is the right approach."

When she finished speaking, Dafne leaned in close to Baier and seemed to study his eyes as though she lost something somewhere inside him. Baier was too startled to react. Her closeness left him speechless and incredibly uncomfortable. His eyes went wide, and his mouth turned dry. He licked his lips almost instinctively. His limbs, though, were frozen.

After a brief pause, Dafne lifted her left hand rose and stroked Baier's bruised cheek, then his forehead. When Baier remained still, she leaned in close and kissed Baier's cheek where it was bruised. Surprisingly, he felt no pain. Only relief. He noticed the light brown freckles sprinkled along her shoulders, which sloped downward toward her breasts and long legs. Her whole body seemed as though it were about to melt into his, so he leaned in closer and kissed her on the lips.

After no more than a few seconds, Dafne broke back from him and stood. "No, this cannot happen. I cannot allow it. And neither can you."

Baier stood and reached for her arm. "I am so sorry, Dafne. Of course, you are right." He shook his head and studied the floor between them. "There is just so much that is wrong here. I never should have done that. Please forgive me."

"Please do not misunderstand me, Mister Baier. I find you very attractive."

"Dafne, there is no need for flattery."

She shook her head and took his hand. "No, I mean that. I am sincere. But I cannot allow myself to fall into this. My superiors would surely learn of this, and then I would forever be marked by this. My career, my place as a woman in the new Turkey would become shallow and constricted."

"Yes, yes, I understand completely. And I agree. And I hope this will not end our work together. We can still help each other."

"Yes, of course we can," Dafne reassured him. "Especially since nothing happened. And we agree that nothing ever will."

"Yes, of course."

She moved toward the door, her eyes not leaving Baier the entire time it took her to walk away and out into the hallway. Baier knew it would not be easy to keep his promise, but he reminded himself of all he had to lose by falling into the temptation this remarkable woman presented. And, dammit, he was married and a professional. He'd have to make sure that he kept those emotions in check, just as he was supposed to do. For his marriage and for his career. Hell, for his mission, his Agency, and, yes, his country.

● ● ●

Later that evening Baier stared out the window as dusk fell over the Turkish capital. He had spent the entire time at dinner and the hour or so back in his room trying to clear his head of the swirling confusion that left his emotions and focus in a daze. The pounding in his head from his beating earlier in the day certainly did not help.

He stood and walked to the bathroom to grab a couple aspirin. As he did so a thought swept over him. He suddenly realized that he had been approaching this case from the wrong angle. He and Headquarters thought that the deaths and disappearance of their Soviet assets in Ankara had been an end. Baier now knew that they were all standing in the middle. Dafne's presence and persistence, the heavy-handed warnings from the Soviet side, the intense interest from the Turks, and Breckenridge's impulsive mood swing would not have happened if all that mattered was an operational history. No, the operation was still going on. It must be. And in all likelihood, he would need the help of someone, or some people, perhaps a body outside the station or the CIA, maybe even the Turks, to find out who all was involved and how. And just where it was supposed to be heading and why. He hoped he had not burned his bridges with Dafne. She seemed to be his most likely ally, along with this Sadak guy. But that was only one angle. He would have to be very careful. The whole thing could come crashing down around him—no, on him—if he took a single misstep. And if he was right about the importance of the operation and if it was tied to events elsewhere in the world as he suspected, then he had to move fast. Based on what he had been hearing from the Ambassador and in the Station, not to mention what he had been reading in the press, there was not a whole lot of time left.

# CHAPTER THIRTEEN

"Man, but you have pissed off the station chief good, "Ralph Delgrecchio said. "I mean, Karl, you have struck out on your own a number of times, but this is a personal best for you. What the hell did you do?"

Delgrecchio stood in front of the armoire in Baier's hotel room. He had just completed his own sweep for listening devices, unwilling to trust Baier's reassurances that he had been doing the exact same thing every night for the last three days. Ralph had always been a stickler for personal security, which, Baier had to concede, was no doubt a good thing. Especially now with at least two services aware of and intensely interested in his presence in the Turkish capital.

"Well first of all, Ralph, thanks for coming to the rescue."

"I haven't rescued shit yet. As you well know."

Baier returned to the bed in his hotel room and propped himself against the pillows. The last two days had been ones of rest and inaction on Baier's part. And he was still in bed early that morning when his friend and colleague Ralph Delgrecchio stopped by on his way in from the airport after his early morning flight from Frankfurt.

"Be that as it may, I am glad to see you. I'm surprised that Breckenridge agreed to let me send my own cable back as a follow-up to his. I guess he couldn't say no when I had it slugged for you guys in the Counterintelligence Division, and you in particular."

"It also demonstrates fair play on his part. Give the guy some credit. He isn't stupid, you know. Sending you home at such a critical moment was bound to set off some alarm bells."

"Critical moment?"

"Oh, hell yes. The President is giving a nationally televised address tomorrow. Rumor in our building has it that he has opted for an embargo on offensive weapons to Cuba as a way to pressure them to get those fucking missiles out."

"An embargo? How is he going to enforce that?"

"With a naval blockade."

"And the Soviets will go along with that?"

"We'll see. If they don't, we could be at war even before I leave this place."

Baier thought back to when the first hard evidence of the missiles in Cuba had appeared, the U-2 photographs, which had been taken on the 14th. There had been suspicions of what the Soviets were up to way back in August, but nothing concrete beyond some rumors and sightseeing on the island. Now, in the space of eight days we were stumbling toward a possible world war.

"And just what is your timing for the visit?"

"That depends. How far have you gotten?"

Baier swung himself off the bed and walked into the bathroom to take a pair of aspirin. He had finished the bottle the hotel supplied, so he tapped into the stock of bottled water Fred Badger had picked up at the U.S. air base outside Ankara. He offered a bottle of the same to Delgrecchio. Baier's visitor took the offering and nodded his appreciation with a short toast. Baier responded in kind, then sat in one of two armchairs across from the bed.

"As I noted in the cable and you can tell from my face..."

"Yeah, sorry about that," Delgrecchio interrupted. "But it looks like the bruise is clearing up. I take it that it's still sore. Hence, the aspirin."

Baier nodded. "That's about right. But it was this little run in that convinced me that we've been going at this the wrong way. The Soviets didn't close things out with these killings and the kidnapping. They're protecting an ongoing op, and perhaps someone here as well."

"Like what and like who?"

"That's what I haven't figured out yet. But it must hinge on what their officers were reporting to us about and what the KGB guy may have known or possibly found out while he was still here."

"And? What does the reporting from these sources tell you?"

"It doesn't tell me much, and it can't really be called 'reporting.' At least not in the official sense. But the one guy who was shot up in Istanbul did have a Latin American background and even served a tour in Cuba at the end of and right after the Revolution, from '59 to '61. That was his posting before he came here."

"That sounds kind of unusual, taking him away from his area of expertise."

"Well, it's not like we never do the same," Baier reminded him. "And the State Department is even worse than we are."

"Point taken."

"But it would give him a certain cachet with us, given all that's going on in the Caribbean right now."

"Are you saying that the guy was a dangle? That his case was all a set up by Moscow center?"

"Not necessarily. One thing I did find in the files was that his reporting always checked out in the past."

"Yeah, but that could have been part of the deception. You know, build his credibility by giving away some stuff the Russkies figured they could afford to lose or that they figured we'd get eventually anyway. All in order to prepare us for the big stab."

"Yeah, could be. But he might also have been discovered and then pressured into playing a new role. That happens, too, you know."

"Once again, point taken," Delgrecchio agreed. "But what else do you have? What's the story with the other two. Do they fit into this scheme of yours?"

Baier shook his head. "No, I haven't been able to place them in all this. The KGB guy did say he might have something big to report when he last met with Fred Badger."

"Like what?"

"Like something had come into the rezidentura that talked about some big operation. He thought it might be about the missile crisis. But he wanted to make sure. He allegedly hadn't seen the report itself but was going to try to get a look at it before passing along any details."

"Then why the hell didn't I see anything like that in the traffic back at Headquarters?" Delgrecchio pressed.

"Because our wonderful station chief never sent the report back in. Or at least not that part of it."

"He what? He sat on that?"

Baier nodded. "That's right. And that brings up another issue. The guy has been acting pretty erratically, just between us."

"You know nothing is going to stay just between us," Delgrecchio warned.

"No, I guess not. But he's been flying off the handle at the slightest hint of disagreement. And more important to me, he seems to be pretty damn indifferent to the loss of those three Russians."

"Did he ever say anything about his home life? You know he's here unaccompanied. His wife is from Texas, and I gather she did not look forward to spending a couple years in Turkey. Too far from daddy and mommy probably."

Baier shook his head. "No, I hadn't heard about that. That would certainly be tough on anyone." Baier thought for a moment. "Texas, you say? Where did they meet?"

"She was a Congressional staffer for some Congressman from east Texas. I take it, daddy got her the job."

"Interesting. But probably useless."

"More to the point, though. are you sure it's not you who's been erratic or wandering off the reservation? That's how he sees it. He told me when I called to set up my trip here that your activities bordered on insubordination."

Baier sat forward, his hands gripping the arm rests. "In what fucking way?"

Delgrecchio pointed at his friend and colleague. "Karl, you look to be pretty quick to anger as well. You've been here too long to put it down to jet lag. Is it the assault and injury?"

Baier waved him off and sat back against the cushions.

"The chief claims you've all but sabotaged the station's relationship with the Turks by playing the lone wolf and endangering his standing with their liaison chief," Delgrecchio added.

"Oh, that's a load of crap. Our chief of station leaves most of the liaison work to his deputy. Claims he himself has yet to master Turkish. Besides, the Turks approached me—after running a honey trap by me in Istanbul, I might add..."

Delgrecchio chuckled. "Oh, I read all about that one. I knew it wouldn't go anywhere, though."

Baier did not respond for a moment. He stared at the floor before looking up at his friend.

"The Turk who braced me claimed to have information useful to my investigation. But he wanted something in exchange, of course."

"Like what. Did he mention anything specific?"

"He asked me to keep him apprised of my search," Baier said. "He also suggested we were looking in the wrong direction and said he could be helpful."

"The same as you suggested earlier, about an ongoing op?"

Baier shook his head. "No. Something else. He claimed we were mistaken to be looking at the Soviets for the hits in Istanbul. He claimed that the Moscow Center had friends in the area it could turn to."

"Anyone in particular?"

"Not that he said. But he did claim they had picked up some entries and exits that sandwiched the killings. I guess he wasn't about to hand everything to me gift wrapped. At least not until I came forth with some nuggets of my own."

"I'll have Headquarters look into it. Moscow does have the East European services on a pretty tight leash, and I don't doubt that they could find someone more than willing to do them the favor of removing some troublesome officers. I'm not sure which ones would have the experience and comfort level to act down here, though."

"How about someone from outside the Warsaw pact?" Baier asked.

"I doubt it. But you never know in this part of the world. It's not like stable friendships are a staple of international relations here." Delgrechio thought for about half a minute. "So that leaves the Turks."

"As the killers? Are you kidding?"

Delgrecchio smiled and shook his head. "No, not for that. But why their great interest? And why approach you directly, and only you?"

"Well, you can imagine how unhappy they might be to have people getting bumped off on their turf."

"Yeah, no shit. I'd be pissed off, too. But why take a run at you?"

"They probably see me as someone who could fill in their own gaps about what happened. I got the impression that they are determined to get to the bottom of this, just like us. Maybe they see me as the vulnerable outsider here in a strange land. And then there's the broader picture."

"Which is?"

"Man, they are scared shitless that we're going to sacrifice the Jupiters as part of deal with the Kremlin. They obviously do not want that. But if it's going to happen, they would like a heads up."

"For what? What can they do about it?"

Baier shrugged. "I don't know. Maybe make their own pitch to Washington to keep them. They do not want to lose any relevance in Washington. Especially not now that their relations with the Greeks are heading downhill with the crisis over Cyprus. Some Greeks there are pushing for enosis, or union with the Greek mainland."

"So I've heard. It would be nice if your British friends handled all this a bit more professionally and not so nostalgically."

"Yeah, well, be that as it may, it's probably one more piece of refuse from their days of Empire that we'll have to pick up. The sun is certainly setting now, and they don't know what to do about it."

"But I still don't see how the issue of the dead Soviets fits with their concern over the Jupiters."

"It is a stretch, I admit. But I think if there is a link it's probably indirect. Their uncertainties over the missiles are spilling over into other areas. They want to be sure they have a firm handle on everything that's going on here."

"How did you leave it with your new friends?"

"How did I leave it? I left it by not promising a damn thing. How the fuck do you think I left it, Ralph?"

Delgrecchio held out his hands to ward off Baier's anger. "Okay, okay. I believe you. So, what do you propose as a next step?"

"I propose that you and I march into Breckenridge's office and get things settled between him and me. I sure as hell do not want to leave this job unfinished."

"And then what?"

"And then we all go see the Turks and press them for whatever they have that can help us in our investigation. They're not doing shit at the moment, anyway, now that the two bodies have been shipped home to Moscow. Not that I can see anyway. Except maybe from leaning all over me."

"Do you think they'll have more to tell us?"

Baier stood while nodding. "Yes, I do. And then we need to get Jim to lift his embargo on approaching the Soviets here. They've got something going on, and we need to find out what it is."

"I doubt anyone in the rezidentura is going to open up to us."

"The we'll grab some prick from TASS or Amtrog, or wherever else they've got their little assholes stashed."

"And how's that going to work? They already appear to be all over you."

"I don't know. Not yet anyway." Baier paused and glanced out the window before turning back to his friend. "Did you know Spronk is here?"

"Say what? That creep? What for?"

Baier shrugged. "Hell if I know. But I wonder if it isn't affecting Breckenridge's approach to this case and my presence."

"How so?"

"I really can't say. But I just don't trust that guy."

• • •

A heavy gray light covered the early nighttime sky outside Baier's hotel room like a shroud. It was not quite dark and somber enough to remind him of a funeral, but his mood was not far off from that. He peaked once more around the corner of the curtain, not sure of what he was looking for.

"Please, Karl, I do not have much time," Dafne pleaded. "My office does not know that I am here. She had been waiting in a corner of the reception hall downstairs when he and Delgrecchio had returned from dinner. Ralph had suggested drinks in the hotel bar, but Baier had dodged the invitation with complaints of a renewed headache. Dafne had showed up at his door about half an hour later.

He let the curtain fall back into place and turned to look at this beautiful creature who continued to visit his hotel room. Try as he might, Baier could not make the temptation disappear. But the more he thought about it, the more he realized he needed Dafne. She seemed to care about him, maybe even felt an attraction for him. She could be a valuable ally within the Turkish service, but he also wanted to be sure he did not endanger her. That would solve nothing. In fact, it would jeopardize his own position in Ankara. It would also be monumentally unfair to the beautiful woman who appeared to like him enough to want to help. Perhaps by giving him more than she had been allowed.

"Then why have you come?" Baier asked. "You are taking a tremendous risk. If your people find out that you've been here on your own, you know what they will assume. It would put us in an impossible position."

Dafne swung her head away from Baier before looking back at him. "Yes, I know. That is why we must talk quickly."

"First, tell me something, Dafne. Do you know anything about the young man who approached me in the lobby? He was a handsome lad, and well-built."

She turned her head to face Baier. "What do you mean he approached you?"

"I was sitting in the lobby, waiting for my colleague to come down for dinner when this young stranger came over and sat across from me. He started asking all kinds of questions about me and my stay here in Ankara, and whether I was lonely and needed company."

Dafne took a step forward toward the window and Baier, then stood stock still. The impact of her statuesque figure was not lost on Baier.

"Oh my God! Then they actually went ahead with it."

"With what?"

"I told them that you were not interested in sleeping with me, and they speculated that you may be a homosexual. They talked about sending someone to see if that was true, but I did not think they would be silly enough to actually do that."

"Well, I guess they are, because they did. I might add that that is one helluva way to go about this. First there is you and my meeting with Sadak, and then your organization tries again with a little boy honey trap. Just who is running the show over there?"

"There is more than one person or one group involved in this." Dafne blew out a breath of frustration. "I should not tell you this, but there are others, less friendly toward you Americans, who are also involved. Mucip is under a great deal of pressure. It is why I urge you to help him, to help us."

"I see. But be honest with me, Dafne. Isn't that why you came here in the first place? I mean up in Istanbul. Outside my hotel room."

"What do you mean?" She stared at Baier for several seconds, then shook her head. "My God, no. They never actually pressed me to sleep with you. I think they just thought that you would become more confused and distracted if I flirted with you, hinted that there might be more to my presence."

"Well, that is true, in a way."

"But don't you see? There is also some good news in this."

"How so? Just what is so good in your organization throwing these little traps at me?"

"That they ran that poor boy by you. It is a good thing for us.

They cannot suspect us of sleeping together. So we can continue to meet, to help each other."

"Okay, I can see that that is a good thing. But are you sure you have not been followed when you come here?"

She shook her head vigorously. "Yes, yes. I know how our people do those things. I know exactly what to look for. I am sure."

Baier stared at the ceiling, if only to avoid Dafne's piercingly dark eyes. "Okay, for now. But we still need to be very, very careful." He finally gave in and met her eyes with his own. "What is it you wanted to tell me?"

"I want to tell you something important. Something useful to you."

Baier could not imagine what that might be.

"The assassins. I know who they were. Or at least where they came from."

Baier instinctively grabbed Dafne by both arms. "What? You know that much? Why haven't your people told us?"

"Because they do not believe you have been forthcoming with what they need. But I will give it to you myself. Perhaps you can use it to learn more."

"Well…?"

"They were Bulgarian. But I do not have specific names. They came from that service."

"And how does the NSS know this?"

"You remember that Sadak told you about the tracks left by foreigners who came to Istanbul and left around the time of the two killings?"

"Yes, of course."

"We also have an asset in the Bulgarian service. He told us afterwards."

"How would he know? Where does he work?"

Dafne turned her face away from Baier. "Please, I cannot say anymore. I do not dare jeopardize this source. He is very important to us. I have told you enough already to help move you along the right path." She looked back at Baier. "Are you going to meet with us again?"

"That's part of my plan. My colleague and I are going to push for that tomorrow when we meet with our chief."

"Then please protect me." She slid her arms around Baier's neck to draw him close. "Please. You know what they will do to me if they find out what I have said."

Baier let himself slip down into her embrace. His body responded as she pulled him closer. His arms folded her into him as he lost himself inside the dark depths of those eyes once more, the smoothness of her skin, and the press of her tight body and the curves of soft flesh.

"Yes, I will protect you. I will not let anything hurt you. Promise me the same."

Dafne broke away. "Yes, yes, I know. But I have been here long enough. I must leave now."

Just in time, as far as Baier was concerned.

# CHAPTER FOURTEEN

"What the hell?" Breckenridge barked, his voice about an octave lower than a shout. "You think I'm going to agree to let you sniff around the Russians and the Turks?" He threw a finger in Baier's direction. "This guy has already done enough damage on that front."

Baier knew the station chief would be a hard sell for what he and Delgrecchio had in mind. They had discussed it on their walk to the Embassy that morning, neither one drawing much from their exchange in the way of encouragement or optimism.

"You know how station chiefs can be, Ralph," Baier had warned.

"Yeah, I know," Delgrecchio replied. "Some of them like to think that they own God's little green acre wherever they're sitting on a given moment. But I guess that's our fault as an organization. We've let them get all puffed up, more so than is really necessary."

"Yeah, and it's how you were in Vienna…"

"And you when you were acting as chief after I left."

"So, what do we do if he stonewalls us?"

"We'll do exactly as we should, especially in this case. Tell him he's under orders from the seventh floor to shove his pretentions."

"That doesn't mean he'll like it."

"I don't give a shit if he likes it."

"Or that he'll agree to it."

"I'll remind him that station chiefs can get recalled, too."

An hour later the two men sat together on the sofa in Breckenridge's office. Breckenridge sat upright at his desk, his elbows firmly planted atop his desk blotter, his body stiff and tense, like it had been cast in concrete. At Baier's request Fred Badger had joined the group, and he stood with his back against the doorframe just inside the office. Baier wondered if any of the station underlings, regardless of grade or experience, were allowed to sit in the presence of their boss.

"For one thing, I don't even see why you're still here, Karl," Breckenridge continued.

"Because Headquarters did not see the wisdom of your request to send him home, Jim," Delgrecchio answered.

"Look, Jim, it's worth a try." Baier added. "You have three experienced officers who are familiar with these lost assets sitting on their asses here. That means they're also familiar with the Soviet target here and how they work. More so than usual, at any rate. For their own sakes, we need to get them out on the street again," Baier added.

"And just how do you see this playing out?" Breckenridge pressed. "It won't do any of them any good if your whole scheme goes belly up. They are already on the Russkies' attention list, at the least. You haven't even thought this through, as best I can see."

"I'll admit you've got a valid point," Baier replied. "That's why we should only include Fred here, at least at the outset. He's the one of the group with the most experience and probably the most familiarity with how their rezidentura works here."

"Plus," Delgrecchio chipped in, "this will all be vetted with Headquarters. Once they approve, you should not have to worry about any unjustified blowback."

"Like fun I won't," Breckenridge responded. "You know damn well none of those fuckers will be willing to fall on their swords if we get burned here. Or anyone else's sword, for that matter."

"I'll do what I can to avoid having anyone fall on a sword, regardless of whose it is or where it stands,' Delgrecchio said. "I can probably get even Angleton to agree, although I won't promise it will be easy. I'll take control of the operation back in Headquarters."

"You think the Soviet Division will just sit idly by?" Breckenridge asked. "I've already got that creep Sprunk sniffing around, asking why Karl here," he motioned with his head in Baier's direction, "hasn't come home yet. He's making noises about a clumsy investigation jeopardizing other operations against the Soviet target."

"Oh, that doesn't surprise me. I'm sure I'll have to fight them off at every turn," Delgrecchio said. "But let me worry about that. CI Division has a natural role here, and I will argue that we should continue to lead on this operation. Besides, the Director is already deeply interested in this affair. They won't be able to tell him to piss off."

Breckenridge went silent for a moment. Baier had the impression that he was desperately trying to marshal new arguments but was not having much luck in finding any.

"But what good will it do to run Fred by the other side?" the chief asked. Thanks to his handling of Levkovsky and that guy's exposure, Fred is a well-known commodity in their office. And he's probably just as well-known back in Moscow by now."

"Actually, we're counting on that," Delgrecchio said.

"Oh, this sounds like a real winner," Breckenridge responded. He shifted his weight in his chair, and the elbows finally became unglued from his desktop. He sat back, ran his fingers through the long brown hair that sat atop his head like a pop singer's, then reset his elbows on his blotter. Baier had to ask himself if there was any lining left at that point. The cheap cardboard filler must have been worn down to the leather binding by now. "And who is supposed to handle the Turks?"

Baier raised his hand. "I'll be happy to take that on."

"You," Breckenridge exclaimed. "That's sweet. You've already fucked yourself in their eyes. What's your play this time? Actually sleep with the honey trap?"

Baier caught his breath, but only for a second, maybe two. "No, although I'd like to, to be honest. But I think I can actually use that to our advantage. They ran a boy by me to test me on that front as well. So, in addition to their other attempts to lean on me, I think I can go in with some leverage. You know, the 'that's no-way-to treat-an ally' argument. And I'll argue that we need to start over in the interests of overcoming this obstacle in our relationship. We need to stop playing games against one another and act like the allies we are.'

"I doubt they see our loss and confusion as an obstacle," Breckenridge replied. "What happened to those three assets was not their fault."

"Not that we know of. But in any case, it has soured our cooperation here. We're not going to be able to give them what they want on the Jupiters, at least not according to what I'm hearing from Ralph here and the Ambassador. So, we have to come up with something else to demonstrate our solidarity in the face of a common and aggressive enemy."

"Yeah," Breckenridge concluded. "Good luck with that. They already know we were running Soviet assets unilaterally on their home field. Thanks to you, I might add. It's going to take a lot to convince them that we are now serious about opening up to them."

"I intend to insist that they open up as well. They've been hiding things on their end, perhaps more so than we have."

• • •

From the chief's office, Baier and Delgrecchio walked down the hallway to Steve Garner's office. His was situated across the hall and about three doors down. The big advantage was not its size—little more than a glorified closet—but the view. Garner at least had a window that looked over the Embassy's front lawn and down onto Ataturk Boulevard. Baier guessed that Breckenridge and his predecessors probably wanted to have the width of the Embassy compound between them and the streets outside in case the military decided to rebel again and met more resistance the next time around. Nobody likes to see their windows shattered by small arms fire. If the big stuff came into play, it wouldn't matter all that much anyway. Until then, though, Garner had the disadvantage of the noise from the traffic, but a wide-open view of the green spaces and modern architecture and the open park beyond the street.

"Steve, let me introduce Ralph Delgrecchio," Baier said as they walked through the doorway.

Garner, who had been sitting at his desk proofreading a cable, stood. "Oh, sure. The deputy chief of CI. What's it like working under Angleton?"

"Buckets of fun," Delgrecchio said, "as long as you remember to bring your snorkeling equipment."

Garner smiled. "I've heard something like that from others, but mostly those who work in other divisions." He paused. "Can you give me any background on the President's speech? I gather he's going to lay an embargo on Cuba and stop any Soviet ships heading there to inspect their cargo for offensive weapons... whatever that might be."

Delgrecchio shook his head. "I'm afraid you probably know as much as I do. In any case, a navel embargo is a lot better than what our military leaders were pushing for."

"And that was?" Gardner asked.

"A full-scale invasion with an all-out bombing campaign." He shook his head. "Those guys are still stuck in the last war."

"I see," Gardner said. "Anyway, what I can do for you?"

"Steve," Baier began, "I've read the file on your operation with Topokov. What I'd like to do is probe into the stuff that isn't in the reporting."

"Like what? I didn't hold anything back from my ops traffic. And there was nothing else going on."

"Oh, I don't mean to suggest that you've done anything wrong. Not at all."

"Well, that's good. Because I'm pretty sure I followed the book." Gardener looked over at Delgrecchio. "And I'm sure your office has had a look at the case."

Delgrecchio nodded. "Not to worry there, Steve."

"What I'd like to ask about, though," Baier continued, "is the stuff between the lines. For example, was he ever nervous? Did he ever appear to be looking for another presence, perhaps his own people? And if so, when?"

Gardner sat down at his desk and pushed aside the cable he

had been reading. As though it was an afterthought, he slid his local morning newspaper, the Cumhuriyet, over top of the report. Then he looked up at his visitors.

"No, not really. He did seem a little bit more uncomfortable than usual during his last two meetings. On the day of our last scheduled get-together I never had the chance to meet with him, you know. That's when he was shot, if you remember."

"Yeah, I do," Baier replied. "And I'm sorry."

"But he was always a nervous guy. I just attributed that to his natural temperament. Now that you mention it, though, I guess that could have been unusual, seeing as to how he had been working with us for several years or so. But I had only been handling him for around year, so I can't claim to know him that well." Garner stared at the newspaper as he thought for a moment. "He was concerned about his family. Quite a bit, actually. He spoke of them often and the challenges of living in the U.S.S.R. They had to stay behind in Moscow."

"Wasn't that unusual?"

Gardner nodded. "Yeah, I believe so. They had been with him in Latin America."

"Turkey isn't some kind of danger or hardship posting for the Soviets, is it?" Baier looked at Garner and Delgrecchio when he asked this.

"Not that I'm aware of," Garner said. "Others in their Embassy have families here."

"Did he have any contact with the security or intelligence folks in his Embassy?" Delgrecchio asked.

Gardner shrugged and shook his head. "No more than the usual, would be my guess. I mean, he didn't like them much. He often complained about how intrusive and suspicious they were. The GRU team in particular."

"Not the KGB?" Delgrecchio asked.

"Oh them, too. Always getting in his face, he claimed. But he really hated the GRU assholes. In fact, that was the word he used most often to describe them. And he gave me the English version. It actually sounded kind of funny when he said it with his accent.

I got the impression he had a personal grudge against them. But then again, I'm guessing nearly everyone from the Foreign Ministry did. Or does."

• • •

"Do you really have a plan for the Soviets here in Ankara?" Baier asked on the way back to their hotel later that afternoon.

Delgrecchio laughed. "Not really. You?"

"Nope, me either," Baier said. "It would have been nice to talk to Hughes as well about his former asset. It's too bad he's away down in Adana."

"What's he doing there?"

"Trying to build up his contacts within the Kurdish community. The consulate in Adana is plugged in there, and the station wants him to take a look at that community to see if we should be active there looking for additional reporting on Turkey's domestic politics and stability. I gather the Kurds are not a happy bunch in the new Republic. At least, that's what he told me."

"Do you think he had much more to reveal on this case?" Delgrecchio asked.

"No, not really. It would be more of a box-checking exercise. But he had mentioned that Kosrov was closer to the Turks than he had realized. He said it was a bit of a surprise."

"How so? Wasn't the Turks' regional policy Kosrov's bailiwick."

"Yeah, but he said the guy even had contacts with Turkish intelligence."

"What kind of contacts?" Delgrecchio pressed.

"I've been meaning to follow up. He noted it as an aside when we spoke right after I got here."

"Let me know what you find out, either way. But getting back to the Soviets, I'm sure we can generate a reaction of some sort. Especially given how much they've displayed their unhappiness with you. I mean, the sort of heavy-handed approach they used is unusual against us. They might try to use their billy clubs again, at least at first. You know, hoping to reinforce their earlier message."

"Lucky Fred Badger," Baier said. "We probably should have warned him what sort of reaction he might generate."

"Oh, we'll be near enough to avoid any serious damage. Besides, they'll probably reserve the rough stuff for you. You'll be going back to Washington eventually. Whereas Fred is likely to stick around for a while. I doubt they want to have someone working here with too much of a grudge against them. And they can't beat every American they encounter. There's enough animosity in the relationship with Moscow as it is."

"That could also play out the other way. You know, try to beat someone into submission to undermine his efforts while he's still here." Baier paused to think. "You're probably right, though. Unfortunately for me," Baier said. He glanced over at his friend. "It so nice of you to see me as a convenient piece of bait."

"No need to thank me. And if they go that way, we can use the Turks' behavior to pressure them as well."

"Meaning?"

"Meaning," Delgrecchio answered, "that if the Turks are willing to play hard ball we could try to get them to turn the heat up on our Russian friends. Something's pretty certain to break out then." Delgrecchio laughed again. "Even the Russians have got to want to avoid a Turkish prison."

"Good Lord, who wouldn't?"

"Speaking of which, do you have a plan for the Turks?"

No. I'm afraid we're winging it there as well. Although based on my past conversation, I have an idea on how to get the proverbial ball rolling."

"And that would be?"

"Let me surprise you. I doubt you'll be sticking around for long anyway."

"Probably not. Not if Headquarters agrees to our proposal. I tried to keep it general but not too vague in the cable I sent back today after our meeting with Breckenridge. I just hope they don't ask for specifics."

It was Baier's turn to laugh. "They do have a way of asking inconvenient questions like that."

# CHAPTER FIFTEEN

After three days of futile effort, Baier was alone again in Ankara. Or pretty much so. He and Delgrecchio spent about 48 hours trying to make contact with a Soviet diplomat or intel officer, but to no avail. And even that was stretching Delgrecchio's allowance. Headquarters had sent its approval to their proposed operation to attract attention and throw some cold-call pitches at any Soviets they could find in town within 24 hours. But the haste came at a cost. Headquarters gave them only two days to work together on the project. Delgrecchio was needed back in Washington, now that he had gotten everyone in the station on the same page and the investigation was moving forward. Or so Washington thought.

He and Baier had squeezed an extra day out of his TDY, or Temporary Duty Assignment, as it was known in official parlance, through some creative timekeeping. Just when did the day start exactly, they had asked themselves. It was an old trick, but it still worked. They knew from experience that there was more than one way to skin the bureaucratic cat.

Unfortunately, there were no Soviets to be found in Ankara at this time, apparently. At least not by these two Americans, no matter how experienced they were. It was as though the enemy had retreated behind his barricades, refusing to come out to engage the besieging forces. Baier and Delgrecchio made numerous runs in the morning, afternoon, and evening by the Soviet housing compound and Embassy in hopes of sighting movement by someone, hopefully from their rezidentura, but if not, from the Embassy staff, with whom they could make contact, however unwelcome that might be. Anything to rattle them. In the evenings they tried local bars and restaurants, and during the day shopping venues, parks, and tourist sights—although there were few enough of these in Ankara. But what there were could usually be counted on to attract stopovers by official visitors. This would have given them an opportunity to pick out an officer for an approach, or possibly more than one. The station had a pretty good idea of who the resident intelligence officers were, along with the real diplomatic staff, but there was simply no movement by anyone of note to catch sight of. Either the Soviets assigned to Ankara did all their socializing behind the closed doors of their compound—which was not inconceivable—or they had been ordered to stay below the Americans' radar. Which at this point was pretty damn low itself.

If that was the case, then they were likely to remain there as long as the missile crisis over Cuba lasted. And that was heating up, now that Washington had decided to apply an embargo against Cuba. It was not a full-fledged embargo, naturally, as that would be an act of war. Instead, President Kennedy had announced an embargo on the shipment of offensive weapons to the island nation. U.S. Navy ships would stop all sea traffic to Cuba to inspect the ships and allow any not carrying the threatening cargo to proceed. Of course, there was always the chance for a mistake or slip-up. And in this environment that could lead to a nuclear war. As so many feared. But as yet, the United States still enjoyed the support of its allies in Europe and most of Latin America. For now. And for their part, the Soviets were not budging either, not in Moscow or, apparently, in Ankara.

Nonetheless, the news from that front was not good. It was almost as though Kennedy and Khrushchev were engaged in a pissing contest, and neither one at the moment was ready to back away. Notes had apparently been exchanged—some of them made public—in which each side justified its own hard line. But in Baier's view, Kennedy's was the most understandable. Numerous reports and photographic evidence pointed to continuing construction work at the missile site, of which at least three had been deemed operational. And Delgrecchio claimed to have heard from Headquarters that the President was becoming more and more convinced that a military invasion just might be necessary after all. At least the embargo was working, as over a dozen ships had been stopped or turned back of their own accord.

\*\*\*\*

So, Baier decided to play his Turkish hand. Weak as that was. Especially now that the Ambassador had received a cable from his superiors at the State Department, instructing him to inform the Turks that the Jupiters were now on the table. And there were also newspaper editorials coming out proposing the same thing. So, it was all out in the open now.

Baier knew the Turks would be even more interested in his activities, and not just because they had braced him and run several seduction attempts past him in the past. Their surveillance had also been steady and persistent as he and Delgrecchio had gone hunting for Soviets. They had even been quite open about it, letting the Americans know that they would not be able to pursue their operation without taking Turkish interests into account.

After seeing Delgrecchio off at Esenboga Airport for the morning flight to Frankfurt, Baier contacted Dafne on her office number and asked her to set up a meeting with Mucip Sadak at his convenience. She called him back that afternoon and said Sadak would be prepared to meet with him after an hour. It would take that long to free up his schedule, which was fortunately not quite full until later in the afternoon. A car would be by Baier's hotel to pick him up and deliver him to the headquarters of the National Security Service.

When the black Turkish sedan—one of the old Fords manufactured in Turkey until the Depression brought the work to a halt in the early 1930s--drove through the front gate, Baier had an eerie feeling, similar to the one he experienced whenever he entered enemy territory. True, Turkey was not the enemy. There was plenty of evidence for that. But this operation, his temporary assignment to Turkey, had been more than a friendly visit. It was almost like he was entering a prison. The pink marble posts and black slab overhead that welcomed the staff and visitors had a certain impenetrable aura surrounding the entrance, an image reinforced by the armed and uniformed guards that could freeze any unwanted intruder with stares of iron and steel. Up ahead lay a campus of white concrete buildings that, despite the rows of windows that seemed to allow plenty of sunlight, struck Baier as cold and uninviting. The service had come a long way from the old two-story building next door to a mosque that had housed the NSS when it was first conceived by Ataturk in the 1920s.

Fortunately, his driver took a quick left inside the gate and drove to a smaller, brick guest house, which Baier assumed was meant to serve as a visitors and reception center. That was all fine and good, as far as Baier was concerned, since he did not relish the thought of spending time deeper inside the campus of an alien—and presumably tough, even brutal--security service. Maybe he was being overly pessimistic about the Turkish service, but one did hear rumors about Turkish prisons and the like. Then again, his colleagues stationed here in Ankara had shown no such trepidation or even concerns about dealing with the locals. Maybe it was just him. Or this particular job.

After a quick check-in at a reception desk, Baier was escorted to a large conference room, where Mucip Sadak awaited. He had two other colleagues with him, whom he did not introduce. Not a good sign, Baier assumed. But Dafne entered shortly after he arrived, carrying a notepad and pen. Maybe this time she would actually take some notes. She was wearing an Oriental-style dress with an array of red and yellow flowers floating on a field of white. The dress showed off her figure to its full advantage, and Baier had to hold his breath for a moment to regain his composure. None of the Turks appeared to notice Baier's discomfort, or Dafne's presence. The two new men were both dressed in dark brown suits that stretched comfortably over thin shoulders and long legs. Both officers must be civil clerks who spent their days at their desks, Baier guessed. For some reason, he assumed that anyone the Turks put on the street spent his free time lifting weights. Sadak was wearing a navy-blue suit with thin lapels and a vest that rested on the beginnings of a pouch above his waist.

"Welcome to our compound, Mister Baier," Sadak announced. "As you might imagine, I was pleasantly surprised by your request."

He took a seat in the middle the table at the head of a u-shaped configuration. He motioned to his side at an empty chair. Baier chose one closer to the corner of the head table, near the right side of the room. The others took their seats to Sadak's left at the longer table that ran almost to the opposite wall. Baier wondered if more people were expected. He hoped not, since he already felt outmanned.

"Thank you for receiving me on such short notice, Mister Sadak…"

"Please, call me Mucip. There is no need for such formality between professional people of our rank."

"Of course, and thank you. My name is Karl." Sadak nodded in appreciation. "And I might add that I am pleased to see us start our conversation on such pleasant terms."

Sadak signaled to a middle-aged woman who had poked her head through the entrance to the room, and who quickly disappeared. She wore a stiff white shirt and a long black skirt that fell to mid-shin. She looked to be middle-aged and stood stiffly, her hands together at her front, while she waited for some kind of order.

"Would you like coffee?" Sadak asked.

Baier nodded. "Yes, thank you."

"Turkish or Nescafe?"

"Oh, Turkish, please."

Sadak smiled as he called to the woman and gave her further instructions. Then he turned back to Baier. "Your request is unusual. Your countrymen normally ask for Nescafe."

Baier wasn't sure which he disliked more, instant coffee or the Turkish concoction, so it mattered little to him. "I always try to keep with local traditions, and I admire the strength of your coffee. Besides, perhaps we can read the future of our cooperation on this venture in the grounds that remain in our cups."

Sadak smiled and nodded in appreciation at Baier's awareness of what was a casual Turkish habit. "So, what can we do for you?"

"Good. We can get right to the point. I know your side has been following my activities of late as a colleague and I have been trying to raise some attention from your Soviet guests here in Ankara."

"Our guests?"

"Yes, the diplomats and intelligence officers Moscow has sent here."

"I see. And, yes, we are always interested in what our American friends are up to. I am sure you are aware of that by now."

Baier paused to make sure he used the rights words and conveyed the proper sentiment. "I would expect nothing less. And I hope you have not been upset by my efforts."

"Should we be?"

"Not at all. You see, I believe we are pursuing the same ends here."

"And what would those ends be?"

"An end to this damn missile crisis over Cuba. It is clearly a threat to world peace, a peace that has lasted since the end of the previous world war. And I do not need to tell you what a tremendous impact a war between the United States and the Soviet Union would have on the world, and especially on Turkey."

They were interrupted by the woman who returned with a tray that carried four small cups and four glasses of water. There were also four plates, each with a collection of cookies, and some chocolates. She set a cup and a plate in front of each of the male participants, then disappeared once more as quickly as she had come. Apparently, Dafne did not count. At least not for this meeting.

"What sort of impact do you think this would have on us, specifically?" Sadak asked.

"Well, as a member of NATO you would inevitably be drawn in. And the presence of the Jupiter missiles would make your country an early target of a Soviet strike, probably a pre-emptive strike."

"But is your government not planning to remove those missiles?"

Baier shook his head and took a sip of his coffee. It was as strong as he had expected. Sadak took the opportunity to drink some of his coffee as well.

"I am afraid I cannot speak to that," Baier replied. "Although I am aware of what is now appearing in the press, I am too far removed from the decision-making circles in Washington to say what exactly will happen." He paused to give his next words a greater effect. "But if we do remove those, you will still be under our strategic umbrella. That is one of the benefits of NATO membership."

"I see. I will take that as a 'yes.'" Baier did not respond, which he knew would confirm their assumption. "And what can we do for you, Karl?"

"You had mentioned once before that we were looking in the wrong direction for the killers of the two Soviet diplomats in Istanbul."

"Yes. Have you had any luck looking elsewhere?"

"Let me run an idea by you."

"Go ahead."

"That the killers, and probably the kidnap team, came from Bulgaria."

"And how did you come by that notion?"

"Well, you had mentioned Soviet allies as one possible avenue, so I thought about the relationship each service has with Moscow, and which ones would be most capable of carrying out such an operation. The Bulgarians seemed like the most likely service to me."

"And how did you come to that conclusion?"

Baier studied the faces of his hosts. Dafne's was buried in her notebook as she wrote furiously, probably to hide her nervousness. Sadak's had a look of curiosity, almost amusement. The other two men, neither of whom had spoken a word or touched their coffee and rolls, stared at Baier with looks just a notch below the hostility of the guards at the entrance. Baier wondered if either of the two men spoke any English at all. And what their real purpose in being there was.

"There were several reasons," Baier continued. "For one thing, they have proximity and easy access, geographically. They also have an interest in Turkish affairs, given their location on your border and with a sizeable Turkish minority in their country. That suggested to me that they would be a logical candidate in the minds of the KGB and GRU."

"Is there anything else?" Sadak asked.

Baier nodded and finished his coffee. "Yes, there is. We know that they are in the process of establishing an assassination bureau in Sofia. And what better way to get in some practice and build your expertise than by responding to a request from Moscow in such a close neighborhood."

It was Sadak's turn to remain silent. He took the opportunity to finish his coffee in what struck Baier as a long and unnecessary method, one that actually gave him an opportunity to formulate his response. But none was forthcoming. Baier took that as the same kind of affirmation he handed to the Turks earlier about the Jupiter missiles.

After an uncomfortable interval, Baier spoke. "I had mentioned our common interest in a peaceful resolution of the missile crisis, and one that would get the damn medium-range missiles the Russians have placed in Cuba back off the island."

"Yes, I can see your point."

"My request is a bit unusual, but please do not take it as offensive."

Sadak smiled, and his look of curiosity returned. "You have my interest, Karl."

"I would like to propose an exchange."

"An exchange? Do you have someone in custody?"

Baier shook his head. "No, no. Nothing like that. If you are currently running any Soviet assets who might be able to provide information on Soviet planning and intentions, we would love to know about that. Or if you have had any reporting along those lines in the past."

"So, now the Americans must come to us for this important information?" Those words came not from Sadak, but from one the two companions who sat at the corner across from Baier. At least one of the brown suits spoke English.

Baier turned to him. "This is a desperate time, and we are flying blind, as we say in my country. We can use all the help we can get."

"Yes, I see." Sadak had regained the role of spokesman for his side. "And your station here and your superiors in Washington are aware of this request."

"Yes," Baier lied. Once again, Baier had gone out on a proverbial limb, and this was perhaps the weakest in his career. But if he got the kind of information he suspected the Turks were holding, something that could be of tremendous quality, then he doubted he would have much trouble convincing Headquarters of the wisdom of his move.

"I will have to take your request to my superiors, as you no doubt are aware. It is, however, a very interesting—albeit difficult—proposal. And what would we receive in return?"

"I would propose that we share our intelligence on whomever we recruit from the Soviet side here in Turkey in the future."

"Again, you have the approval from your superiors in Washington for this?"

"Not just yet," Baier said. "But if you help us with this, I can promise you that my people in Washington will be very receptive."

Sadak stood, followed almost immediately by his two brown-suited companions. Dafne took a moment longer as she rushed to complete her notes. "We will get back to you with our response." He nodded in Dafne's direction. "Our usual liaison officer will call you. Unless you hear from me, of course. There are others in our organization who may want to discuss this further."

Baier stood and walked over to Sadak, his hand outstretched. "Thank you, Mucip. I hope we can cooperate on this matter. It is of vital importance, not only to our two countries, but also to the world."

Sadak nodded in agreement and his body posture stiffened. Baier almost expected him to click his heels. "Yes, I agree. And I will recommend that we accept."

When Baier turned toward the door he noticed that Dafne had already disappeared. Instead, he was left with the image of the woman who had delivered their coffee, removing the cups and saucers from the conference table as dishes clattered on top of the tray.

Baier thought again of his friend Delgrecchio, whom he had warned earlier of his proposal. Whether Ralph would be able to protect him if things went south was an open question. And Baier, as yet, had no answer from anyone.

• • •

Dafne did not stay away for long. She was waiting for Baier at his room when he returned that evening. Her face carried a look apprehension, fear even. She had trouble standing still as she paced the room, wringing her hands in front of her waist. She looked as though she might erupt in tears at any moment.

"You were right before, Karl. We must be very careful," she said.

"I know, I know. And we will."

"I also worry now that we could be in danger," Dafne continued.

Baier stepped toward her, hoping the get her to stand still. He wanted to talk to her calmly and quietly, to reassure her. He took hold of her wrists. "More than before? What has happened? Have you been followed?"

She shook her head vigorously. "No. no. It is not that. It is the atmosphere at work."

"What do you mean. Are people suddenly suspicious there? Of us?"

"No, I do not mean that."

"Then, for God's sake, Dafne, what is it?"

She hesitated. Baier's fears began to intensify. Had she given herself away? Let something slip?

"It is some people at work. They have been ostracizing Mucip. I think they may be working against him. And I am associated with him, so their suspicions—if that is what they are—will also be turned against me as well. That means new scrutiny."

"Has anyone said anything to that effect?"

"No. Not directly. But there have been meetings on our relationship with you and our policies with our Western allies that Mucip has been excluded from. That is not right."

"How do you know this?"

"Rumors mostly. But I know one of the officers, who attended them. His family is Circassian, you know Turkish people from the Caucasus region. We have spoken in the past with each other about the challenges we face as minorities here."

"But I thought you were okay with that, that you had your niche in Turkish society."

"It is still difficult. At times. Especially now with relations with Greece going so poorly. Anyway, he told me of the meetings and warned me to be careful."

"I see. Is there anything else?"

"Yes, but maybe I am being paranoid or just insecure. But it is the way some people look at me and Mucip now and those in our office."

Baier moved back in closer to Dafne and took her in his arms. "I understand. Thank for telling me this. And you are right. We will be very, very careful. In fact, I do not want you to take such enormous chances by coming here alone again. We should only meet when Mucip or others are with you. Let them take the lead."

He noticed then that her cheeks were wet, and that new tears streamed down her face. He realized at that point just how much of a risk she had been taking by attempting to operate alone with him, to give him as much as possible to build his case, as it were, to complete his mission. It was one more reason to move as quickly as possible.

# CHAPTER SIXTEEN

If nothing else, Baier was looking forward to not having to sit across from Jim Breckenridge in the chief's office once this assignment was over. He even took a place at the opposite corner from the one he had occupied throughout his visit, but it didn't lift his mood at all.

Baier wasn't sure why their relationship had turned as sour as it had. He recognized the strong sense of turf Breckenridge had shown. Yet that was something all station chiefs had in common. They saw themselves as lords of their domain, and they resented any sort of interference, including those at Headquarters. Those intrusions, of course, were to be expected, as every recruitment, nearly every operation had to be approved by the mandarins occupying the desks in Langley before they could move forward.

His own arrival, Baier knew, was even worse, and not only in the eyes of Jim Breckenridge. Every station chief he had ever known would have been resentful. Perhaps not as much as Breckenridge, but Baier knew it did not take long to wear out one's welcome, especially on as sensitive a case as this one. He would have probably felt the same way. Baier also knew that he was lucky to have the full backing of Ralph Delgrecchio back in Washington. If anything, that man could also play James Angleton to ensure that Baier's efforts would not only get to the bottom of the loss of the three Soviet assets, but also prevent the emergence of new counter-intelligence barriers that might result. Indeed, this setback was likely to make Angleton even more concerned—if that was possible—about Soviet dangles or provocations, as well as increasingly suspicious of any new sources of information from that side. He already believed Moscow was playing some sort of master chess game against the United States as it was, and that all Soviet recruitments or volunteers were nothing more than potential penetrations of the Agency. Baier believed such a fear was fictional, if not actually paranoid, but as long as he received the room he needed to maneuver in Turkey he could care less about Angleton's delusions. At least for today.

"So, you want to go to Istanbul?" Breckenridge asked. It was a rhetorical question, of course. "Tell me why you can't complete this fantasy ride you and Delgrecchio cooked up right here in Ankara."

Baier shifted his weight on the couch. "I told you already, Jim. The Soviets have locked themselves up tighter than Fort Knox here in the capital. It's probably because whatever they're running is focused here. And, as a result, they're being especially defensive."

Breckenridge stood and paced to the window behind him. When he turned back toward Baier, he was shaking his head and his face wore a broad smile. "And you think they'll be more open up there? If they're running such a sensitive operation here in Ankara, why would anyone up there know about it?"

Baier shrugged. "I can't say that they will be open or even informed, or that they won't. But if there's going to be an opening, it's more likely to happen up there. Unless they're also running this operation in that city, which would show how serious it really is."

Breckenridge sat back down. "But you don't even know if they are running something, here or up there. What makes you so sure?"

Baier sat back. "Well, getting punched around in the back seat of one of their Zils and warned off twice makes for a pretty strong suggestion, as far as I'm concerned."

"Warned off from what?"

"From poking my nose into any more corners here. And I'm trying to find out just what they're so sensitive about. Goddammit, Jim, there has to be something there."

"And do you also have a strong feeling about what it might be?"

Baier nodded. "Yes, I do, Jim. Given what's going on in the Caribbean, my guess is that it has something to do with Cuba."

"But we already know they were lying to us about only putting defensive, short-range stuff on the island. The U-2 photographs have proved that. So, what else could they be up to? We already know all we need to know."

Baier looked toward the door, as though help might arrive any minute from that quarter. The door stayed shut, however. His most important ally, Ralph Delgrecchio, was back home.

"Jim, this crisis in Cuba is far from over. Neither side knows how far the other one is prepared to go to resolve this thing. In their own favor, I mean. Just what are the plans and intentions in Moscow? He studied the chief's face. "I take it you've heard that the Soviets or one of their Cuban friends have shot down a U-2? The pilot was killed in the crash."

"And you think that will affect your plans how?"

"Well, I'm not sure. It could make them even more defensive. But it could just as easily get them to open up. I mean, we're on the path to war here, Jim. Do you have any ideas as to what Moscow might be up to, how they're planning this out?"

"No, I don't. And neither do you, apparently."

Baier sat forward. "You're right. I don't. But it is incumbent on us to try to find out."

"And what if you draw a blank? How do we explain that to Headquarters?"

"We explain it by telling the truth. We were doing our jobs. And it's not like they're going to tell us we were wrong to go after new sources among the Soviets."

"Oh, is that so? Then why did Headquarters tell us to stand down on the Soviet target after we lost the three assets here?"

Baier shook his head in disbelief. "That was a response to your recommendation, Jim. We can easily come up with a justification to reverse that."

Breckenridge stood again but moved this time toward the door to his office. "I am going to send another cable back to Washington, Karl. And I have to be honest with you…"

"Fair enough," Baier said.

"I am going to recommend against going any further because of the risks involved

"Which are?"

"Which are that we risk exposing our station's operations to the Soviets even more so than before. And we risk alienating our Turkish hosts as well."

"But I would still like to go to Istanbul to scout the lay of the land as it were." Breckenridge frowned. "Just in case Headquarters approves," Baier finished.

Breckenridge sighed, as he opened the door. "I suppose I can give you that much."

"Thanks, Jim," Baier said as he left the office.

He moved as quickly as possible through the door before Breckenridge could change his mind. And since when are we supposed to avoid risks, he mumbled to himself as he stalked down the corridor. They're inherent in the business we've chosen. Especially when the world stands at the brink of a nuclear war.

• • •

He had visitors waiting for him in his hotel room once again.

"Don't you people ever knock?" Baier asked. He did not bother to hide his exasperation. He threw his suit jacket on the bed, where it fell against the back of one of the thugs who had been there the last time Mucip Sadak had come to call. "Or use the telephone? Or how about waiting in the lobby like civilized people do?"

Sadak rose from the chair by the window and approached Baier with his hand out. Baier took it and shook, almost on instinct. Not as a sign of welcome.

"Excuse the intrusion, Karl. We are still using our first names, correct?"

Baier nodded and let his hand fall. "That may depend, though, on the purpose of your visit."

"I am sure you will appreciate it, Karl." Sadak raised his eyebrows. "I chose to come to your room first to avoid drawing attention to my presence here by waiting for you below. You see I could not be sure when you would return."

"Okay. I guess. Did you help yourself to a bottle of water, or a cocktail from the minbar while you waited?"

Sadak smiled and shook his head. "No, we did not want to get too comfortable. And your phone is not secure, as you are no doubt aware." Sadak surveyed the room. "Your space here is another matter, though. You appear to have removed whatever devices had been installed, so I believe we can speak freely here."

"You haven't installed any new ones while you waited, I hope."

Sadak smiled. He almost laughed when he shook his head.

"I take it this room is the usual one reserved for official American visitors." Sadak simply smiled. "And your colleague here…" Baier motioned toward the other guest still sitting on the edge of the bed. "Is he trustworthy? For whatever it is you have to tell me?"

Sadak studied his colleague. "He speaks no English. And I have my superiors' approval to speak with you."

"Do you have their approval to say what I hope you are going to tell me?"

Sadak shrugged and smiled again. He appeared to be in a very good mood. "What I have to say is in the interests of both our countries."

"Good. Then I will listen carefully."

Sadak paused for a moment, as though he was gathering his thoughts and choosing his words with care. And caution. "I would like to give you some observations on our Soviet friends, Karl."

"Observations? Or information?"

"You could say a bit of both. It is an observation based on information we have acquired."

"Acquired? From our mutual KGB source?"

Sadak nodded and stared hard at Baier. "Yes, but also more. You will understand if I do not reveal from where else."

Baier shrugged. "I understand. Of course, it would help me evaluate the information better if I had some idea of the sourcing."

"That I am afraid you will have to do without knowing just where it has come from."

"Understood."

"I believe that Moscow is actually running a double operation in Cuba."

"Come again? A double operation. What do you mean by that?"

"It is not just about the missiles. Of course, if those remain it will be a considerable victory for the Russians. They will have shifted the strategic balance. Not completely in their favor, of course. But they will have reduced the distance between themselves and your country, while gaining significant leverage."

"And that is precisely what my country is determined to prevent."

"Of course, you are. But what are you prepared to give in return? The Jupiters?"

"That again? I have told you in the past Mucip, I do not have access to the decision making on that issue. I do not know what my government is thinking. You know as much as I do on that." Baier sighed. "But you know, don't you, that those missiles will soon be obsolete? They will disappear, in any event."

"You cannot replace them with something else?"

"I doubt it. There is no need with the new Polaris submarines. Those are capable of launching nuclear missiles from anywhere on this globe."

"My government will not be pleased. Will there be discussions with us over where we go from here?"

"I am sorry, Mucip, but I just do not know. But I can assure you that your country remains a valuable strategic partner for us. We will still need our bases here, especially the air bases."

"Yes, of course."

"But what is the other part of the Soviet plan? You spoke of a double operation."

"It has to do with a tradeoff."

"For what?"

Sadak shrugged. "I am not sure. But it has to do with offering a trade in another part of the world. And it might not even come to a trade. Depending on what your government decides, the

Kremlin may conclude that is has the need—indeed, the right—to move elsewhere in the world."

"Where?"

"I do not have that information."

"And what sort of objective does this operation have?"

"I am also unsure of that. I think the original objective has changed. The original was to hide the nature of the missile deployments by feeding false information." Sadak shrugged and studied his colleague for a moment. "Your intelligence sources…" Here, Sadak pointed upwards to the sky. "…have upset that particular apple cart, as your countrymen like to say. Now, however, it must be something else. But it is continuing. We are certain of that. We are trying to learn more."

"And the three deaths? Are they tied to this operation? And if they are, how so?"

"Our KGB source, this Levkosky fellow, had warned us of as much. We encouraged him to tell you as well, and he said he planned to do so. But he wanted to learn more himself."

"So, you think he was uncovered when he tried to collect more information, more specifics?"

Sadak nodded. "Yes, unfortunately. His organization may have suspected him earlier but only decided it was necessary to act when they did. Things may have been coming to head, as you say."

"And the others?"

"I cannot be certain, but the diplomat, Topokov, must have been a part of this plan."

"'Must'? Why? Because of his background in Latin America and tour in Cuba?"

"Yes, of course," Sadak answered. "How else do you explain his assignment here?"

"They could have sent him anywhere, for that matter. Dangle a potential asset like that in any capital in the world, and he is going to look very attractive."

"Perhaps. But perhaps Moscow thought he would be more attractive in a country that was already concerned about how things would play out. After all, there were already rumors about your government's willingness to sacrifice the Jupiters, which was bound to upset us."

"So then, if we didn't bite, then you would?" Baier asked.

"It makes sense," Sadak replied.

"But what about Kosrov?" Baier continued. "What role did he have to play in all this?"

Sadak shrugged and shook his head. "I am afraid that remains a mystery to us."

"I see." Baier paused to study Sadak's companion. "Was Kosrov even necessary? I mean, was he a part of their plot as well?"

Sadak looked over at his colleague. "In a way, he must have been. It's the only thing that explains his death."

"How so?"

"He must have failed in his mission, or betrayed it. Did your people learn anything from him?"

Baier glanced toward the window, then the floor, trying to think of anything he heard from Hughes or read in the files that would have hinted at something like this. He even noticed that he was chewing his lip when he looked back up at Sadak, shaking his head.

"No, no. Not that I have seen. But your logic makes sense," Baier added. "Naturally, I will look into it. In any case, thank you for the information you have provided. It will certainly help me."

Sadak nodded. "Of course. It has been my pleasure actually to help you. That way I can explain my presence and this discussion as in keeping with my instructions and the approvals I was given."

Baier smiled and extended his hand. "Then thank you, Mucip. I appreciate all that you have done. Let us hope that our efforts have been worth the trouble." He thought of Breckenridge. "And the risk. If I learn anything on my end, I will be sure to let you know."

Sadak shook Baier's hand with extra vigor and purpose. "I am counting on that, Karl. I am counting on that a great deal."

# CHAPTER SEVENTEEN

It happened in the blink of an eye.

It was an expression Baier had heard before, of course, but he had never given it any thought until now. Literally, in the time it took him to blink his eyes, the note had been dropped in the side pocket of his suit jacket. There had also been a slight bump, but Baier realized moments later that it had almost certainly been intentional. His new friend—if Baier could call him that—had undoubtedly wanted to be sure Baier found the note.

"Galata Tower. Nine o'clock."

The author had failed to mention AM or PM, but Baier would be sure to be there for both, starting this evening. He checked his watch. Seven hours yet. He and his colleague Robert Hughes would easily find something to do to keep themselves busy. Baier had a pretty good idea whom he was scheduled to meet. The real question was why.

The two Americans had spent the better part of the last 36 hours, not quite two full days, wandering past the Soviet consulate and enjoying food and drinks at Rajans, the popular smoke-filled Russian hangout since the days of the Tsar, where vodka was the drink of choice instead of raki. Their visits there, they were sure, would announce their presence to the Soviet mission in the city, and hopefully, draw them out. It was a form of the 'cold call' approach, where you simply knocked on a door or telephoned a target to make your pitch without the usual spotting, assessing, and personal development that were essential parts of a recruitment. Baier simply did not have the time for a the traditional and more careful approach.

Apparently, it had worked. He hoped. Within hours of their arrival in Istanbul, he and Hughes had drawn a set of surveillance teams that kept the two Americans blanketed for the rest of their stay. Fortunately, the Soviets, while thorough, were also predictable. The author of the note resting in Baier's pocket had selected a time of day when the surveillance appeared to slacken, and the gaps in coverage widened. Nonetheless, the two Americans would still practice their best counter-surveillance run, which would require at least an hour strolling through the streets of the Galata district and circling Taksim Square, and even wandering more widely through the Pera district in an effort to identify their tails. And elude them, if necessary.

Oddly, Baier was not sure the latter would be necessary. He had caught a glimpse of the man who bumped his arm and he looked remarkably similar to one of the surveillance team members that had been accompanying the Americans during their stay in Istanbul. Granted, Baier had only caught a glimpse of the man from behind when he had dropped off the note. But he had definitely not been a Turk. And his clothes looked a lot like the cheap polyester and cotton mix one could find on the racks of the finest department stores in Moscow. Or East Berlin, and probably Warsaw and Kiev.

Once Baier and Hughes finished their dinner at the restaurant in the Pera Palace, where Baier and Hughes had once again found themselves ensconced in rooms previously occupied by Leon Trotsky and King Victor Emmanuel of Italy, respectively, the two Americans began their hike through the nearby streets of Galata. Clearly the room selections were more than a coincidence. So, the two men had given each room a thorough check for listening devices and were surprised not to find any.

It was easily Baier's favorite section of Istanbul. One of the Byzantine emperors had awarded the district to the Genoese commercial community many years ago—centuries, in fact—to help promote the city's and the empire's role in the trade between Europe and Asia. Baier found it to be a form of poetic justice that the Genoese had been chosen, since they had supplied perhaps the largest contingent of European volunteers defending the old capital of the Byzantine Empire when it was finally conquered by the Turks in 1453.

In any event, the Emperor's gesture had provided an unexpected benefit for the Americans years later when the United States had purchased the baroque palace—albeit a small one—of an Italian merchant to house their embassy and later the consulate in the old capital. Conveniently, it was also right next door to the Pera Palace of Orient Express fame. The streets throughout the district ran up and down steep hills lined with steps to assist the pedestrians, and with balconies resting on the facades of stone buildings that seemed to reach out to their neighbors across the street and provide what were almost ceilings to cover avenues that were often little more than alleyways. The majority of Istanbul's Greek population had lived in this area, as the Greek community in the old capital had been granted a waiver from the expulsions of so many Greeks living elsewhere in the old Empire in the 1920s. Most of those who remained after Turkey's war of independence had fled, however, during the last wave of anti-Greek riots in the mid-1950s when the dispute over Cyprus broke open and reminded the Greeks and Turks how much they had come to dislike each other over the last century and a half.

Baier mourned the loss of so much history in what had once been one of Europe's most enduring and charming cities. The Italians were gone, too, and long ago in fact. Most of the Armenians as well. Istanbul had turned its back on the Ottoman legacy of relative openness and was fast becoming more Turkish and less cosmopolitan. Still, Baier had surprised himself at how quickly he had developed an affinity for this city. Unlike Ankara, where the lines of history marked the boundaries of entire parts of the city, in Istanbul the centuries and their periods of the past merged together almost seamlessly in what was the closest thing to a living history museum he had ever encountered.

The narrow streets and alleyways also made countersurveillance much easier. Not only were the passageways small, dark and winding, but they also provided plenty of opportunities to stop and check for tails with the many shops, cafes, and restaurants. There was even a print shop where Baier had purchased some wonderful lithographs of old Constantinople, with its crumbling medieval walls, its waterfronts and islands in the Bosporus, and the moonlight casting a hallowed glow like some sort of cathedral setting.

An hour and a half later, and after an exhausting—but thorough--hike, Baier took up a spot in the small cobblestoned square to the side of the brick tower that stretched something like nine stories into the sky above the old city. He was actually a bit surprised when a young middle-aged Russian emerged from the shadows of the Galata Tower to approach Baier, who had stopped to check the other pedestrians after a stroll around the Tower that had lasted maybe five minutes. It was just a few minutes after nine o'clock, remarkably punctual for a man from a county not known for punctuality. Hughes waited a block away, also hidden in the shadows cast across the darkened doorways of the stone and brick stores and residential buildings that looked as old and worn as the city's history, and ready to go the way of Istanbul's diversity.

"You may tell your colleague to go." The Russian's build matched that of the man Baier had seen briefly on the edge of Taksim Square several hours earlier. "He will not be needed."

Baier studied the eyes of his antagonist. They looked almost friendly. The collar on his padded jacket was lined with fur and had been pulled tight around his neck to ward of the beginnings of an evening chill, which surprised Baier. The weather was still pretty warm for the time of year, but even then, he would have thought the Russian found the climate almost balmy. Apparently not.

"His room at the hotel is not all that comfortable," Baier answered. "The plumbing is atrocious. He would prefer to stay."

The Russian shrugged. "That is up to you. But you have nothing to fear from us. No one will assault you. Or kidnap you, for that matter."

"It has happened before."

"Yes, I am aware of that. But that would no longer serve our purpose."

Baier glanced up at a moonlit sky that held no secrets. It reminded him of the old prints he had purchased, and he wondered at the sense of history in this meeting between the two antagonists. He decided to press on. "Just what is your purpose?"

The Russian smiled. He moved within two feet of Baier. Baier turned and looked for Hughes. He hoped that his colleague did not choose that moment to leap to his defense.

"I could ask you same question," the Russian said. "You see, we asked ourselves why you were here when you first came. We found your presence in this city"—the Soviet officer spread his arms wide and surveyed the square around them—"unusual and unpredictable. It was almost threatening. But this time you and your friend appear to have given up your earlier efforts to inspect places where our people were lost."

"And whose fault was that?"

The Russian continued as though he had not heard Baier. "But now you two are just wandering around as though you are lost. Or making clumsy attempt to contact us. At same time, you do not appear to be operational here. More like silly and disoriented tourists. But you do not visit any tourist sights."

"I have already seen those. Now I need to speak with someone from your side. But someone who will be honest with me."

"Honest? About what?"

"About your operation here. In Turkey. The one you tried to scare me away from." Baier paused to study the Russian again. The man's smile had not changed. Not a muscle had moved. It was almost as though the smirk had been glued across his face when he left the Consulate, where Baier was sure the local residentza was planted. "Tell me, does it have to do with the crisis in Cuba? Because if so, it is time to stop playing games."

"Ah, yes, the missile crisis," the Russian responded. "That is good guess on your part. It is why I am here tonight."

"Indeed. Do you have something for me? And please, do not try to reassure me about the defensive nature of the deployments in Cuba. Your premier's promises to that effect have rung hollow from the start. Especially now that we have the photographs."

The Russian shook his head, and the smile faded. "No, no. No more of that. By the way, that was very effective move, to show those pictures at U.N."

"Thank you. I wish I had thought of it."

"No, I am here not only because of my English language skills."

"Which are very good. Where did you learn our language so well?"

"Thank you. I had tour in New York city with our delegation to United Nations. It is fascinating city, I must admit. Perhaps it is most interesting city in entire world." The smile returned, only it looked more genuine now. He even raised a finger in the air between them. "And I have lived in Paris and Rome, you know."

"No, I didn't know."

"But that does not matter. No, I am here because I fear we could easily stumble into nuclear war. Overnight."

"You and everyone else."

"We know you side continues to prepare for invasion, and that your military leaders actually prefer that."

"I have nothing to say to that. Did your superiors send you to this meeting with that lame message?"

"It is true that my people know I am here. I also came alone. That is why you and your colleague were not able to find any surveillance this evening."

"Interesting. So, now I am supposed to trust you?"

The Russian's smile faded away entirely, finally. "That is up to you. You cannot be certain, of course, but this almost always the case, is it not?" He laughed. "No, my superiors know I am here. I would be foolish to try to hide our meeting. But they do not know what I am about to say."

"And that is?"

"That we have already come close to war. Closer than you realize. And that is why I want to give you my message. I hope you will share it back in your Washington."

"You keep talking about how close to war we are. What is so new about that? I read it in the newspapers every day."

"But it nearly happened. You do not realize it, but there was almost attack on one of your ships in blockade."

"An attack? What sort of an attack?"

"One of our submarines was following one of your destroyers. Your foolish captain dropped small anti-submarine mines to force it to surface. Once it rose, the commander of the ship and of fleet in those waters came to bridge, where they met captain of your ship. During their conversation stupid helicopter appeared and lit the bridge with flash and noise bombs. Our submarine started to submerge and to load its nuclear torpedoes. It almost fired one to destroy your ship in response. Fortunately, our fleet commander heard your captain hollering apology and trying to explain. So, he cancelled order to fire."

"What do you mean almost fired?"

"On our ships these kinds of attacks, nuclear attacks, must be approved by three most senior officers before firing. Two agreed, but third refused. That man was fleet commander." The Russian's eyes grew wide, and he raised his hand toward the sky. "Can you imagine what would have happened?"

"No, I cannot." Baier shuddered, not from a lack of imagination, but from the realization of what might have followed.

"That is why I am here," the Russian continued. "This has to end."

"And how will that happen?"

The Russian glanced at his surroundings. He hesitated, as though frightened by the unknowns lurking in the city's darkness, the burdens of its history. When he spoke it was in a whisper that Baier had to strain to hear.

"My superiors think I am going to give you punch line of our operation, as it were. Our objective."

"What is that? But more to the point, why would you do that?"

"That our real objective has been West Berlin. That is the seed we have been wanting to plant. To get you thinking about an alternative to war. But one that we allegedly would wish to happen. Our intention was to plant the seed in your minds, to help move along the compromise we wanted."

"Oh hell, haven't we been down that road before? Several times, in fact."

"Yes, we have. And I do not mean to claim that we did not want to find way to move strategic balance, now that you have Polaris submarines."

"And putting intermediate range missiles on our doorstep would do that?"

"Yes, that was our early planning. But there were many who believed it was foolhardy to expect that you would allow it. So, it was hoped we could find trade-off for compromise to end the standoff."

"Getting us out of West Berlin in return for you getting missiles out of Cuba?"

The Russian smiled again. "Yes, exactly. That city is far more valuable to us than some island in Caribbean. No matter how close to Florida."

"I see. And just how was this supposed to happen?"

"By planting seed of this idea, as I have said. It would be how we avoid nuclear war. That was real purpose of operation here. In Turkey."

"And you know this how?"

"Because I am here to oversee operation."

"And the means of running this thing?"

"By turning your asset Topokov. He was to tell you of our desire for compromise, of pressures on Khrushchev. But also of buildup of our forces around city to make its fall seem inevitable. Your President Kennedy had already given up on eastern side by accepting Wall."

"So, what happened?"

"He refused. Topokov. His family was threatened, but he still refused. His poor wife now works in arms factory in Urals. And he had to be eliminated to protect our plan. I am still supposed to be running it." He glanced around once again before locking onto Baier's eyes. "It was also a warning to others on our side. But I doubt that surprises you. Not after adventure with your old friend Chernov."

The man's reference to Baier's nemesis and now ally left him stunned and speechless for almost a minute.

"What did you say?"

The Russian shook his head. "Never mind. It does not matter here. There are more pressing matters than desire for revenge on my part. That can wait."

Baier studied his new ally. The man's face betrayed no emotion. It was though he was daring Baier to take the next step, which, of course, he had to do. "Then what about Kosrov? Was he part of your plan? Is that why he was poisoned?"

The Russian shook his head. "No, no. Not at first. But Topokov told him of plan. Of that we are sure. We could not let him survive. The risk was too great. We knew he was also working for you, and we wanted to make use of him as well. But he had outlived his purpose and had actually become danger for us here. Like Levkovsky." The smile returned, but this time it was one of triumph. "He was also working with Turks, you know."

Baier held his tongue just long enough to avoid displaying his surprise and disappointment. "Then it looks like you have a bigger problem than you realize. It seems just about everyone you send here is drawing a double salary. Even triple at times."

"Not really. Kosrov was acting on our orders. Let us say he was one of our liaison officers with the Turks."

"You used a diplomat for that? Or was he here in a cover position after all?"

"No, we used actual diplomat. Someone we thought would do better job hiding his relationship with National Security Service."

"And the KGB officer you called home?"

"The same. He had heard about the cables outlining the operation. And we knew he was also working for you."

"What, did someone leave them lying around on his desk?"

"No, he gave himself away by insisting on seeing them. We had planned to use him to pass our message along as well, unwittingly. But that, too, became too risky."

"So, what happens now? We will never sacrifice Berlin. We have too much invested there. It is far too valuable. To both our sides."

"I know. I just wanted you to know so your side is prepared. If you force our hand, we will concede. The military imbalance between us is too great. At least right now. Besides, Cuba is not important enough for us to take such risk. I have feeling it will become drain on our resources at some point, in future time. Besides, those leaders are fanatics. Did you know Castro really wanted us to go to war? Yes, to start nuclear war. He has no idea."

"And your people do?"

"Of course. We also know that history is on our side. So, we would like to have something left when we gain victory."

Baier's eyebrows arched. "You sound pretty confident."

The Soviet officer shrugged. "You must study history, like we do. It is inevitable."

"Well, I guess I read different books."

The Russian laughed and shook his head. Then he nodded toward the Tower. "Impressive, no? You know it was once tallest building in Istanbul. Ottoman rulers used it to look for fires. So it is fitting, yes? We may have put out biggest fire of our time right here." The smile returned and seemed to cover half the man's face. "Maybe one day they replace cone on top of tower in honor of our work."

The Russian turned to go. Baier grabbed his arm. "Wait. Can I at least have your name? In case we need to talk again."

The Russian shook his head. "No. Just think of me as temporary friend." The smile returned and widened in a display of confidence. "I believe perhaps we give this one to your side. But it will not always be like this. We will catch up. Of that I am sure. In fact, I promise you we will."

"But tell me how you know about those three men who you claim worked for us. I always thought it strange that we never picked up on your presence, especially at those last meeting sites. Your people seemed to be waiting for us, for everyone."

The Russian stared at Baier's face, as though trying to gauge the depth and sincerity of the American.

"We have source. He gave us what we needed."

Baier tightened his grip on the man's arm and pulled him closer. Their faces were just inches apart. Baier could smell the vodka on the Russian's breath, and he felt the strength in his arms.

"What did you say?" Baier almost spat his words at the Russian. "An American? Who is it?"

The smile evaporated as the Russian pulled his arm free. "That you will have to discover on your own. Our meeting here is finished. You have enough already. Your superiors will be very pleased." The smile returned. "But be careful about your woman. She is in danger, too. I can give you that much extra."

Baier stepped back, his breath caught somewhere in his throat. He watched the Russian walk away into the darkness, then wheeled to find his companion. But Hughes was nowhere to be seen.

● ● ●

Baier sat on the edge of his bed, the one in which the great revolutionary Trotsky had allegedly slept. But by then he was no longer a revolutionary. At least not in deed, although he still had his dreams. He still pursued a world revolution, but he must have realized at that point that his goal had been squashed by Stalin, who demanded that his Soviet regime focus on building communism in the movement's heartland, its one successful seizure of power up to that point. By then the international workers' movement had given way in Europe to fascism and xenophobic nationalism.

The noise of the heavy traffic outside drifted up to his window, carried by the depths of a night whose darkness penetrated his room. And his mind. Just what had Trotsky and his revolutionary friends set loose, not just in the world but also in Baier's life. And what could he do about it? He had found himself immersed in the struggle between two articles of faith that now stood on the brink of global annihilation. Maybe, just maybe he could use this meeting tonight to help avert that, and not as the result of some great operational victory. If there was one thing he had learned living and working in a world of competing political and ideological certainties, it was that it was also filled with surprises and measured by compromises.

"Come in."

Baier had barely heard the knock. He wasn't even sure if it had been the first one that he did hear. Hughes strode into the room, holding out a piece of note paper.

"An officer from the consulate dropped this off at my room. You'd better read it."

Baier took the note and stared at it. It took him a minute or two to comprehend what were only two short sentences. He looked up at Hughes.

"I guess we'd better get back to Ankara. It seems Jim Breckenridge has something he wants to discuss. Immediately."

"I'll book us a flight back tomorrow. I think there's one running around noon that we can get on."

"Thanks." Then Baier's voice rose, as he worked to control his anger and curiosity. "What happened to you tonight? Where did you go?"

Hughes shuffled his feet and studied the floor before looking at Baier. His eyes seemed vacant, as though he had something to hide. "I thought I spotted some movement behind us. It sounded as though we had been followed." Hughes glanced at the door, then back at Baier. "At first I thought the damn Russians had double-crossed us." The words were flowing now, as though Hughes was afraid to stop. "But then I figured maybe it was the Turks. In fact, that was actually more like it. It's just what they would do."

"Do what?"

"Hound us, Sir. You know, cover us like a blanket."

"Why would they do that?"

"Because they don't trust us. They don't trust anybody."

"Well, who was it? Did you find anyone?"

Hughes shook his head. "No, unfortunately. They must have been too quick for me. I guess they got away."

"I see."

It was all Baier had the energy to say. For now, anyway.

# CHAPTER EIGHTEEN

He did not bother to take a seat on the sofa. He wanted to keep this meeting as short as possible. So, Baier stood before the station chief's desk, his feet planted at shoulder width on the blue and red Turkish carpet that covered the center space in Jim Breckenridge's office. The early morning sun cast a harsh light across the office walls, leaving Baier's view of the station chief with a backdrop of halos and shadows. He had to blink and look aside more than he cared as he stood there, already on the defensive.

"This time you are going home for sure." Breckenridge hurled his decision at Baier. He had nearly shouted it. "There is no fucking way you are staying here now."

"What's your excuse this time, Jim?"

"Your buddy Sadak has been arrested."

Baier's feet shifted before reclaiming their spot on the rug. He started to stutter, paused, then spoke again. "Arrested? What... what for?"

A smile of triumph spread across Breckenridge's face. "They claim he was tied to the Menderes government, part of the plot against the Republic and Ataturk's legacy. That's bullshit, though, if you ask me."

"Has anyone asked you?"

"Don't play the smart ass with me, Karl. You know damn well that he was no Menderes stooge. The Turks have thrown him in the clinker because of his relationship with you."

"And what sort of relationship is that?"

"Fuck you, Karl. Against my express wishes you have tried to run that poor guy as a brand-new asset. I hope you got something worthwhile out of it. For his sake and yours."

"Just what are you implying, Jim?"

"I'm not implying anything. I'm asking you what you did to get him to play along with your game here. I just hope you haven't given away something truly harmful. It could mean the end of your career this time."

"My game, as you and Headquarters are well aware, has been to get to the bottom of the deaths of three Soviet assets on your watch, Jim. That's all there is to it."

"And?"

"And I found that out in Istanbul. I also got the information I was after on the Soviet operation here in Turkey. You may not be interested, but Headquarters certainly will be."

"What the hell is that supposed to mean? I'm not interested? Just what was this big operation you claim they were running?"

"Moscow wanted to promote a trade-off to end the missile crisis. The missiles in Cuba for West Berlin."

"Oh, really? That sounds pretty far-fetched. How good is the sourcing?"

"Pretty good. If you have a rogues' gallery of the Soviet presence here, I'd like to see what I can find on the source. I'll explain it all in the cable back to Headquarters."

"Alright. I'll look forward to that. And once you're finished drafting, you can pack your bags. I've already sent the cable demanding your recall."

"Demanding? You've got a pretty inflated sense of importance, Jim. You might want to be careful."

"Is that a threat?"

Baier smiled and shook his head. It felt good to finally have a reason to smile on his own for a change. "No, Jim. I'm not threatening you. I'm just doing my job."

• • •

He had left the cable as a rough draft, promising Breckenridge that he would finish it the next day. Baier had been uncomfortable all afternoon, trying to decide what to include and what to leave out. The information about the Soviet influence operation on West Berlin as the trade-off for a resolution of the missile crisis favorable to the Americans was too important to withhold because of his pissing match with the station chief. But the revelation—or insinuation, really—about a source within the Agency was too sensitive to stick in the immediate report. It was something Baier wanted to discuss with Delgrecchio when he returned—as Baier would request in this cable--and together they could, hopefully, steer the investigation around his friend's boss and into more realistic and secure channels. Especially if Baier's suspicions were correct.

The review of the rogues' file the station kept had been more profitable, though. His interlocutor the night before had indeed been a KGB officer, a Major Dimitri Bukharin. Baier wondered as he stared at the picture, if the man had been related to the famous Soviet revolutionary who ran afoul of Stalin and is more remembered today for his execution during the great terror of the 1930s than his role as a more conservative opponent, and then later an ally of Trotsky. Stalin's Terror had made for some strange bedfellows. Baier had studied for several minutes the grainy photo taken at nighttime with a full accompaniment of shadows but failed to see anything convincing on a family resemblance either way. But the photo alone did suggest that the information had a credibility strong enough to report it, even without a complete source validation. Lord knew, there was not enough time for all of that. But the guy was clearly a high-ranking KGB officer.

Baier was pondering just how to finish his draft the following day as he strolled back to his hotel when a dark blue Buick sedan pulled up next to the curb on Ataturk Boulevard. The same two human giants who had visited his hotel room with Mucip Sadak the very first time climbed out of the car with a slow and menacing purpose as though they owned the street. Baier really did not expect any assistance from the other drivers or pedestrians making their way along the crowded street. One of the hulks motioned with his head toward the back seat, and Baier had been in Ankara long enough to know it would be so much easier if he simply obliged his new hosts.

This time, when they drove through the gate to the NSS headquarters the driver did not bother to stop. Nor did the guards give any extra attention to their car as it sped through the square stone gates and then up toward one of the white sandstone and marble buildings just beyond the visitors center and the large parking lot that sprawled across the front of the compound. The car did not stop in the parking lot, either. Instead, it raced to the front door of a building on the left, where two more escorts—slightly smaller and thinner than the men in the car, but also wearing black suits stretched tight over bulky shoulders and upper arms—and a woman waited. The female officer was not Dafne, however, and Baier's heart sank. It had nothing to do with any romantic illusions Baier might have harbored. Remembering the ominous words of parting from the KGB officer the night before, he suddenly feared for her safety. And he hoped he had not been the one to jeopardize it.

The party hustled, almost ran, to a room that resembled more of an interrogation center than an office. The only furniture there was a small table and four chairs, all of them metal and without cushions, either on the seats or the backs. Baier was certain the spartan setting was intentional. There were also no windows. One of the new escorts motioned—also with his head—toward one of the chairs, and Baier dropped into it. Again, he realized any sort of resistance would be useless. He also noticed that his armpits were growing moist from sweat.

Baier waited about fifteen minutes for someone else to show. He was not alone, of course. The two new escorts remained with him, and one even offered him a cup of Turkish coffee. Not knowing what was coming next, Baier passed, thinking he should put as little pressure as possible on his stomach and bladder. His hosts apparently had no such concerns, as they both ordered coffee from a waitress of some sort who poked her head in the room. She backed out when Baier shook his head. One of the escorts stepped quickly to the door, opened it, and shouted something down the hall. Minutes later, a different woman, thin and wearing a brown skirt and white blouse, but without the apron, brought in a tray with two small cups of coffee and two glasses of water. Baier wished now that he had accepted the offer, but he decided to wait things out to see where this all was leading.

When someone did arrive, he was surprised to see it was the man who had been present at his first meeting in the NSS headquarters, the one run by Sadak. Baier had not paid much attention to this individual at the time, since he spoke only once and appeared to be below Sadak's rank or standing. He realized now that he might have made a mistake. The heavy forehead, thick black eyebrows, and flat nose held a menacing look that Baier had missed during their first encounter. At least, Baier could not remember him as such. Apparently that, too, had been a mistake. And this time he appeared without a suit jacket, just a white shirt and blue tie, which suggested he was very busy and did not appreciate the interruption by this American guest. Or prisoner.

"We meet in a different situation today, Mister Baier." His English had not improved in the interval. Baier leaned forward, straining to understand the heavily accented words. "But thank you for coming. Nonetheless."

"I had no choice that I could see. What do you want with me?"

The Turk leaned back in his chair and pulled a cigarette pack from his shirt pocket. He tapped one free and offered the pack to Baier, his face relaxing enough to frame an unspoken question.

Baier shook his head. "No, thank you. I do not smoke."

"Ah, good for you. That will help you to live a longer, healthier life." He paused to light his cigarette. "That is, if you act more carefully in the future."

"What are you talking about?"

"Your relationship with Mister Sadak, of course. We know you have been running that man as one of your agents here in Turkey."

Baier stayed silent, staring at his host while the smoke he had exhaled drifted toward the ceiling. It circled the ceiling light fixture, then disappeared.

"I do not know where you got such a ridiculous idea. The man has acted only as a liaison partner, which I believe were his instructions."

"How would you know what his instructions were?"

"I know because he told me as he tried to learn about our plans regarding the Jupiter missiles, which your government believes are so precious."

"Are they not?"

"Precious? They were once. But now they are outdated and in need of replacement."

"Which, as we suspected all along, is not going to happen."

"As I told Mister Sadak, that decision is way above my pay grade. I am sure that if your representatives in Washington speak with our officials at the State and Defense Departments and the White House they will learn much more than if your people speak to me."

"I see. Can you also explain why you and Mister Sadak have become such close friends? I understand that you are on a first-name basis."

Now, this was getting truly frustrating for Baier, silly even. "We both care about the mutual interests our countries share. So, naturally our exchanges were friendly. They had a common purpose."

"Which was?"

"Our nations' mutual interests in this part of the world and our continued support for each other."

"Ah, but they were also revealing for you, were they not?" He took several more puffs on his cigarette before crushing its stem in a silver metal ashtray in front of him. "I mean, your words sound so nice. But I doubt you played—what is it you call the game—pattycake?"

"I am not sure I understand your meaning."

"He revealed the identity of the killers of the two Soviet diplomats…"

"He did not."

"And he revealed our relationship with the KGB officer, with whom you were also meeting."

"And can you tell me why your organization has been keeping that information from us? I thought we were friends and allies."

Baier had tried to avoid answering the accusation directly, but he could not deny it. The NSS clearly knew the answer already.

"To an extent, Mister Baier. To an extent. We were prepared to share what we knew, but only if we received something in return. That never happened."

Baier opened his mouth to speak, then shut it. He realized that the less he said about whatever understanding he had reached with Sadak, the better. He had already started down that particular rabbit hole and did not want to go any further. If that was even possible. He looked down at the table, folded his hands in his lap, then laid them on the table. He did not want to say anything more that could be construed to support the accusations against his former interlocutor. He was also uncertain of his standing in this room, this compound, since he was traveling only on an official passport, not a diplomatic one.

"I could not give your side the information you desired because I did not have it. If you had been more open with me we could have investigated these cases together and shared what we learned."

"Why should we cooperate in what was an internal matter for the Turkish police? Are you admitting that you had Soviet agents in Turkey and failed to tell us?"

"I am not admitting anything. Is this an interrogation? If so, then that is not the proper way to treat an American diplomat, and you know it."

The Turk smiled and extracted another cigarette from his pack. "Diplomat? That is unworthy of you, Mister Baier. We do not need to play those games. Not now. Besides, we already have our answer. Why else would you even be here?"

Baier's face grew hard as his mind grew tired from sitting in the hot stuffy room with no ventilation and on a hard metal chair that was beginning to make his butt feel like it was made entirely of bone. Plus, the damn cigarette smoke was starting to bother his eyes and breathing. That was probably why the man continued to puff away like some damn internal combustion engine.

"Then why even bother to ask?" Baier said. "So, let's cut the bullshit."

"Excuse me." The Turk's face had a questioning look at first, then turned angry as he processed what sounded like an insult.

"It is an expression we use in America. It means let us stop avoiding the real subject and get to the point of this discussion."

"You have already confirmed the point of this discussion, Mister Baier," the Turk proclaimed as he stood. "That Mucip Sadak is a traitor."

Baier stood in turn. "Mucip Sadak is a patriotic Turk who is trying his best to serve his country." Then Baier recalled something from his earlier conversation with Breckenridge. "Besides, I thought he had been arrested as a Menderes supporter, part of the coup's aftermath. Not as a spy."

The Turk smiled. It was an unpleasant smile, more of a threat than a greeting or agreement. "There are those of us here who decide who is a member of the Menderes clan, and who is not." He walked to the door. "Good day, Mister Baier." He turned to the two escorts. "Take our American friend to the car. Then drive him back to his hotel. He needs to pack for the flight home tomorrow."

He spoke these words in English, clearly for Baier's benefit. Whether the two thugs understood or not was immaterial. They had known what their assignment was earlier that morning. And it had not changed.

Their route back to the car was different than the tour they had followed upon arrival. It ran in the opposite direction down the hall and took longer with a detour down a separate corridor. This route took them past an office with a door open and from which Baier could hear shouting and pleading in different Turkish voices. He could not understand what was being said, but it was clearly not a friendly discussion. And it ended as they drew near to the door.

Baier found this odd. But then he understood as they slowed and both escorts took hold of each of Baier's arms. Inside the door and tight against the opposite wall sat Dafne. Her makeup was streaked with tears. Her hair was also disheveled, with strands standing out in different directions as though currents of electricity had run through them. Her dress was wrinkled and clung to her legs. It looked as though she had spent the night in a cell, or possibly that very chair. Her hands were folded and handcuffed, resting in her lap. When she saw Baier, her eyes grew brighter with a glimmer of hope and surprise. But then they turned vacant, and her glance slid to the floor. A hand from a hidden arm and unseen body slowly shoved the door shut.

# CHAPTER NINETEEN

"You want me to do what?"

Baier was standing in front of Jim Breckenridge the following morning. Once again, he had forsaken the sofa and remained upright in front of the station chief's desk. Breckenridge was also standing. It remined Baier of a showdown in the Wild West, something out of the OK Corral. But without the guns or the cowboy hats.

"I want you to help me get an NSS worker out of Turkey."

"You've gotta be fucking crazy. And shouldn't you be back at your hotel packing? What time does your flight leave?"

Baier thought back to his final confrontation at NSS headquarters yesterday after he had stumbled across Dafne and her apparent incarceration. He had swung himself free and ran down the corridor, back the way they had come. His interrogator still stood by the door of the office they had recently occupied. His look of surprise turned to annoyance when he saw Baier and the two men running after him. The Turk squared himself in the corridor facing Baier, but his focus shifted beyond Baier's shoulders to the men running after him. His anger was clearly aimed at Baier's escorts for letting their prisoner return.

"What is the meaning of this?" He stepped forward and moved to the center of the hallway.

At the time, Baier could not be sure if these words had been addressed to him or his escorts. The Turkish official continued to look past Baier for the most part, while his eyes darted to Baier just about every other second. Both men reached Baier at the same time and took a firm grip on his arms.

"Just what the hell are you playing at?" Baier shouted. "She had nothing to do with any of this. She was simply a translator."

"Oh come now, Mister Baier. We know that you seduced her, and that she became much more."

"That is a lie."

"Then why do you care so much what happens to her?"

"If you ever want to get anything out of my visit here, any information at all…if you do not want to have doors shut in your face in Washington, you will let her go." Baier knew he sounded desperate and that he would probably never be able to enforce this. But he did not know what else to say. How else he could sound threatening enough to make his point, to get what he firmly believed was justice for an innocent woman who had simply tried to help his investigation? Hadn't that been her assignment?

"And what then?" the Turk asked. "We no longer want or need her now. She has outlived her usefulness, as far as I can see."

"Exactly. Let her go. I will see that she leaves Turkey and finds someplace new to live."

"And where would that be? In America?"

"Wherever it is, it will not be in Turkey. "You need not worry."

"You know, Mister Baier, because you created this mess I am tempted to let you clean up after it. But her future is not in my hands."

"Then let me speak with whoever has those hands."

"Perhaps. But now I have other matters to attend to. Good day."

He nodded at the escorts and turned away. This time their hands clenched Baier's arms tightly enough to pinch the muscles of each one in a vise.

• • •

He spent of the night tossing from one end of the bed to other at his hotel. He could not remember how many times he rose from the mattress and stormed to the window only to find the night sky as black as his mood. He watched the sun rise with frustration and anger, both at the Turks and at himself.

"I've postponed my departure for another day." Baier pointed to the small pile of paper on the chief's desk. "That's the draft of my cable to Headquarters. I give my reasons in there."

Breckenridge picked the draft up off the desk and began to read. His lips moved intermittently, and his head shook back and forth slowly. He tossed the sheets back on the desk once he had finished.

"You've got to be kidding me. Look, I will forward this stuff to Headquarters, but I and the Ambassador are going to attach our own comments as well. Mine will question the sourcing as untested at best and unreliable at worst. I can almost guarantee that the Ambo will question the substance. A trade-off? Really? And for fucking West Berlin? I don't even see why we bother with that relic."

"Be that as it may, I do not see how you can raise any serious doubts about the validity of the information."

"For Chrissakes, Karl, this is obviously an attempt at disinformation. I know you have a lot of fond memories of Berlin, but it just doesn't carry that kind of weight anymore."

"Oh? Then make sure you tell that to everyone in Washington. It's still the number one object on everyone's mind when it comes to our Cold War with the Soviets."

"And what about Cuba?"

"It may be a crisis now, but once it's settled that island will remain an inconvenience for us but hardly a threat to the future of Europe. That's where the Cold War will be decided."

Breckenrdige laughed. "Yeah, dream on. Maybe you can swing another posting there if you tell enough people that." He picked up the papers again, then tossed them back at the desktop. "And your request and rationale about sticking around in light of your screw up with the NSS is not going anywhere. Not with anyone who knows shit all about our business."

Baier hesitated before responding. He wanted to make sure that he chose the right words and that they would have the impact he desired. The important thing was to keep the threat implied, not explicit. He did not want to force Breckenridge into a corner, where he would become overly defensive and infuriated—not to mention forewarned.

"There is something I left out of this cable. And it's something you need to be aware of."

"And what would that be?"

"It has to do with something else the KGB officer said two nights ago. And it's something you should have been pursuing well before I got here."

"What's that, Sherlock?"

"I told him it seemed as though they had advance notice of the meetings that had been arranged when they moved against those three officers of theirs. He claimed that was because they knew in advance when and where the meetings were scheduled to take place. And when I asked him how they knew that, he told me it was because they had a source on our side."

"Well, who is it? Did he give you what's really important?"

"No, he did not. He told me he had betrayed enough, and that it was my or our job to find all that out on our own."

"Well, isn't that convenient. Now we're supposed to spend our valuable time and resources searching for some phantom traitor? Don't tell me you can't see through that, Karl. Someone of your experience?" The chief fixed Baier with a stare that was filled with disappointment and just a step short of contempt. "Even so, don't you think that is important enough to make it into your cable? Why the hell would you leave that out. especially in light of the other crap you put in here?"

Baier stared back for what seemed like a full minute. "It's the sort of thing that will set off alarm bells the minute it hits the cable secretariat, and you know it. I want to discuss it first with Delgrecchio and whomever else in CI he sees fit to bring into the investigation."

"You are so full of shit, Karl. While you're chasing that particular rainbow you won't have your Turkish girlfriend to keep you company. You'll have to settle for your wife."

"What are you talking about?"

"This broad you want me to rescue from the Turks. Well there is no fucking way I'm going to ruin our relationship with the Turks by snatching one of their own and smuggling her out of the country."

Baier could feel the heat rise. He hoped it did not show in his face, but already his cheeks were burning. He took a step towards the desk.

"Goddamit, Jim, that girl deserves better. I don't know what sort of fantasy you've let loose in that meager, little brain you've got, but she helped me by pointing me in the right direction on a number of aspects of the investigation. And she got nothing in return."

"Nothing?"

"No. nothing. Except nights in a cell and days of interrogation."

A moment of silence hung between the two men like a weight. Baier chewed his lower lip while he pondered his next few words. Breckenridge's eyes did not move from Baier's. It was then that he remembered the parting words from the KGB chief that day Baier had been kidnapped and beaten. Their station chief had wanted our side to be aware that Baier had been grabbed by the Soviets and warned off again. And more seriously this time around. The entire episode had been a set up to send a message to someone in particular.

"I'm pretty damn sure it was you, Jim. In fact, I know it was you. It all fits."

"What was me? The traitor?"

"You were the one informing the Soviets about the assets we had and the meetings that were arranged."

"How the hell do you figure that?"

"Because you were the only one in the station with the knowledge of all three cases. The background and the operational details of those recruitments and reporting streams were far too valuable to share beyond the most limited need-to-know basis. Neither Hughes, Garner, nor Badger knew about the other cases. Nor did they expect to. All that only came together with you. At the least, it will make you a person of interest in this case."

"That's pretty specious, Karl." His hand rose from the desk, the index finger pointing at Baier like a knife. "You'd better be damn careful before you go throwing out accusations like that, my man. I hope you have more than that kind of simple speculation if you're going back to Washington to make a case."

"Oh, I'm sure there's more. But what I can't figure out is the why of it all. It runs against the course of your entire career. Hell, it runs against the course of your life."

"Who the hell are you to challenge my principles like that, my motives?" His words seem to trip a shift in focus and memory. Breckenridge's face betrayed a heightened emotion as his jaw muscles clenched, his eyes narrowed, and his breathing became harder and quicker. "I'm not admitting anything, and certainly not to you here and now. Or anytime, for that matter. I don't have to. And you had better be damn sure that there aren't others in the building who authorized everything I did here."

"Others? Like who? Spronk? Is that why he was here? And for what?"

Breckenridge smiled as his facial muscles relaxed. His gaze roamed the room for a moment before settling back on Baier. "Spronk? That fucking worm? He's nothing more than a nervous Nellie." The smile widened. "But I guess you'll be able to find all that out when you get back home. Which will be sooner than you realize. The Turks don't want you here either."

"That's no surprise. You're probably in cahoots with them as well." Baier thought back to the KGB officer's comments in Istanbul about Kosrov's double role and Hughes sudden disappearance when he thought someone else might be at their meeting the other night in Istanbul. "Oh shit, you are working with the Turks as well. Or at least one faction. They must have been in on this little game as well. Just what the hell have you gotten yourself in to? Just who do you think you are?"

"Don't tell me you haven't questioned the wisdom of our leadership over the past few years. Look at the fumbling that's been going on ever since Kennedy took office. And now he's brought us to the brink of a nuclear war. Someone needed to do something."

"Like what?"

"Like reach out to the other side. To establish a channel of communication, build some trust. Something needs to be done to reduce tensions to a manageable level so we can find a way out of this mess." Breckenridge's look had shifted over the course of this monologue to one of lost logic, confusion almost, and a sense of pleading. His eyes almost seemed to glaze over with faraway look in search of a lost logic and rationale. "Do you really think those clowns in charge in Washington can solve this? Thank God we have friends like the Turks. Or at least some of them."

Baier was too stunned to speak for about half a minute. When he did respond, his voice had dropped several octaves, and he spoke in a slow and careful cadence.

"I'm not at all sure, Jim. I guess I'll have to raise that when I get back to Washington."

"Yeah, okay. You do that."

"But in the meantime, what can we do for the girl?"

Breckenridge seemed to awake from a dream. "Oh, her again? I doubt there's anything we can do to help her at this stage. You might want to raise that as well when you get home."

"Thanks, Jim." Baier pointed at the draft cable. "Don't forget to sign off on that thing and get it sent along to Washington."

Breckenridge retrieved the papers and stared at them. It did not look like he was actually reading the document, as his eyes and lips stayed motionless. Instead, his mind seemed to be back in that lost place, somewhere else, far away. Baier stepped quietly to the door, opened it, threw one more glance at the station chief, then closed the door as softly as possible.

# CHAPTER TWENTY

Breckenridge had been right about one thing. The Turks wanted him gone. At least, some of them did. The ones with the power and authority to make that decision and make it stick.

Baier sat at the end of a row of white plastic chairs, hooked together by a series of thin metal rods. These seats were as uncomfortable as any of those he had occupied at NSS headquarters. He wondered who had the uncomfortable chair concession for the country and how wealthy he must be. Baier stared out the large window that covered most of the wall to his right with its view of the runways outside. A Lufthansa flight taxied in from the outermost runway, its sleek metal body gleaming from the sunlight that rolled off the mountains behind it while reflecting a glare that seemed to hide so much of what had happened in this capital. He assumed this was his plane for the flight to Frankfurt, although no arrival notice had been posted as yet. It could be early, which would be normal for the Germans' vaunted punctuality. If so, he figured it would be clean and orderly inside as well. He hoped the crew would be friendly, too. He could use a friend this morning.

The sound of high heels clicking on the linoleum floor announced her arrival. She was dressed today in a modest wool suit, checkered in grey and black, with a hem that fell midway between her knees and heels. She also wore a matching jacket that helped tuck her figure behind the folds of cloth, but it could not hide her body completely. Not from Baier.

She took the seat next to his, her body angled in his direction. He sat back and turned his head toward her.

"You seemed to have recovered well," he said. "I hope your colleagues were not too hard on you."

Dafne smiled and shook her head lightly. "No, it wasn't so bad. I was just a pawn in their bigger match."

"I see. The match against Sadak?"

She nodded. "Yes, in part. But also against you."

"Was I really that important?"

"I suppose you could say it was more what your represented. You were a threat."

"Really?" Baier could not hide his look of disbelief. Nor did he want to. "How was that?"

"You threatened to upset their plans. You also threatened a connection they wanted to protect."

"And what plans were those? And whose plans were they?"

"A nationalist faction within our organization. They call themselves the Karakol."

"The what?"

"The Karakol. They took that name from a group of former military and intelligence officers formed after the First World War. They operated mostly out of Istanbul and gathered intelligence on the Allied forces here and smuggled weapons to Ataturk's army in the east."

"Why?"

"You see, they were opposed to the Western Allies' plans to break up what was left of the Ottoman Empire and either give it away and keep some of it for themselves. They believe their group is facing much the same challenge today."

"But we don't want to break Turkey up."

"Some appear to doubt your sincerity. Others see the problem as a similar one, even if your claim to respect our territory is true. They want to loosen what they see as our dependence on your country. And the cooperation with the Soviets here fit into that nicely."

"Of course. I guess it was one of the conflicting dynamics I was told about. Will they be the ones in control now?"

Dafne shrugged. "Who can tell? Things change. I think the military will end up blocking them eventually. They usually get their way. And those people do not worry about becoming too dependent on you."

"But what if the military, or some inside that institution, also favor this other way?"

"I doubt there would be that many of them. Not enough to make a difference."

"But what if they have help from outside?"

"Outside? Like where? Surely not your people."

Baier stayed silent. He explored her eyes with his own, wondering how much she knew. He reached over and took her hand. He was glad, primarily, that she had survived. At least thus far.

"And what about you? What will you do now? Do you still have family in Greece? Up north in Thessaloniki perhaps? Or on Crete. I understand that's where many of the Pontic Greeks who left Turkey were sent."

"Yes, I do, up north. But I will stay here for now. I made that decision long ago, but I am less certain about that now. I will stay long enough to see what kind of future I have here."

"What do you mean by that? Professionally? Or as someone with a Greek heritage?"

Dafne was silent for a moment, her eyes focused on the Lufthansa plane just beyond their window. It had begun to deboard, a long, silent stream of passengers marching down the steps set by the front door near the pilots' cabin and onto a bus that would carry them to the terminal's passport control area.

"I suppose both. If things take a more nationalistic turn, life could become very uncomfortable for me."

"Will you be punished for working with me?"

Dafne's gaze shifted back out to the runways again. She studied the planes as they rolled along the concrete as though she was trying to guess at which gate they would park. When her eyes moved back to Baier they seemed to glisten with moisture and the sunlight of the morning.

"No, I will not be punished. I did nothing against my orders. I was told to get close to you. And I did. Closer than some were comfortable with, but they are unlikely to press that issue. Some are probably suspicious that more happened between us, but a woman gets used to that."

Baier sat back. "Was that it then? About us, I mean. Did you ever feel that there was something more? Or were you just following orders?"

She leaned forward. "Of course, there was. You should have felt that, just as I did."

"Oh, I felt it alright. It was very unprofessional of me. I am glad, though, that we were both able to resist doing something so unprofessional and just plain wrong."

"Yes, that is how I feel, too. And now it is over." She paused and leaned back against her chair. "What will you do when you go home? Have you spoken with your wife? Will you tell her of our cooperation, our friendship?"

"She will know anyway. At least, I think she will. She is too smart not to know. But I doubt anything will come of it."

"And at work?"

Baier smiled. It was his turn to take in the airplanes and their routes to the terminal. "I'm not sure." The smile faded. "I will have to pursue what I think is the right course."

"And that is?"

"I will have to go after a man I believe is a traitor. He betrayed our organization and our country, whatever reasons he may have believed he had."

"Is that man here?"

Baier nodded.

"Was it someone in your own organization?"

Baier nodded again.

"Was it your chief? Was he working with us? I mean, against what you had been sent here to do?"

Baier shrugged. "I will have to see where things lead."

"I wish you luck, Karl. You know I only wanted to cooperate with you on this operation. I knew nothing of any other agendas. Or what your chief here may have wanted, if that is the man you believe is a traitor."

"I can't speak more about my suspicions yet. Not here and now." He paused. "But you, Dafne, have been one of the few things I can be certain of."

"Whatever else you may say, I am afraid your chief may have been your biggest nemesis all along."

"It has not been an easy assignment. I suspect it will get even more difficult once I return to Washington. An even bigger issue is if others have been involved back there."

"You know, Mucip much preferred to work with Mister Badger. I think he trusted him more."

"Why was that?"

Dafne dropped her hands into her lap and shrugged. "He never explained it to me. But I always had the impression that your chief did not care for Mucip either, that he preferred to work with others in our service."

"Was it this group you mentioned? The Karakol? Do you have any names?"

"No, not really. Not any specific names. But I believe you met one of them when you came to that first meeting in our building. He attended the discussion with us but said very little."

Baier sat back hard against the cold plastic seat.

Dafne waited a moment, but when Baier said nothing further she stood and held out her hand. "I really do wish you luck. You know, it is best that you are leaving now. Best for both of us. But I am still sorry to see you leave. I will miss you."

"And I you."

Baier stood, took her hand, then pulled her close. He left a lingering kiss on her cheek and a nod against her forehead. Then he watched her disappear down the corridor and away from the waiting room as his flight was posted for boarding.

# CHAPTER TWENTY-ONE

"No, Dafne. Wait." Travelers hurrying to catch their flights moved aside with looks of amusement or concern as Baier hurtled down the corridor. Baier heard the boarding announcement for his flight to Frankfurt and wondered half aloud just what he hoped to accomplish. He slid around a corner and caught a glimpse of Dafne as she strolled through the airport's front entrance. He had just minutes to catch her before she disappeared into the parking lot across the street. He pushed himself through the door with his shoulder and called out to her again.

She paused and turned slowly, a look of utter confusion clouding her face. But at least she had stopped.

"Karl, what is it? You will miss your flight. You really do not have time for this sort of drama."

"No, Dafne, wait. There is something else."

She shook her head. "Between us? No, there can't be."

He raced on and halted just short of her. His momentum almost brought them together, but Dafne stepped back to give him more room.

"I realize that, Dafne. But there is something else I need to know. And I need your help."

"But what about your flight and your luggage? And what about your chief here? He will not be happy if you suddenly show up again at his office this afternoon."

Baier nodded and gasped for breath. He was really going to have to start exercising. "I can always collect my bags in Frankfurt tomorrow or the day after."

"And your chief?"

"I do not plan to go back there. That is one way you can help. Can I stay at your place for a day or so?"

She stepped further back and threw Baier a look of amusement. "Just what sort of help do you need? Do you not think it is time to go home to your wife? I thought you wanted to pursue this case back in Washington."

Baier shook his head and waved his hand in front of himself, as though to banish the thought. "No, no, I can explain. But first, I need a place to hide. Your people do not want me here either."

The amusement disappeared, replaced by worry, fear almost. "My God, Karl, what are you asking? My people? Which ones?"

"That's what I need to find out. It is probably some of those people you mentioned. That Karakol bunch. I need to find out what their entire agenda is and how someone on my side may be helping them. I'm afraid this could go deeper than you realize, Dafne. I need to know before I return to Washington."

She grabbed Baier's arm and pulled him toward her. She took his hand and led him down a row off to the right and to a blue Ford that looked like one of those heavy-set Fairlane's now crowding the streets in Turkey. At least it wasn't yellow. It was the first time he bothered to study one up closely. The size looked smaller than the cars found on American streets, and the lines were rounded on each side to make the body more compact. Plus, there wasn't nearly as much chrome.

"Here. We can talk in my car. It is better than standing out in the open where we will draw attention. Your exit from the airport was not exactly smooth, you know."

"Yes, yes, of course." Baier dropped into the passenger seat while Dafne marched around the front and sat behind the steering wheel. "I could also use your help in getting me to talk to some people in your building."

"Like who? And why would I do that?"

"Because this affects you as well, Dafne, and your country. If these people want to reorient Turkey away from the West and toward the Middle East it will reverse the changes Ataturk tried to bring to Turkey through his revolution. And you know that will be bad for everyone we care about." He paused to study her face. "And it would probably be bad for people like yourself."

"But why, Karl? I don't see what difference you're staying here makes for you and me. Why should we both jeopardize our careers, even risk our lives, for some kind of feeling or suspicion you have?"

"But you are the one who told me about this faction in your service. You know they are dangerous." He paused to catch his breath. Baier had not realized how fast he had been speaking, that he had not bothered to take the time to breathe as the words had just flowed forth like water over a broken dam. "It's important, Dafne. It's what we do. It's the life we chose years ago, and that path can bring us to these kinds of decisions. And now is one of those times."

Baier could see how much she was struggling with her decision. He could see the tears in her eyes and the quivering in her lips.

"Believe me, Dafne, I would not ask you to do this if I was not pretty damn certain that there's some fire at the bottom of all this smoke. And that it can burn both of us and both our countries."

She started the engine and slipped the car into reverse. Dafne threw her head around to see if anyone was behind her. She pushed the stick shift into first but then paused before starting to drive away.

"Please, Karl, please do not make me regret that we worked so closely together, that we ever cared for each other."

Baier reached over to dry her tears with his handkerchief, then stared straight ahead. "That is the last thing I want to do, Dafne. You mean too much to me."

• • •

"So, just how do you plan to go about doing whatever it is you think you need to do?"

Dafne had brought Baier to her apartment, a modest one-bedroom flat in a new high rise—Baier guessed about ten or eleven floors when they drove up—clearly thrown up after the war. In fact, he figured sometime in the last few years. Maybe even sooner. The red sandstone and modern, neo-classical architecture suggested as much. And then there was the absence of any landscaping to speak of, including trees. Dafne's place was on the fifth floor, which for some reason gave Baier a sense of security. Not too easy in terms of access, but not too high to require a sprint down or up all those flights of stairs. Sure, there was an elevator, but Baier trusted his luck in any kind of pursuit to the stairs. More options and less of an imprisoned feeling.

"Well, I haven't really worked out the details yet."

Dafne's face lit up with anger. "What? Are you running this thing—whatever it is—on the fly? You've jeopardized my career, my life on a hunch? Without any sense of your next steps?"

Baier walked over to her and pulled her away from the window. "Let's stay away from places like that. We really do not know who may be watching."

"I checked for surveillance on the way here. And I noticed that you did as well."

"But where does your office think you are right now?"

"On the way back from the airport after seeing you off. Imagine their surprise when word gets out that you have missed your flight."

"Yes, of course. So, we will need a plausible story of what has happened."

"Well…?"

Baier paced the room, then let himself drop into one of the chairs that surrounded a small dining table set across from a modest kitchen, more a gally actually. "Can you tell them you never found me? That you spent all this extra time looking for me in the airport, but that I was nowhere around? That would explain the time that elapsed before your return."

Dafne frowned. "I suppose that might work. But what if someone saw us together?"

"You said you had come to the airport alone, right?" She

nodded. "Then the chances of that are pretty small. Small enough to take." He paused and blew out his breath. "It's not like we have a lot of options here."

"Good enough. I am assuming you will be safe here while I return to work. Try not to break anything."

"Is there food and something to drink? Like bottled water?"

"There should be some yogurt and bread in the kitchen. And, yes, bottled water, Mister American-with-the-sensitive-stomach."

Baier spread his arms wide. "Hey, so I'm spoiled. It is an affliction I share with most of my countrymen." He stood and moved toward her. When he reached Dafne, Baier's arms encircled her waist, and he kissed her forehead. She did not move away, but neither did she respond to his closeness or his embrace.

"I will stop on the way home and pick up something for dinner. We will eat in, of course."

"Of course."

"How long will you be staying?"

"I promise, no longer than a day or two."

"Good, because you will probably be caught after that."

He brought his arms up to her shoulders and leaned back. "You do not have to worry, Dafne. I will not try to pressure you into anything, anything that you do not want or that might endanger you."

She took his face in her hands and kissed his forehead in return. "You already have."

"In that case, there is just one more favor for today." Dafne's eyes rolled. "Can you contact Sadak? He is not in prison, I hope. I think I am going to need his cooperation."

Dafne broke from his arms and sat in the armchair set across from the window on the other side of the room. "No, he is not. Remember, I told you that he was released after a day of some pretty rough interrogation. I guess they were satisfied that he did not overstep his orders more than was necessary to keep track of your investigation. Those who arrested him must believe they have him neutralized now. They probably realize that if they pushed further with him, they would most likely be overplaying their hand. They are not that strong yet. Or at least I hope not. But why do you need to talk to him?"

"I need him to help me navigate some of my suspicions about your place, about the officers who might be behind what has happened. And any part people in my office here are playing."

"Tell me then, just what do you think has happened..."

"Is happening. Like I said, it isn't over yet. It's why I felt I had to come back, why I'm taking this chance."

"Okay, what is happening?"

Baier walked over and sat on the arm of her chair. He took her hand. "I suspect that some of the people behind Menderes and his efforts to bring Islam back are still at work within your country's institutions. They are even willing to turn towards the Soviet Union if it means creating more distance from us and the West in general. And you suspect it as well. That's why you told me about this Karakol group."

"And your organization's part in all this?"

"It isn't my organization per se. But certain people right here in Ankara. I doubt they share the same goal. In fact. I'm sure of it. But they are being played."

"And who might they be?"

"That's where I hope Mucip can help."

# CHAPTER TWENTY-TWO

In the end, Baier could not just sit and wait in Dafne's apartment. Nice as it was and nice as the view of the mountains outside Ankara was, he came down with a case of cabin fever. His anxiety about staying behind in Turkey and having to go into hiding to escape detection by both the Turkish authorities and his own organization was simply too much. He needed to be active, not sedentary. To be doing something to move this case along, to confirm his suspicions, and to force a resolution. Somehow.

He loitered at the back entrance for fifteen, maybe twenty minutes, checking on his surroundings and any suspicious presence. When Baier felt secure enough to leave the complex, he took the back streets. That in itself was no guarantee, of course, but it did reduce the chances that he would be recognized. And apprehended. He had enough of a map of the area in his head and knew that if he traveled parallel to Ataturk Boulevard, he would eventually reach the long park that ran away from that main thoroughfare and the US Embassy. It was in that park that Baier had walked with Fred Badger on an earlier afternoon, in part because Badger had recommended it from his own hikes through the area. It was a convenient and pleasant path through the city to his own residence on the other side of a series of hotels and the Iranian Embassy, a pretty nice residential district, according to Badger.

So, Baier thought he would wait and pretend to be enjoying the pleasant fall weather, which was fortunately not very cold at all, despite it being late October. Certainly not to a native of Chicago, at any rate.

That began to change once the daylight started to fade and the warming afternoon sun disappeared. Thankfully, Badger appeared, presumably on his way home, around 6:30. So far, Baier's luck had been holding. But when Badger's face dropped from the unprepossessing innocence of a lonely walk home to the shocking discovery of his presence, Baier wasn't so sure that would continue. Badger stopped in mid-step, his right foot hovering in place before finding the ground again. He did not move forward. He did not move in any direction, which Baier took to be a good thing. Potentially. But the lines in his face showed a troubling mixture of confusion, anger, and concern. Badger had stopped about ten feet from Baier. And he started to retreat slowly when Baier attempted to approach.

"What the hell do your think you're doing?" Badger asked, his voice shaking with anger. "Just what the hell is going on here?"

"I couldn't leave. I had too much unfinished business."

"Oh really? Like what? Do you have any idea of the shit storm you've unleashed here? People are looking for you everywhere."

"Well, hopefully, not here."

Badger relaxed his posture enough to take a long look around the park. When he turned back to Baier, his face showed more anger than concern. "What the hell are you trying to do to me? My career? I should run back to the Embassy right now and alert the Marine guards, tell them to call Breckenridge."

Baier held up his hands. "Please don't do that. Let me explain why I've jeopardized everything to come back here. Why I think this is so important."

"You've got five minutes."

"Someone here has strayed off the reservation. It's that simple. And if I'm right he has—wittingly or unwittingly--endangered our position in the region and undermined our policy against the Soviet Union."

"That is one hell of an accusation. Who is it?"

"I think you know already. Or you can probably guess as much. That's why I'm turning to you, Fred."

Badger did not respond. Since Baier assumed Badger was waiting for a name, he told him. "It's your chief, Breckenridge."

"Oh, is that all?" The sarcasm in Badger's voice could have shredded a kebab.

"Maybe he's had some help, but he is the principal figure."

"Like who? Someone in the station? Those guys are all first-rate officers and patriots. That is one hell of a slur you're throwing around. Sir." The last word had been added as an afterthought, and empty of any sincerity.

"Look, Fred, I know this is a lot to process..."

"I'll say."

"...But I need your help. I already know some of what's been going on from what the Russian told me the other night."

"Which was?"

"That they have a source in our office. He didn't give me a name, telling me that it was up to me, to us, to follow through on this."

"Why would he do that? A source inside our place would be a dream come true for those pricks."

"Probably because that source is expendable now. They've gotten what they needed here, and they no longer see any use for him."

"Again, why would they do that? Why wouldn't they just put him on hold to see what sort of jobs or responsibilities he got in the future?'

Baier shrugged. "I think the Soviet officer may have spoken out of term. He wanted to convince me of the legitimacy of his information."

"That makes him sound very much like a dangle."

"But the guy was speaking of a much bigger purpose. It seemed to me that he sincerely believed he was helping avert a nuclear war. Besides, his side probably figured the source's game was up. That we would cotton on to him sooner or later. It's how they knew about the meeting with our three assets before they even happened. They knew we would focus on the one guy who had the access to information about all three operations. So, they decided to throw him under the bus to get what more they could out of him and his betrayal."

"And that would be?"

"Think of the shit that will fly from the fan back in Langley with this. But more important for this moment, is that they wanted to give a sign of their sincerity when they told me about the incident with their submarine."

"What are you talking about? What submarine?"

"The one that almost launched a nuclear missile at our destroyer that was trying to force it to surface," Baier answered. "They are scared shitless that World War III was about to break out. That it still could. The Russian tossed that tidbit in when we met in Istanbul the other night."

"So?"

"So, they know they are badly outgunned."

"Why am I only hearing about this now?"

"Oh, hell, Fred, why do you think?"

When Badger did not respond, Baier continued. "Besides, they had gotten what they really wanted. The identity and proof of their own officers' betrayal. I guess they figured there were bigger fish to fry in the current atmosphere."

"Anything else?"

"As a matter of fact, yes, there is. The Russians also hinted at another operation here, one that involves infiltrating and working with the Turks at the NSS. Or, at least some Turks."

"Okay, but what does that have to do with our station here? I mean, other than working to figure out what's going on and moving against that with our own Turkish friends?"

"It's our pressing business because I think we may have been pulled in as accomplices."

"No fucking way. Sir."

There sounded to be a little more sincerity in that final word this time around.

"It turns out the Soviets were using Kosrov as the link."

"But that guy was a diplomat," Badger protested. "Why would they do that kind of end run?"

"Because no one would expect that. I know you guys must have done a deep background check on the guy and his career, but let's not fool ourselves by assuming the Soviets couldn't have hidden his own ties to the KGB or GRU. I mean, you know they're not complete idiots."

"Fair enough. But how would Hughes not have figured that out? You're not saying he was complicit in this?"

"It's something I need to find out. How deep or wide this goes. My guess is that Breckenridge was running this thing and that Hughes may be just collateral damage of sorts. He could have been convinced that it was all necessary and above board."

"Or that it all had the approval of some superiors at Headquarters," Badger suggested.

"Yeah, and if that's really the case, then we have a bigger problem that I ever imagined."

"Then you're fucked, Sir."

"We all are, Fred."

Badger stared at the ground by Baier's feet for almost a minute. Then he studied the park's surroundings once more and moved in closer to Baier. His voice, when he spoke, was little more than a whisper.

"So, what do you want me to do?"

"You're supposed to be the main man for liaison exchanges and cooperation on operational stuff with the Turks, right?"

Badger nodded. "Yeah, that's right."

"But what has Jim been doing? Has he interacted at all with them?"

Badger shrugged. "Just when he has to. The occasional dinner with visitors in town or an office call on their director now and then. He claims he doesn't like those guys."

"Well, I'm pretty sure there's been more. I'm going to try to find out more from my end, and you need to let me know what Breckenridge is up to on that front as well."

"And Hughes?"

Baier nodded. "Hughes, too."

"Okay, I'll see what I can do. I'm still not convinced, mind you, but I can give you the benefit of a doubt. At least for now. Where are you staying?"

Baier shook his head. "Let's leave that for now. It's probably best that you don't know. We can use the park here, practice our dead drops to communicate. Is this a good spot?"

"Let's use the benches further up. There's a grove of trees that provide better cover. One of us can leave a chalk mark on the bench farthest from the road back there…" Badger's head bent toward Ataturk Boulevard. "…To minimize the risk of exposure."

Baier surveyed the area Badger had indicated. "Okay, good. And one more question."

"What else?"

"Do you have your exfiltration routes up to date?"

Badger took another step back. "Are you kidding? Is it really that serious for you?"

"It's not just for me. We may have to bring out a Turk or two as well."

"Jesus, Sir, you are asking one hell of a lot. What sort of guarantees do I have that I'll survive this affair?"

Baier looked hard at his colleague. "Well, none actually. You've probably guessed that much already. But I don't plan to leave us hanging out on a limb all alone. Or not completely alone, anyway." Baier pulled a slip of paper from his pocket. "You'll need to find some kind of opportunity to contact Ralph Delgrecchio. Give him the information on this note, and if you have time, explain what it is we're up to here. He'll understand and help where he can."

"Okay, okay. I'll see what I can do."

"And, Fred, the route out of here? I hope it's to the west?"

Badger looked up from the note. He was clearly trying to memorize the message, probably intending to destroy it once he got home.

"Yeah. It's around Antalya. Why?"

"Because that will make things easier, should we need it. You never know how long the territory around the region here will stay friendly."

• • •

"Where have you been?"

Dafne's voice was calm and low. She did not yell. She stood there in the middle of her apartment, oblivious to Baier's warning about the window and potentially preying eyes, in her dark grey skirt and jacket, feet planted firmly apart at shoulder width like an ancient statue that had been reborn into the modern age. But her face betrayed an anger and bewilderment that was unmistakable. And very much in the present.

"I...I had to go out." Baier wanted to sound confident in his response, but he faltered in the face of her disapproval. "It was important for me to reach out to someone."

"Who? Tell me."

"One of my colleagues. I need to work with someone from our side as well."

"Which one?"

"Fred Badger. He's the deputy there. Your people know him. He's someone I'm pretty sure I...we can trust."

Only then did Baier notice the figure seated on the sofa behind her against the wall. Mucip Sadak. His light brown plaid suit looked like it had not seen a dry cleaner in months. It looked exactly as one would imagine it would if the owner had slept in it. The shirt also had traces of brown around the collar, and the tie had disappeared. Sadak's face did not look much better. His eyes were red and the right one wore a black and blue bruise at its outer edge. His upper lip also carried a thin scar that ran vertically from top to bottom. Other than that, he was the same Turkish intelligence officer Baier had worked with when he arrived and with whom it looked like he would be working again.

Baier moved forward, his hand extended. Sadak started to rise.

"No, please," Baier said. "Do not stand up. Not for me, at any rate. Are you okay? How badly were you treated?"

Sadak slid back down into the sofa's cushions. "Not too badly, considering. And it was really only rough the first day, when their suspicions were strongest."

"I am so sorry..."

"It is not your fault, Mister Baier. If it was, I would not be here. It is the fault of others. And it is because of them that I have come."

"Yes, I see. And whom do you believe is responsible?"

Sadak sighed as he looked to Dafne and then beyond to the world outside her window. "There are several. I doubt I can expose all of them."

"Is it this Karakol group?"

Sadak nodded. "So, you know of them. How did you learn this? From Dafne?"

Baier stayed silent, watching his new Turkish ally and friend.

"I see." Sadak paused for a few seconds, then continued. "Well, there are a few I hope to undermine, to make others in my government and service aware of what they are up to."

"And what is that?" Baier asked.

"They oppose my country's orientation to the west, the close alliance with your country."

"And why is that?"

"They believe it betrays our nation's history and its heritage. Basically, they believe that Ataturk created something altogether new, a bastard nation, if you will."

"I would imagine that would not get very far now."

"Ah, but that is why they have decided to work with the Soviets, or shall we say the Russians. They are all the same to me and many of my countrymen. They want to work with them to create distance between us and show some benefits or advantages from finding friends and allies elsewhere."

"And did that apply in the case I was investigating? The three Russian who were killed here?"

Sadak shook his head eagerly. "Yes, yes. They wanted to demonstrate that they had things they could deliver. That they had leverage."

"Were they ones who betrayed the men to the Soviets?"

"No, but they allowed the Soviets to do what they thought necessary to take care of those poor men."

"And what did they get in return?"

Sadak smiled and uttered a short, sharp laugh. "Not much. From what I can tell. But there may have been something else, something beyond what I know."

"I see."

"But do you?" This question came from Dafne. Baier had actually forgotten her for a moment, as he focused on Sadak. He turned toward where she stood in the same spot she had occupied when he entered her flat. Her body was more relaxed now, and her hands had fallen from her waist to her side. She raised those now as she stepped toward Baier. She came within a few inches of his body, and he could already feel the heat rise from his legs to his chest. He took a step back.

"What do you mean?"

She leaned forward to cover the distance Baier had created. "Do you understand all the ramifications? Who else have they been working with besides the Russians? And not just in our government, which is something that people like Mucip and myself have to consider. What about others from the region, and even from your side?"

"Do you mean my colleagues?"

"Yes, I do. That is something I know you want to pursue. And without that sort of help, however unwitting, these people would have no hope of success. So, you see how we must work together."

Baier nodded. "Yes, of course. I agree completely. Besides, I clearly need your help. I cannot look into what my side has been up to alone, especially not on foreign soil. Not here."

"Good." Sadak stood and moved across the room toward Baier. He rested his hand on Baier's shoulder, like a good priest or a close friend. "Our best hope is to catch them together."

"Who?" Baier asked.

"Whomever my people meet with. But for your purposes, it would be best if they met with some Americans."

"So, we're dependent on what they set up? There's nothing we can do to find some evidence of what you have described?"

Sadak shook his head, and his hand dropped to his side. He glanced at Dafne, then back at Baier. "No, I am afraid not. Neither of us has the kind of access we would need to find that material. Besides, I doubt they have put much in writing. That is too dangerous."

"How will we know when we can move on this?"

Sadak nodded in Dafne's direction. "She will know. I will make sure of that." Sadak walked back to the sofa, where he retrieved a small parcel wrapped in brown paper and tied with a string. "Here, I brought this for you."

Baier took the package and unwrapped it. A dark grey sweater, light blue shirt, and pair of dirtied and faded tan slacks fell to the floor. Baier bent to pick them up. He looked first at Sadak, then at Dafne. "What is this?"

"We agreed that it was too risky for you to continue to wear the clothes that everyone could easily recognize on you," Dafne said. "Mucip agreed to bring some of his own older things for you. They should help hide you a little better."

"Yes, yes, of course." Baier examined the clothes. "They may be a bit small, but I'm sure they will work just fine." He glanced at Sadak. "Thank you, Mucip. That was very thoughtful."

Sadak started for the door. "Of course. Anything to help. But please, do not take any unneeded risks. Only leave these rooms when it is absolutely necessary."

"Yes, of course. I understand. But one more question, if I may, Mucip."

"What is it?"

"Why did they let you go? Or did you escape?"

Sadak smiled at the thought. "No, escape is not really an option." He paused before continuing. "It seems they decided I was no longer a threat. Besides, they might face some uncomfortable questions if they held me too long." He smiled. "They do not control my organization. Not yet. We still have allies. I am sure of that."

"But if they still face opponents inside your organization, why did they did not have to explain their actions thus far? Would not those have already raised suspicions?"

The smile broadened. "Not when you say you are investigating a possible CIA penetration. And they judged that while I worked closely with you—although not as close as my colleague here—I did not overstep my responsibilities as your liaison officer. At least there was no proof of that."

"Because it doesn't exist. And what now for you? Aside from this, I mean."

Sadak shrugged. "That will depend on what we discover. If we fail, I will be lucky if they assign me to a backwater out east."

"And if we find nothing or cannot prove it?"

Sadak smiled some more, then let it all fade away. He did not answer. He slid out the door and let it shut quietly behind him.

• • •

Later that night, Baier awoke with a start. The air outside looked dark, as though bathed with a sense of uncertainty and fear. He struggled to focus, sensing that someone stood next to the sofa on which he had made his bed. When he did find focus, Baier saw the tall and wonderful shape of Dafne before him. At first, he thought he was dreaming. But then realized with a start that he was fully awake. Her white cotton nightgown hung in soft folds off the curves of her body like an image from the mythology that pervaded this part of the world. The image and the figure before him seemed just as unreal. A ray of moonlight shone through her nightgown, outlining her figure and bringing his mind back to the present.

She reached down and took his hand from the cushions and pulled him up from the furniture. Then she turned and led him to the window. She was silent as she stared at the world outside for nearly a minute. Later, Baier could have sworn it was longer, much longer. She took his hand and placed it against the glass.

"Look over the tips of your fingers," Dafne instructed.

Baier did as he was told but saw only a collection of cars by the building opposite hers, half hidden in shadows cast by the moonlight that crept over the tops of the mountains in the distance.

"Do you see them?" she asked.

Baier struggled to see anything of importance. "Do you mean the cars or the fields and hills beyond? Is it something in one of the buildings?"

"No. It's the small black sedan in the lot below. It is one of ours."

Baier stepped back from the glass. He gasped for breath. "Are you sure?"

"Not absolutely. But I have never seen it before. And it has been here all night."

"What should we do?"

"I think we should do nothing. Not right away. But you will need to be extra careful. If it is someone from my organization, it could be a blessing."

"Say what? How does it work that way?"

She looked at Baier as though he were a child. "Because, Karl, we know now where they are. So now we can avoid them."

"I suppose so. As long as it's the only one." He pondered the car and its meaning, the potential threat. "There could be others. Ones we don't see."

Dafne smiled. "No, I am almost certain there is just this one. Whoever is behind this is only checking on my residence to be sure. If they were certain you were here, we would not be standing together in my apartment. Not any longer."

She stared into Baier's eyes and stroked his arm, then let her hand drop to her side. She tossed another smile at Baier and turned toward her room. The moon light that slipped through the window seemed to carry her away.

Baier sighed and returned to his sofa.

# CHAPTER TWENTY-THREE

It took two days. Baier was surprised that things appeared to be coming together after only 48 hours. But the information from Dafne and Mucip about a meeting of several members of their service who they suspected of belonging to this Karakol group with someone from the foreign intelligence community indicated that something was up. The more he thought about it, the more sense it made. True, it could be almost anyone, but the late-night, clandestine arrangement suggested it was well out of the routine, certainly for a normal liaison gathering. If his suspicions were correct, then whoever was involved could not afford to wait too long. In fact, Baier guessed, his own continued presence may have even forced their hands.

He had tried to stay put in the apartment, as Dafne and Sadak had instructed. It made perfect sense, of course. Minimize his exposure and the chance of discovery. Especially since the NSS had known of his relationship with Dafne. But he had no other way to communicate with Badger. And the car Dafne had pointed out was there only at night. So once each day Baier performed the most thorough surveillance detection run of his career and then walked to the park where he and Badger had last met, searching for the telltale chalk mark in the hope that Badger would have something to impart, something that could move the case along.

Baier was torn throughout. He needed to follow through to see if his suspicions were on the mark. Not to do so would betray his organization, not to mention his country. If an Agency officer had engaged in treasonous activity—whatever his motives—he had to be stopped. But what did that say about the institution and the people who served there? In all the years he worked at the CIA and with all the people he had to come know and respect, he would never have imagined something like this to be possible. Still, he had to see it through.

Each day he gave himself half an hour to wait for Badger's arrival. And each day it was late in the afternoon, when the park was crowded with pedestrians on their way home or to an early evening out. It was the time of day he would normally have chosen. Plenty of people to provide cover and a chance to get away if he was discovered. And a convenient time to be out and passing through if you needed to leave a message.

Which is what Baier found on the second day. A yellow chalk mark sat about a foot off the ground at the base of an oak tree with a hedge of waist-high shrubbery surrounding it. You would not have noticed the mark, it was so well hidden, if you did not know what to look for. But try as he might, Baier could not find any kind of message in the bushes or on the underside of the bench, as the two men had agreed.

Thinking of no other workable alternative, Baier walked up the street to an intersection where a row of shops and restaurants ran in either direction to his left and right. He found a telephone booth about a bloc away and stepped inside. When Baier dialed Badger's number at his office, his colleague answered on the first ring.

"There was nothing there." Best to get right to the point, Baier thought. Less time on the phone meant more security for both of them.

"I didn't want to leave anything in writing. I didn't think it was secure enough. Too damn many people."

"Fair enough. So, what is it?"

"Tonight. At nine o'clock. The Citadel, believe it or not."

"Our guy"

"Yep. The one and only."

"How do you know?"

"He wrote it on a note at his desk."

"He wrote it down? And then he left it there in the open? He must be losing his touch, getting nervous."

"Not quite. I had to decipher it from the impression on his note pad."

"Who's he meeting?"

"It didn't say."

"No, of course not. He can't have gotten that careless."

"So, are you going to be there?" Badger pressed.

"Hell, yes."

"Alone?"

"Can you come with me? It might help prove me right. Or wrong for that matter."

Baier heard a sigh over the telephone line, followed by a pause filled with shallow breathing.

"I was afraid you'd ask me that," Badger answered. More silence followed. "I guess I should. In for a penny and all that shit."

"Good. I think it's best. Can you meet me at our new place at 7:30? That should give us enough time to get down there and check out the site for surveillance and any other company there might be."

"Alright. Should I come armed?"

"Better not. That could easily escalate the situation. We need to play this with cool heads and easy hands."

• • •

Baier reached the apartment at half past six. Dafne and Sadak were already there, waiting. Sadak had changed out of his beaten suit into something more comfortable and less conspicuous, a pair of brown cotton slacks and a light green sweater over a white shirt that looked to be freshly laundered. He also had on comfortable-looking walking shoes, probably something like a Turkish version of sneakers. It all made Baier envious. With his luggage hopefully waiting in Frankfurt, he was completely reliant on the set of clothes Dafne and Mucip had provided. His own blue shirt, woolen slacks and sports jacket were not only potential give-aways, but already felt thin and jaded. To say nothing of his socks and underwear. Fortunately, Dafne owned an iron that he could use to bring some sort of crispness to his appearance. At least he felt a little better.

But once again Sadak, ever the gentleman, had brought along a new shirt and thicker sweater for him to help ward off the evening chill. And feel somewhat cleaner and healthier. Dafne looked as beautiful as ever, even in her loose, cotton, black and grey sweater. Her hair had been pulled into a braid that trailed halfway down her back. Both Turks slid into their lined raincoats after Baier changed.

Good," Dafne announced. "You are finally ready. We must go. There is a meeting tonight, and we should move."

"At the Citadel?"

Dafne nodded. "Yes. You know about it?"

"That's right. Fred Badger informed me."

"Good," Sadak added. "We have to get to the meeting place before the others to check out the site."

Baier's heart felt like it was about to burst through his chest. Dafne and Sadak turned to him in surprise when he breathed in loud enough to hiss.

"Is something wrong?" Sadak asked.

"No. Just nervous. Let's go," Baier said. "But we need to make a quick detour." He explained where he wanted them all to go. "I need to pick up my colleague. He needs to be there to see this."

"Why is that?" Dafne asked.

"Trust me."

When their party got to the Citadel, Baier and Badger spread out and surveyed the streets surrounding the old fortress. A few of the shops had stayed open, mostly those offering spices and carpets, in a bid for some additional tourist business. The moonlight reflected off the damp bricks that ran along the streets, casting an eerie sheen that leant an air of mystery to the night. The darkened windows that stared out from the upper floors of the buildings lining the streets and alleys gave the entire enterprise a foreboding air. Baier chalked it up to his own feelings of anxiety and uncertainty and wondered if he was alone. Ever since they had left Dafne's place he found his mood on the verge of despair. It was not the first time in his career he had confronted anxiety, but this time it was tinged with a sense of desperation and uncertainty that he found nearly overwhelming.

When Badger and Baier were reasonably certain that they were alone, the two Americans marched up to the spot where Sadak had claimed their officers were supposed to meet with their asset. It was the first time Baier had imagined he would ever use that word for a colleague, if indeed their meeting was really with the man he suspected. The term implied control over someone in a subordinate position, and Baier had been shocked when he first heard Sadak use that term.

Sadak and Dafne were waiting together at the far end of the fortress, the opposite point from the entrance where Baier had had his coffee and sandwich shortly after his arrival in Ankara. All four gathered in the shadows between two buildings that apparently housed a tourist office and shop window filled with copperware. No one said a word, and Baier thought at one point that his head would explode from the weight of the silence.

They suffered through about twenty minutes of that when Baier heard the sound of footsteps and Turkish being spoken. He glanced over at Sadak, who nodded. When the new visitors passed through the light of a streetlamp, Baier saw two men in raincoats, one of whom was the man from Baier's initial meeting with Sadak, the same one who had interrogated him at NSS headquarters. Their supreme confidence struck Baier as somewhat foolhardy. They seemed to be oblivious to their surroundings, as though they did not have a care in the world. When they stepped beyond the edge of the light, the two Turks stopped to pull a cigarette from the packs that each carried in his coat pocket. The glare from the matches showed both faces smiling, as though they were out for an after-dinner stroll while their wives cleaned the dishes.

The two men finished their smokes and tossed the cigarette butts into the street. They let loose a light laugh, then looked around. The Turks did not have long to wait, however. Nor did Baier and Badger, for that matter. Another figure entered their circle, emerging from the shadows after avoiding the arc of the streetlight. Like a true professional, or someone who was less certain of his place and surroundings. When the third party spoke, Baier recognized the unmistakable voice of Jim Breckenridge.

And he was speaking Turkish, a language he supposedly disliked and had claimed he could never master. But he sounded pretty damn comfortable and fluent to Baier's ears. The voices rose and fell a few times, and Baier looked over at Badger. His colleague raised a finger as he leaned forward to listen to the conversation, nodding periodically. Sadak and Dafne considered Baier every once in a while with looks of sympathy and concern. Twice he heard his own name, the only words he picked out of the entire conversation. Baier felt like waif and a fool.

Then after about thirty minutes, maybe thirty-five, the meeting broke up. All three initially made their way together to the fort's entrance, but then split apart as each one took a separate path down the hill toward the city center.

His first impulse was to rush after Breckenridge. Baier even broke from the shadows and started to trot in that direction. But Badger's hand seized his arm and restrained him. He was smiling.

"What the hell is so funny?"

Badger kept his grip on Baier's wrist. "It's alright, Sir. We've got him."

"What do you mean. What we're they talking about?"

Badger let go of Baier and plunged his hand into his coat pocket. "You'll know soon enough. I think I got it all here."

He raised his hand. It was holding a small tape recorder, a miniature device that the techies must have built for agent meetings. Baier had seen them before, but in his anxiety about the evening's event, he had not thought to tell Badger to bring one along. Thankfully, one of the two Americans had kept his cool and taken steps to preserve what they discovered. The two Americans started to walk down the street that ran through the middle of the old fortress, heading for the same exit the Turkish officers and the American Chief of Station had taken.

"So, what did they say? And why did they mention my name?"

"The first time it was to explain that they had not been able to locate you." Badger looked over at Sadak and Dafne who stood immobile on the curb behind them. "It looks like you chose your hiding place well, Sir."

"And the second?"

"That was a little more worrisome. Jim said they needed to find you before you blew the lid off the whole damn affair."

"And the other two? My Turkish friends over there?"

Badger shook his head. "They were not mentioned by name that I heard. But they did say something about when they found who had helped you, then it was not going to go easy for them."

"So, it's a good thing you still have the exfiltration route set up."

Badger nodded. "Yes, it looks that way, Sir. Will there be two or three of you?"

Baier looked over at his Turkish friends. "Two at least. I'm not certain about the third. But I guess you should probably plan on all three of us. For now."

• • •

"You can probably put those plans on hold, Karl."

They had reached the street that ran across the front of the Citadel. Baier's head shot up, and he stopped with an abruptness that left Badger a few feet in front of him. But then he noticed that his companion did not stop at all. Badger kept walking straight ahead until he stood next to Jim Breckenridge. The two Turkish officers moved with a silence from the shadows across the street like they were ghosts from the ancient past, spirits from past invaders that still haunted this city.

Baier was too stunned to speak for almost a minute. He tried to assemble the events of the past two days so that they would make some kind of sense, a pattern that did not betray the expectations he held of those involved in this particular drama, of his American and Turkish colleagues, of men he thought were his accomplices if not his friends. He failed.

"What the hell is this, Fred?" he asked.

"I'm sorry, Mister Baier, but your story was just not credible. I mean, it was too fantastic."

"You can still say that after what you heard back there?"

Badger shook his head. "I didn't hear anything that supported your version of what has been going on here."

Baier started to pace back and forth in the street that separated him from his old and new nemeses. He could not believe that he had been so wrong. Not in his estimate of the man he considered a traitor, but in his assessment of the deputy, someone he believed he had come to know and that he could trust. In the end, though, he knew that in this life he had chosen that so much of what he did, so much of what came of his work, his efforts, so much of it had relied on that line of trust in his comrades and awareness of the enemies they faced. But it was a thin line made stronger by the experience and insight you gained into the nature of individual men and women you encountered and acted with side by side and day after day. But it was still stretched thin at times. And here he had been drastically wrong. He just hoped he had not been fatally wrong.

Breckenridge's smile betrayed his confidence and sense of triumph. His eyes showed his contempt for his colleague from Washington. "I am surprised, Karl, that you took the bait so easily and let us smoke you out."

"So, what happens next?' Baier asked.

The smile seemed to turn cruel, twisting Breckenridge's lips into more of a leer. "Oh, you are definitely going home, Karl. But whether it's in a box or upright depends entirely on you."

"And what is it that you expect me to do?"

You will sign a confession we've typed up…"

"We?"

Breckenridge's smile widened. "Yes, my Turkish allies and me. I don't think you could bring yourself to write it all out by yourself, even if some more of my allies were watching over your shoulder. So, we've typed one up for you to sign."

"What am I confessing to?"

"That you have worked with some Soviet comrades, men you got to know over the years from your work with that Soviet creep you got to defect, also part of an elaborate plan to infiltrate the CIA." He laughed. "Can you see it, Karl? Angleton will be creaming in his pants, he'll be so excited." Breckenridge shook his head, laughing some more. His raincoat flapped in the breeze that swept the streets. "It will all be verified by the men here tonight. Probably a few more as well. At least the Ankara parts."

"And if I refuse?"

"Then you suffer a different fate. What's the Hollywood phrase, 'shot while trying to escape'? But even then, the story will be the same." He nodded in Badger's direction. "Fred here will drive you to NSS headquarters."

Baier stood in the middle of the street for a moment, then whipped his head around in exasperation, frustration, and fear. He searched for Sadak and Dafne, searching for a way out, a glimmer of hope. But they had disappeared.

# CHAPTER TWENTY-FOUR

At least, they could have given him a more comfortable room than this prison cell. Baier studied the damp and dirty walls surrounding him. It was too dark to make out their color, but it was definitely not something pastel, or even green or blue. Most probably some kind of grey that had darkened over time with more dirt and suffering. He hoped none of it was blood.

Then again, he did not really know how bad his situation was. The cell was small, of course, but not nearly as tiny as whatever hope he harbored. He cursed the chief and deputy chief of station for conspiring to put him in this situation, one that threatened not only his career but his life. Oddly, he did not curse the day Ralph Delgrecchio had raised the possibility of this TDY to Turkey. That had been honestly and sincerely done, part of a necessary and potentially valuable mission. Goddammit, but if only he could somehow contact Delgrecchio now.

It had been roughly 36 hours since he had been tossed into this prison, somewhere on the outskirts of Ankara. He had not been delivered to NSS headquarters, as Breckenridge had claimed he would. No, this was someplace different, and Baier was not sure what that meant, if anything. It was surprisingly small, not a real prison. Or so it seemed. It was more like an abandoned apartment complex with some damp, dark cells instead of a proper cellar. The NSS headquarters it definitely was not. Of that much he was sure.

They had not bothered to blindfold him, nor had they taken Baier's watch. In fact, Baier had not been subjected to any rough treatment at all, other than to be dragged by both arms down the flight of stairs that led to his cellar holding cell. He had not gotten much sleep, which did not surprise Baier. The periodic pounding on the door and constant glare from the single light bulb hanging from a ceiling wire like a thin snake was pretty standard treatment, especially if an interrogation was on order. Baier assumed there would be one to determine just how much he knew and what he had been able to report back to Washington.

And then there was the depression that had begun to swallow him like a whale of desperation and fading hope the moment he had confronted his American and Turkish nemeses back at the Citadel. Now, it felt complete. That sinking feeling of abandonment and uncertainty had darkened to a hollowness that was blacker and more bleak than the night outside and the cell inside.

When the cell door swung open, Baier glanced at his watch. Just minutes after six o'clock. He assumed the dusk had fallen full upon the city by now, and the Turks probably figured that he had been softened enough to reveal what they needed and to sign whatever they placed before him. To his surprise, it was not a Turkish guard that stood shadowed in the doorway, but an American. Fred Badger to be precise.

"Have you come to gloat?" Baier asked.

Badger was silent for a bit, no more than fifteen seconds, before he spoke. "Is there anything you need to have our hosts return before we leave? Or did they leave everything with you?"

He spoke those words in a rapid cadence that suggested to Baier that he did not want anyone else to understand him, no matter how good or bad their English was.

Baier stood from the bare cot and approached his guest. He glanced to either side of the American and was stunned to find him alone.

"Leave? Where are we going?"

"Away."

"But where?"

"Let's just get a move on. The fewer people that know and the quicker we leave the better."

Baier was not about to press for further details. He started to move—jump almost—but slipped onto his back as his shoes slid across he damp concrete floor. Badger stepped into the cell to help him up, but Baier jerked his arm free. "Thanks, but no thanks."

"Then come on. We don't have much time."

When the Americans walked into the hallway, Baier was struck by the silence. And the absence of any guards. He glanced up and down the hallway.

"Where is everyone?"

"Not here," Badger replied. "And that's what's important. It's all you need to know." He reached for Baier's arm again. "Come on. We really do need to move fast."

The two men trotted down the hallway towards the stairs that Baier had tripped along on his way in. This time he scrambled up as quickly as he could. His right leg cramped some from the lack of movement and exercise in his cell, but he was not about to let the minor pain slow him down any more than necessary. He was still able to keep up with Badger, who headed towards a black Chevrolet sedan that sat just outside the door to the prison block where Baier had been held. Badger jumped into the driver's seat and pointed for Baier to get in on the passenger side. He waved his arms in a fast circular motion to hustle Baier along. Once Baier was inside, Badger gunned the engine as he rammed the key forward to ignite the engine. He wheeled the car toward an open gate that bordered the small courtyard. The tires spit gravel and dust when he roared from the prison lot and out onto the street.

"Do you mind telling me just what the hell is going on here?" Baier asked.

"Not at all." Badger's eyes stayed with the road, while both hands gripped the steering wheel like it was alive. "I'm getting you the hell out of here."

"Where to?"

"Well, Greece, for starters. There's a boat waiting for us at Antalya, or nearby, which will take you away from this place. From there you can get to Washington easily enough." Badger glanced over at his passenger side and winked.

Baier fell back against the seat. "Just whose side are you on, Fred?"

"Yours. At least I am now."

"Then what was all that back at that fortress? A place I never hope to visit again, I might add. I don't care how good the deals are on rugs and saffron."

Badger glanced from the road at Baier and chuckled. His right hand broke from the steering wheel to troll his coat pocket. He pulled out a tape and tossed it into Baier's lap, where it slid down between his legs.

"That should tell you which side I'm on, Sir."

That word again. A good sign, Baier thought, particularly since it had the right inflection of respect. And collegiality. Baier retrieved the tape cassette and stared at it like a piece of precious jewelry.

"Is this what I think it is?"

Badger's eyes stayed with the road. Their path ahead looked as though it was cloaked in darkness and uncertainty. Baier felt oddly comfortable with him at the wheel, however. He marveled at how easily his trust in this man had been revived. The night no longer seemed so dark and forlorn. Anything was better than the cell and the uncertainty.

"You betcha," Badger said.

The man was almost enthusiastic. "Then why?"

"Look, Sir, you can't really wonder that I was hedging my bets. I mean, I had been working with Breckenridge for almost a year, and I had never found any reason to doubt his loyalty to us, to our country. But then you've got a reputation, too. So, I thought I'd play along to see what turned up." He nodded toward the tape in Baier's hand, Badger's one concession to let his gaze drift from the windshield for all of about three seconds. "The conversation between Jim and the Turks last night told me you were right. I had already arranged for our reception with Jim, but I wanted to be sure there was some kind of proof in case your suspicions proved to be right."

"But then why would Breckenridge and the Turks engage in such a sensitive conversation if they knew we were there?"

"Well, they didn't know exactly where we were, and Jim was

getting pissed at them for repeatedly bringing up the subject of their joint efforts with the Russians." He shrugged. "My guess is that they wanted something that would commit Jim to their agenda even more deeply." He laughed. "Besides, nobody knew I was taping the thing." He paused. "And I didn't bother to tell anyone either."

Baier studied the tape again. He let a thin smile escape. Then he turned to look at Badger.

"So, how is this going to work?"

"There should be a sailboat waiting at a beach just west of Antalya to take you to Greece. I can't say which island. That will depend on the coast guard, the wind, and all that sailing stuff."

"How much of a risk are we running?"

"It shouldn't be too bad. The area is not that developed yet, and the city only has about fifty thousand residents. Maybe a few thousand more. There's been talk about building up the tourist industry there because it's so damn beautiful…"

"Lots of ancient Greek ruins?"

Badger shook his head. "Not really. More from the Seljuk and Ottoman periods. Although there is an impressive gate built into the city walls to commemorate the visit of the Emperor Hadrian around 150 AD. Anyway, I don't know if you'll get to see it, but the area has this stunning geography with rocky outcrops and waterfalls falling right into the ocean at spots."

"What about our spot?"

"Oh, there's a real beach there. It's about ten miles or so from the town. Konyaalta Beach. Very nice. So our access should be easy enough."

"And no one will question the boat just hanging around there?"

Badger shook his head. "I seriously doubt it. Sailboats cruise the area all the time."

"Is anyone meeting us there?"

"I'm afraid not, Sir. You'll be leaving on your own."

"Hell, man, I don't know how to sail a damn boat."

Badger chuckled again. "Oh, yeah, sorry about that. You'll

have a skeleton crew. That much has been arranged, of course."

Baier hesitated. He was almost afraid to ask but knew he needed to find out one last bit of information. He would never forgive himself he let it all go.

"What about our…I mean, my Turkish friends? The man and the woman who were with us at the Citadel?"

Badger bit his lower lip and glanced over at his passenger. He slowed the car's speed from the steady sixty to seventy miles an hour he had held since they left Ankara to around forty. Baier had a feeling the news was about to be disappointing. He was right.

"I'm not sure what happened to them, Sir. The gentleman who was there, Mr. Sadak, he was the one who arranged for the change in the prison guards that let us get away. He was supposed to be there tonight as well, but I didn't think we could wait any longer."

"And the woman." Baier's breath caught as he uttered these words. He hoped Badger did not recognize the catch in his breathing and the slight stutter it produced.

"I'm sorry, Sir. But I haven't heard from her. Sadak said he would contact her to see if she was going to leave, too." Badger paused to give Baier time to adjust and control his feelings. "My guess is that the Turks, the bad ones, have them now."

Baier's head fell back against the seat. He stared out the windshield at the road ahead, a dark path that led past rounded shadows off in the distance and a black hole in the sky ahead. They must be the Taurus Mountains out there, he thought. It struck him what an odd thought it was to consider the geography at a moment like this. But then he cursed those mountains, and he cursed this country. He wasn't sure who to blame, but he needed to blame someone or something as he fell asleep in the car taking him away, and only him.

• • •

The surrounding geography came into focus very slowly for Baier when he awoke. At first, he thought he was back in jail, and he searched the air around him for the prison walls. When the car rode over a thin long pothole, it bumped Baier back into full consciousness. He sat up with a bolt that sent his chest into the dashboard, then bounced back against the dry, cold fabric of his seat. He glanced over at the driver and experienced a surge of relief when he recognized Fred Badger.

"We're almost there," Badger said. "Feeling refreshed? You had a nice little nap there, Sir."

Baier rubbed his cheeks, then ran his hand through his hair. "Yes, thanks. I guess I was exhausted from the last few days. It's been a real fucking ordeal, if I do say so."

"I can imagine. We'll be at Koonyalta Beach in another ten, fifteen minutes."

Baier stared out his window at the dark mountains in the distance. A light rain was falling, and he could imagine those hills covered in greenery, probably pines and cypress trees mostly, he guessed. The early morning shade obscured his view of much of the countryside, but the sheer drop of vine and shrub-covered cliffs to the pebbled beaches below suggested a rich and verdant scenery that must be as beautiful as Badger had claimed.

"I can see why the Turks are talking about building up the tourist industry here. It's like we're riding through a brochure."

Badger yawned, then nodded. "Yeah, it is pretty impressive. Too bad we aren't driving through the area in daylight. It would knock your socks off."

"I'm sorry you've had to pull an all-nighter with this drive. Any trouble along the way?"

Badger shook his head, then rubbed his cheeks for a second before grabbing the wheel again. "No, none at all. Your pal Sadak must have done a good job at blocking any notifications going out. I haven't seen a cop or a tail all night."

"Thank Heaven for small favors. It really is too bad he couldn't make it."

"I guess so. But you know, he may have decided it was his real job to stay behind and help steer his country in the right direction."

"You mean, the direction we'd prefer?"

"Well, why not? It's in Turkey's interest, too."

Baier thought for a minute, then leaned toward his driver and colleague. "Any word on how things are playing out in the Caribbean?"

Badger smiled and nodded in Baier's direction. "Oh, hell yeah. The Ambo told us the President has agreed to the Soviet's offer to pull their missiles out of Cuba in return for us taking ours out of Turkey and Italy."

"No shit? That's good news. The Turks won't like it, though."

"Well. They'll have to get used to it."

Baier thought again. "Jesus, what day is it anyway? I've lost track with all that's been going on."

Badger nodded. "I can understand that. It's October 31. Happy Halloween, by the way."

"Gee, thanks. Let's hope this all ends with a treat and not a trick."

Badger swung the car in a soft curve to the left and down a gravel path that led to a cove in the beach. He cut the engine and let the car roll to a stop at the side of the path about twenty yards from a sandy inlet, where gentile waves just about waist-high rolled to the shore with a low rush and tumble. Despite the darkness, the dawn released enough light so that Baier could see a thin blue cover on the sea that looked as though it came from the world of ancient poets and philosophers. More likely, he told himself, it had probably carried imperial navies and conquerors. Pirates, too.

A long rowboat rested against the surf, its front half pulled up on the beach and nestled in the sand. Badger pointed to the horizon.

"That must be our boat. Can you see the outline out there?"

Baier stared, but his eyes were either too old or too tired to focus that far off.

"I trust you, Fred." He turned to the rowboat. "Is that our way out to it?"

Badger trotted through the sand, his shoes tossing handfuls of white and brown powder against his calves.

"Yeah. Let's go. I'll help get you out there. Then I have to get back to Ankara to see what sort of shit has hit the fan." He stopped and turned. "Do you still have the tape? It's not still in the car, I hope. If so…"

Baier punched his pants pockets. "No, it's here."

"Good."

Badger turned back to the sea and finished his trot to the rowboat, the ship of escape and freedom. He threw his arm around in a big wave to summon Baier, who rushed up behind his colleague and climbed into the boat after him. Baier sat in the front and grabbed the oars.

"I insist," Baier said. "You've been driving all night."

When they were about fifty yards from the shore, Baier, who had been rowing with his back to the open sea, glanced over his shoulder and found the outline of a large sailboat bobbing on the waves that had turned clear blue against the rising sun. He recalled the phrase from Homer about a wine-dark sea and thought that the poor poet must have seen a polluted stretch of ocean. This water shone like jewelry, a light turquoise that spoke of natural wealth, opulence even. When they finally reached the sailboat, a rope ladder fell over the side, and the two Americans clambered up. It took Baier a several minutes longer than it took Badger, since his muscles were already tight and tired from the exercise. Blisters were also forming on his hands, which the wet hard rope and the knots set against the edges aggravated further, leaving raw, red spots along his knuckles and palms.

The pain all fell away when Baier discovered Ralph Delgrecchio standing by the rail next to the ladder. Delgrecchio leaned over and reached for Baier's hands. He grabbed Baier's wrists instead and hauled his friend and colleague onto the deck.

"Welcome aboard, matey."

"My God, but it is good to see you, Ralph." The two men embraced for what must have been thirty seconds. "But you can cut the sailor lingo. You're as much of a landlubber as me. I just hope you found someone who can sail this thing out of here."

"Not to worry, my friend. We've hired a pretty capable crew

and will get underway shortly. But first, there's someone I need you to see."

Delgrecchio turned to his side and led Baier to an open stairwell that ran into the ship's hold. Before he could step down, however, an image drifted toward him as it ascended the stairs.

"My God. Dafne."

# CHAPTER TWENTY-FIVE

"You can see why Karl has been such a success in our profession," Delgrecchio proclaimed. "He has a remarkable and quick grasp of the obvious."

"Thanks, Ralph. I'm sure Dafne has figured that much out by herself," Baier replied.

"Good, then. I will leave you two to yourselves and get things ready to move out of here."

Delgrecchio's footsteps echoed on the deck behind them. When Baier moved to wave him off, he noticed that Delgrecchio's head and shoulders looked round and damp in the morning light, where they shone with a dull glow of achievement. It made the chilly rain that now blanketed the boat suddenly more bearable. He turned back to Dafne.

"How did you find your way here? I thought you told Fred that you were staying behind."

"I am," she said. Dafne spoke with a tone of sincerity and longing blended with disappointment and sorrow. Her dark eyes shone with affection and tears as she reached out to take Baier's hand. "I knew I would never forgive myself if I did not come to see you off."

"See me off? What do you mean?"

"I am staying in Turkey, Karl." She squeezed his hand hard enough to cause Baier to wince. "No, I must. I want to help Mucip and the others build a Turkey that remains western and secular. To do otherwise would be to betray my ancestors. They lived here for centuries, and I cannot simply walk away from the legacy they built in this land. I am more than just a Greek living in modern

Turkey. I am part of the Byzantine and Ottoman heritage that populates these lands, Karl. I may not stay here forever, but I know I have to stay for now. I know that may sound too theatrical and even melodramatic, but if you got to know me, my family, and our history better, you would understand."

"That's a lot to take in, Dafne. And it is a helluva burden to place on yourself. Especially in a country that looks to me like it is building its identity on an exclusive Turkish and Sunni culture and outlook. I will worry about you if you stay." He smiled. "Hell, I would worry about you anyway."

She took both Baier's hands in her own. "No, Karl this is the right thing for me to do. Besides, can you not see that we would only end up tempting each other and possibly betray our work together and the friendship that came from that? You have your wife and your work at home. You cannot simply walk away from those any easier than I can from my background and life here."

"Dafne, I appreciate all that, and I thank you for it. I know you are right. But are you sure you'll be safe? We can arrange a new life for you in Europe. There are many Turks living in northern Greece, around Thessaloniki. You told me that yourself."

She raised Baier's hands to her lips, then let them fall. "Perhaps some day, but not now."

"Hey, you two," Delgrecchio yelled from above. "Time to make up your minds. Either stay or go. We've got to get moving."

Baier and Dafne reached for each other. His arms slid surrounded her shoulders, and she seemed to fold into his chest. Her lips brushed his neck, then found his mouth. When they broke apart Dafne's eyes were wet and red. Baier told himself it was from remorse, but later whenever he looked back, he could never be sure.

"I will never forget you, Karl. Be brave, and be strong. As strong as you were here."

"You, too, Dafne. I think you will need that more than me. And I will never forget you."

Baier followed her across the deck and watched as she climbed down the rope ladder and sank into the boat with Badger. He watched her return to the shore like he was watching a ghost return to a place of spirits between Heaven and Hell.

• • •

"Before I forget, have you brought anything resembling hard evidence to support your suspicions?" Delgrecchio asked.

The two men sat in a tight room that resembled a cross between a mini-lounge and a galley kitchen. Baier assumed this sort of working space was typical of middle-range sailboats like this one. A typical Midwesterner, he really had no idea or experience with life at sea. The light, chilly rain that had been falling back by the shoreline had pursued them out to sea, but Baier was grateful that it had not transformed itself into a howling storm, like those he had seen in the Saturday matinees as a child. Instead, the gentle rocking—more like a swaying, actually—left an image of a dark but not a stormy ocean as Baier and his close friend and colleague rode to safety across seas that, at this point, did seem to be wine-dark.

"You'll have to excuse me, Ralph, but I've been out of touch for the last few days."

"Yeah, I noticed. It sounds like there's a question coming instead of an answer."

"Well there is. What the hell is happening in Cuba? The last I heard we were just a step shy of war."

Delgrecchio leaned back and laughed. "You can rest easy on that one, buddy. A couple days ago...about the time you were grabbed up at that old fort...Kennedy and Khrushchev came to an agreement."

"When was this?"

Delgrecchio searched the sky, as though for an answer in the clouds. "Day is still Halloween, right?"

Baier shrugged. "I guess so. I haven't seen a calendar lately."

"In that case it must have been three or four days ago. I think it was on the 27th."

So the missiles are gone?"

Delgrecchio nodded. "Well, not quite yet. But soon. The

Russkies have agreed to pull them out in exchange for a promise to lift the embargo and not to invade Cuba again."

"So, what are we waiting for?"

"We want to verify that those damn things actually are gone. It will take a few weeks. But it looks like we're in a good place. At least, better than we were a few days ago."

"What about the Jupiters?"

"Oh, they're gone too, or soon will be. But we will not acknowledge that publicly." Delgrecchio studied his friend. "But back to the matter at hand right here, though."

Baier fingered the tape in his pants pocket. "What's the matter, Ralph. Don't you trust my judgment?"

Delgrecchio smiled and leaned back against the thin wooden slats of his chair. "Of course, I do. But I took a quick look at the reporting from Ankara after our last meeting out here, and there was not a lot to go on, if you want to pursue this case. In fact, there was nothing to go on. And I truly doubt we'll be able to turn up something like a surge in income or lifestyle expenses. Breckenridge isn't stupid, you know."

Baier pulled the tape from his pocket and held it in front of Delgrecchio. "I don't think he did it for money, Ralph. In fact, I'd be surprised if there was any payment at all."

"Then what was it?"

"I believe it was the product of an arrogance that perverted his judgment. He thought he knew better than anyone else what the problem was and what needed to be done to correct it." Baier held the tape up. "This should help explain things."

"What is it?"

"It's a recording of a conversation that Breckenridge had with his Turkish contacts about their work with the Soviets."

"No shit? How in the hell did you get that? Jim must be slipping."

Baier explained the circumstances of the late night gathering and Fred Badger's role.

Delgrecchio shook his head in disbelief. "Holy shit, Karl, you must have been pissing nickels wondering how the hell you were going to get out of that mess. So, Badger came through in the end?"

Baier nodded and leaned forward. "I sure hope so. He did get me out of there and contacted you, like I asked." He waved the tape in the air between them. "I haven't had a chance to listen to what he got on here, but he said he thought the sound quality was pretty good."

"What do you mean you haven't listened to it yet?"

"Well, Ralph, the Turks do not provide tape recorders to their prisoners. At least not that I know of. And it's all in Turkish, so there wasn't much point. We'll have to get this into the hands of the folks in the language school once we get back."

"I think we might be able to find a Turkish speaker among our people in Greece. But if not, we will certainly do that." Delgrecchio thought for a moment. "Tell me, though, why do you think the Turks decided to play this game, and why would they push Breckenridge to commit himself at a meeting like that one, especially if they suspected there were others there?"

Baier sighed and let the soft movement of the Aegean Sea pull his thoughts together. "I think they wanted more leverage on Jim. They no doubt believed that they would be able to keep their hands on me and control me. So, Jim was their entry into one of the power players in Washington and in the region. He was more than just an unwitting asset. He was a form of insurance."

"But why did they need that? What sort of game were they playing?'

"They want to rein in Ataturk's reorientation of their country toward the West. They believe Turkey has become little more than a lickspittle for the United States and that crafting a closer relationship with the Soviet Union—among others—gives them greater opportunities to pull away. I think they're inspired by some Ottoman-like delusions about the continuing role Turkey should be playing in the region."

"But what was in it for Breckenridge?"

"I guess he thought he needed the Turks to chart the independent path through this latest crisis with the Soviets that he thought was the right one. He was, after all, on foreign turf. There wasn't much he could do without some kind of assistance. I doubt he planned on having it continue once he left Ankara. And after he had solved the Cuban missile crisis."

Delgrecchio laughed. "Well, in my experience the Arabs and others in that part of the world do not share fond memories of Turkish rule. And anyway, if you were able to get away like you did, then my guess is that their group is not all that large and influential. I mean, this Sadak guy was able to spring you easily enough."

"I don't know how easy it was, Ralph. But I hope you're right."

"And the girl? What happens to her?"

Baier wasn't sure how to respond to that question. He knew what he hoped would happen, that she either was safe enough in Turkey to go on with her life and career, or that she would be able to escape to Greece or perhaps Germany if not. Baier looked up and confronted a face on Delgrecchio that showed concern and curiosity.

"Hell, Ralph, I wish I knew."

"Do you plan to come back to find out?"

Baier shook his head. "No, Ralph, I don't. That would not help her or me. I think it's in the best interests of us both if I left that in the hands of others."

"If you can, Karl. If you can."

# CHAPTER TWENTY-SIX

"Well, that sucks."
It had been three days, and Baier was back at his desk in Langley. The one at which he had first heard about his trip to Turkey from Delgrecchio. The two men had gathered once again, as Delgrecchio brought his friend and colleague up to speed on the investigation into Jim Breckenridge and his unauthorized collaboration with the Soviets and Turks. The Turkish triangle that had cost the lives of three Soviet assets and the career of an American intelligence officer.

It was a Saturday afternoon, and Baier had come in to catch up on all the work that had piled up in his absence. His own two training courses had been put on hold while he was away, four personal evaluations on course instructors were waiting as well. It was promotion panel time at Langley. The good news was that because it was the weekend the standard practice was casual wear. Baier had gratefully obliged with dungarees and a blue and green sweater. After all, there was a Notre Dame game on the radio.

Delgrecchio was likewise attired. But he was a little more formal with a pair of worn brown corduroy slacks. He, too, had on a sweater, but his was red, the color of his alma mater, Rutgers University. He had taken a seat at the side of Baier's desk this time, his legs crossed and an arm resting on the edge of Baier's desk.

"Karl, surely you knew all along it would come to this. We can't have a public trial on something like this. Can you imagine the fall out if even a little of the information from this case made it out in the open? The deaths, the betrayals, and the information on how we found out about the Soviet schemes? Not to mention the reliability of an important ally? Hell, we don't even want to admit in public to having Soviet assets."

"Yeah, I know. I know all that, Ralph. But it still sucks."

"Hell, man, Breckenridge's career is over in any case. You sure as shit would not want to be in his shoes. He will definitely get fired for his security breach. I think he believes he can hang on here in some make-work job for a couple years, at least until this whole affair blows over. But that is a pipe dream on his part. Hell, he'll probably lose his pension. It's the best we can hope for. You can forget a public trial and prison sentence. It's not like we have piles of evidence."

"The tape?"

"Yeah, the tape. There's some good information that comes through, but the sound isn't the greatest. And don't forget, Breckenridge does still have some allies in the building."

"Like that Spronk creep?"

"Yeah, I'm not too sure about that. Do you think he played a role in all this?"

Baier let his feet fall to the floor. "Oh, hell, Ralph. I can't say for sure. He may have given Breckenridge some sort of green light about an opening to the Soviets as a way to gain some leverage. But I seriously doubt we'll find anything to confirm whatever it was. Or may have been." He thought for a moment. "Have you heard anything about Hughes?"

"No, nothing on that front. It doesn't look as though this Kosrov character played much a part in all this. I can see how he might have been part of the Soviet operation to infiltrate the NSS, but he did not have any assistance from Hughes that we can see."

Delgrecchio sighed and ran his hand through hair that Baier noticed for the first time was beginning the thin along the top. Shit, we are all getting older, Baier told himself. In some ways, he had felt that way in Turkey. The overpowering sense of betrayal and lost direction among a colleague he had never had a reason to distrust. His near betrayal of Sabine. A mid-life crisis or just arrogant stupidity? For both men?

"Like I said, it's not like we have a pile of evidence against

Breckenridge," Delgrecchio continued. "The General Counsel's office didn't think we had a strong enough case to get beyond the reasonable doubt barrier. There was no evidence of any payoffs, and no American lives were endangered. And what U.S. secrets were betrayed beyond the existence of some Soviet sources?"

"Well, my prospects looked pretty dim there for a while. And what about what we lost when we lost those assets in terms of the intelligence they could have provided?"

"Are you willing to go public and take the stand? And some could argue that they were double agents anyway." Delgrecchio shook his head. "No, we will have to take care of this betrayal in our own way. And we will. Believe me."

"Fair enough. So, how is Jim taking it all now?" Baier asked.

Delgrecchio leaned forward with a smile. "He's actually cooperating. We've had several debriefings so far, and the guy isn't holding anything back. He probably thinks that that sort of behavior will win him good marks. But he has to realize—eventually--that it's over for him."

"Is it helping expose the damage he's done?"

Delgrecchio sat back. "Yeah, I think it is. The guy actually considers himself a patriot. Still. There's more to get out of him, of course, but so far, so good. In the end, it won't help him, though. He's still a fucking traitor." Delgrecchio paused and studied his friend. "You, however, are almost certainly facing a much rosier future."

"How so?"

"Well, gee, Karl, you answered the questions here about the loss of the three Soviet assets, as you were sent out to do."

"I'm glad that's recognized."

"And you've uncovered a Soviet penetration, not to mention a Turkish collaboration that went way beyond what was allowed."

"Yeah, so am I getting some kind of reward?"

"For doing your job? Hardly, at least not in terms of a big pile of cash."

"Then what?"

"From what I hear you're in line for a nice posting overseas, probably a chief of station assignment."

"Like in some nice, cushy European capital?"

"Well, I think our bosses on the seventh floor are thinking more along the lines of South Vietnam?"

"Say what?"

"Our country is gearing up for a major military and diplomatic effort to protect that place from a Communist takeover. It could lead to the Agency's largest program ever. And, believe me, it would do a helluva lot more for your career that sticking with this training gig."

"As I told you before, Ralph, there's more of a reward than you realize in this sort of assignment. I mean, the people going through this place represent the future of our organization. At least in the operational side of things."

"Be that as it may, Karl, I doubt you'll be able to hold off the minions upstairs for long." Delgrecchio stood and leaned in close. "Everything okay on the home front?"

Baier stood and moved around to the front of his desk. He let a friendly smile escape as he held out his hand. "Thanks for coming by, Ralph, and for keeping me in the loop. I really appreciate that. Almost as much as I appreciate the faith you showed in my judgment when you came to my rescue out there in the Aegean."

Delgrecchio stood and took his friend's hand. "Hell, Karl, you know I could never let you drift on your own. I'll always be ready to act as your wing man. And I know you'd do the same for me."

Baier shook Delgrecchio's hand, then threw his arm around the man's shoulder. "You're damn right I would, Ralph. Anytime or place."

• • •

"Did your football team win?"

Dinner was over, and Baier glanced at the radio in the stereo cabinet in their living room. He stood and walked over to the set, where a string of football scores drifted across the air. He turned the machine off, then retook his seat by the fireplace. Sabine sat in the armchair on the side. She held a glass of white wine, a German Riesling, in her right hand and studied her husband. He sipped his glass of Jack Daniels, and the ice chimed as it rolled against the glass.

"Yes, they did. Finally."

"They have not had a good year, have they?"

"They haven't had a number of good years. I think they need a new coach."

"Why do you Americans care so much about your university football teams? It strikes me as a bit childish."

Baier took another sip. "I suppose it is. But it's who we are. At least some of us. Like me. I think it's because we let those four years of university define us so much. It's not just four years of studying."

"I see." Sabine was silent for several minutes, as she finished her wine. She studied her husband the entire time, as he stared into a fireplace that held no fire. "Do you love her, or did you, even briefly?"

Baier's gaze shot up from the soot-covered bricks to his wife. He had not said a word about his work with Dafne, but he also knew that he did not need to. His behavior, his moods and distance would say all that was necessary. Sabine would figure out the rest.

"I'm not sure. But I don't think so."

"Why not?"

'It was just a strange moment in time and in a faraway place. I don't think I can explain it any better than that. And it did not come to anything. She wouldn't let it, and I did not want it to."

"Why not?'

"I couldn't do that to you. To us."

"Was she pretty at least?"

Baier was silent while he studied his wife's eyes. "Yes, she was. Quite beautiful, actually."

"Do you plan to stay in touch with her?"

Baier shook his head. "Gosh, no. I was asked that once before, and I explained that something like that would only harm us both. And others. Besides, I see no need to."

"How so?"

He studied the fire. "You know, I wonder now if it wasn't as much the history she represented as her beauty and the help she gave me. I probably would not have survived this if not for her assistance."

"So, what do you want now?"

Baier stared at his wife. His glass of whiskey suddenly felt heavy and cold. "I want what we have always had together. I never forgot that all the while I was there. There really never can be anyone else."

Sabine stood and stepped over in front of Baier.

"I think I will go back to Germany and visit my parents."

"When will you return?"

"I will let you know."

Those final words trailed from her back as she walked to the stairs. Baier watched her rise into the night that enveloped the rooms upstairs. He drained his whiskey and pondered a second glass. He wondered how long he would be drinking and eating alone. And whether his work would be enough to fill his days and nights. He knew it could only do so to a point. In the end, he was glad he could tell Sabine the truth about himself. He realized now more than ever how much he needed that.

# ABOUT THE AUTHOR

Bill Rapp began his professional life as an academic historian of modern Europe before embarking on a new career with the Central Intelligence Agency. During his thirty-five years there, Bill spent most of his time in the Washington, D.C. area, but he also spent over nine years overseas in assignments ranging from Berlin (during the fall of the Wall and the reunification of Germany) to Iraq, where he served as the deputy chief of station for analysis. Among his other assignments Bill was the White House PDB briefer for National Security Advisor Condoleezza Rice and her deputy Stephen Hadley. Bill retired in 2017 as a member of the Senior Intelligence Service, an Office Director, and senior executive at the Agency. He lives in Virginia with his wife, two daughters, and their miniature schnauzers. Bill is currently working on his Cold War Thriller series, which now has five books. He also has a three-book P.I. series set outside Chicago, where he grew up, and an independent thriller about the fall of the Berlin Wall.

CPSIA information can be obtained
at www.ICGtesting.com
Printed in the USA
LVHW030526180523
747245LV00005B/533

9 781684 920792